CAGE ME

AN IMMORTAL VICES AND VIRTUES NOVEL

HEATHER RENEE

Cage Me

Heather Renee

Published by HRB Publishing LLC

Edited by: Jamie with Holmes Edits

Discreet Edition Cover Art by Manuela

Regular Edition Cover Art by Urban Rex Designs

ISBN:

CONTENTS

CHAPTER 1
SPENCER

The sun's glare is a cruel trick, bright without warmth, while the wind slices through Crossroads with an unforgiving chill this morning. My skin prickles against the cold, a silent nudge from my wolf reminding me that I could shift and find comfort. Yet, considering my irritability brewing this morning, that might just lead to an unwanted snap—a literal one.

Depending on the unsuspecting victim and considering we're supposed to be in the land of the lawless here, it's not likely anyone would care, but I've already been banished from my pack thanks to my sperm donor being a royal prick. I don't need another asshole throwing a fit and making me go on the run again.

Hurrying through the busier part of the city, I curl my shoulders forward and keep my head bowed. I've called this place home for about four months, but making friends hasn't been at the top of my to-do list. Trust isn't a luxury I can afford, yet necessity has forced my hand more than once as of late.

A crowd is starting to form ahead, but I do my best not to give the portal beyond them any attention. I have a witch to see first.

Except my gaze still flicks to the left as I keep ushering along the sidewalk. The newly created portal is why I'm still here a month after the deadline I'd given myself. Well, and because this is the first place I've been that has felt...not so desolate.

Power permeates through the air from within the swirling vortex, piquing my wolf's interest and calling me toward it, but I stay on my path. I have no desire to see for myself what's on the other side. None whatsoever.

Tartarus, they call it. Where the God Caius rules and shadow shifters roam along with other sinister supernaturals. Well, they might not all be dark and evil, but the world started as a prison. I intend to keep my judgment *and* my head, instead of assuming otherwise and risking my life.

I take a deep inhale without meaning to, soaking in the wafting energy before I get too far past the portal. The shiver travels down my spine at the same time as my wolf lets out a content grumble from my chest.

Though, her peacefulness is swiftly taken away when the apothecary we're headed toward comes into view and she's snarling on the inside. Too bad she's not in control. I am.

Keeping my eyes forward, I focus on the sign ahead. Spells, Secrets, and Sorcery. The place is owned by a witch named Natalia. Nice enough supernatural, but that's probably only because I give her something she's never had before and likely never will again once I finally leave this place behind.

The blood of an Albino Wolf.

It's something I hide from most people—including my bastard of a father, which is why I'm still banished—but I've also learned when to use it to my advantage, always taking precautions when I do.

Thanks to whatever mutated gene I inherited from my parents when I was born, my wolf can act like a chameleon, changing her coat to blend in with our surroundings. Though, we mostly use it to hide who we truly are thanks to the warning my mother gave me when I was just a pup.

Your wolf will get you killed one day if you trust the wrong people.

Okay, maybe my trust issues didn't start when Daddy Dearest banished me for protecting my little brother from his fists. They might have been embedded in my subconscious since I was old enough to understand my mother's words.

Still, I have to believe in some people if only enough to get what I need to survive in this fucked-up world. One where magic is power and without it, you're better off dead.

Arriving at Spells, as I like to shorten it to, I walk through the front glass door and cringe when the songbird above me chirps out a tune, alerting Natalia to her new customer. Why the sound always grates on my nerves, I'm not sure, but I've never wanted to kill an innocent animal more than that damned bird.

Inside, the space is dark—the daylight from outside blocked by tinted windows. Candles float in the air a couple feet from the black ceiling, but not many of them. Just enough to create an ominous atmosphere of flickering shadows and lights.

Glass shelves line the walls, filled with herbs, gems, body parts, and anything else a standard potion might require, but the stuff behind the midnight purple curtain just past the counter is what's truly valuable in this store.

Between the shelves, I pass by the tables of books, empty vials, cauldrons, and more before I get to the front desk.

Natalia pops out from behind the curtain, a smile on her face and a glint of eagerness in her russet eyes. "There she is. My favorite customer."

I used to think that was something she said to everyone, but after having visited her once a week for the last three months, I'm starting to believe it.

She waves a hand into the air, and I hear the click of the lock on the front door. "I assume you're here for your weekly trade?" Her fingers brush one side of her slick straight ebony hair behind her ear. "What will you be needing today? A coin or some sort of potion?"

Somehow, I hadn't thought about what I might want. I typically change it up so as not to draw even more attention to myself, but the stronger the draw toward the portal becomes, the more distracted my mind seems to get.

"Coin," I tell her, stopping in front of the wood counter.

"Two weeks in a row, huh?" she asks with too much curiosity, watching me closely as I roll up my sleeves. "Planning on going somewhere soon?"

My hardened gaze levels on her. "Planning on still making money off my blood?"

She holds her hands up innocently. "I'm just making friendly conversation, Spencer. No need for threats. I know our deal. One I've honored since the first day you stepped into my shop."

Natalia was the first person I extended a sliver of trust to in Crossroads. Not because I wanted to, but I needed her. Though, I'd made sure she believed it was her who needed me more, while also keeping watch long enough to get information I needed in case things go sideways.

The witch gets a vial of my shifter blood every week for as long as I'm here, and I get whatever I ask for, without question. If she tells a single soul what she's learned by playing with my blood, then I'll kill her. No second chances.

And there's little doubt that I'd know the moment she did because like I've learned and witnessed, powerful magic is too damned tempting for most. No matter if I'm in one of the Houses or if I'm in No Man's Land, supernaturals are greedy. If too many people find out what I am, I'll be hunted. At least, according to my mother, a wolf shifter with her own unique trait of foresight that has proven accurate on numerous occasions, allowing me to heed her warnings throughout my life without hesitation.

When I withhold my wrist from the witch, she sighs heavily. "Am I not allowed to be curious if this is the last donation you'll be making? This isn't about the money or your secrets. I'm making lifesaving spells with your blood."

This isn't the first time she's mentioned that—the families who have benefited from Natalia's enhanced cloaking potions thanks to my blood—but that's not my concern. At least, I try to tell myself so.

As much as I've tried to become the hardened supernatural I prefer to portray, knowing the difference I'm making by being here has also attributed to my longer-than-planned stay in Crossroads. Still, I like to keep the upper hand and don't show the witch that.

"No questions, Natalia," I warn her, then hold out my wrist. "Take the blood, hand over the magic coin, and pretend you never saw me."

"Right," she murmurs as her lithe fingers reach for me, wrapping around my forearm. The cool touch of her olive skin sends a shiver through me, the same as always.

The intensity of her power is why I came to her in the first place. From what I sense, the witch could possibly decimate the entirety of Crossroads. Yet, she chooses to run her little shop, helping even those who can't necessarily pay, only asking them to remember this favor of hers.

With as many *favors* as she's collected, the House leaders should be careful. Especially those now poking their noses around our little city that's supposed to be for those Houseless.

Regardless of all I've witnessed, I've remained distant, knowing that my life isn't just about me. I have my own people to save, but I'm not quite ready yet.

In another month or two, I should have enough magic to trade and build a home in the middle of nowhere, and enough cloaking spells to keep it hidden for generations. More importantly, the right kind of power to get my mother and brother the hell away from my abusive, manipulative, and all-around piece-of-shit father without leaving a trace of my temporary return to Fire and Fluorite.

Natalia twists my arm and uses her sharp black nail to cut cleanly across my wrist. When blood starts to pool on top of my fair skin, she uses magic to guide the crimson into the waiting vial.

I watch closely and yank my arm away just as soon as she has enough.

"You know, I could heal that if you'd allow," she says, corking the container before slipping it into the pocket of her long grey sweater.

"I'll be fine," I say gruffly. My wolf shifter genes will take care of the incision soon enough.

"So you keep telling me," she muses. "Still living in your shed at Kasha's house?"

Kasha, my would-be roommate. The fae and wolf shifter hybrid offered me a room to stay in when she heard about me from Natalia, but I declined. Sort of.

Knowing that I needed somewhere to stay, I at least showed up at her house and told her I would be fine in the rickety shack in her backyard.

She'd thought I was joking at first, but for nearly three months now, I've been sleeping there, perfectly content to maintain my distance.

I don't answer Natalia's question. Not even when she reaches into her other pocket and slides the gold coin imbued with magic across the counter, smiling. "Have a good day, Spencer."

Without returning the gesture or offering my thanks, I grab my trade and head for the front door. My gaze flicks upward, glaring at the red-and-black songbird perched outside her wooden house that hangs above the door.

Moving my attention to the exit, I shove it open and quickly slip out, only catching the annoying tune for the few seconds it takes the door to close behind me.

Without lingering, my steps increase, and I turn left instead of right toward my temporary home. A mistake I realize too late when Corvin Blackwell, the half-fae and half-gargoyle shifter, steps into my path.

His steel-blue eyes glance down at me as he smiles. "Spencer."

"Corvin."

I shove past him, but he's quick to jump back into my path, blocking me once again.

My responding snarl has him at least stepping back. Guilt gnaws at me for being such a bitch, but what he's been offering me these few weeks...it's not the life I can ever have.

Yet, he hasn't given up on me. Though, I don't know why. Even my warning growl doesn't stop him from asking the question I've already heard many times before. "Have you given any more thought to joining me?"

With a sigh, I give him my full attention, taking in his black hair, tanned skin, and muscular build. Attractive, but not my type. Especially when our interactions have had more of a familial vibe than anything else. Plus, I've met his mate. Styx isn't someone I'd want to piss off.

"It's the same as every other time," I tell him, doing my best not to grumble. He might be driving me mad with his friendly persistence, but I'm not too stubborn to admit it's because he seems to truly care. "What is it going to take for you to leave me alone?"

His responding smirk doesn't bode well for me. "You finally saying yes to becoming part of my pack."

"Your pack that barely even exists?" I toss out crudely since packs in No Man's Land aren't recognized by the Houses. "No, thanks. *Again.*"

Giving him my back, I continue walking in the wrong direction, but that doesn't stop him from chuckling and calling out. "You'll change your mind eventually."

I might want to, but there isn't a chance in hell that I will.

He lets me pass, and I brush off the interaction. No sense in wasting time thinking about things I'll never have, like another pack.

Before I know it, I find myself standing just two hundred feet from the new portal. The crowd I spotted earlier has doubled in size, plenty of people curious as to who might come through today and if they're anyone we need to worry about.

It seems whoever is guarding the other side only lets limited amounts of supernaturals in a couple times a week and so far, most have gone back to where they came from, and none that I know have caused any real trouble, but that doesn't mean all newcomers will be the same.

The desire to see what's on the other side still pulses within me as the intoxicating energy thrums through the air. Almost as if it's summoning me forward, to be consumed by what lies within.

With a lofty shake of my head, I clear my thoughts and step further back from the portal. I'm not weak enough to give in to that feeling, but clearly, I'm curious enough to allow my subconscious to keep bringing me back here.

Gods have come through this thing. I can't be faulted for my interest.

I catch sight of Tori, moving quickly past the portal to Tartarus. A fae who seems to avoid others possibly more than I do. Our interactions have been friendly enough, but I've really only chatted with her in passing, typically coming and going from Spells. Though, not lately. I briefly wonder if something's going on with her, but then realize it's none of my business. This is all temporary for me. So I keep telling myself.

The guards in front of the portal move into formation and I take a seat on the bench, refusing to move forward even as others within Crossroads get closer.

"I wonder who it will be today," someone mutters walking by.

"Who knows, but nothing has been as exciting as Caius," the woman with them says with a purr. "Who would have thought that gravedigger Raegan would be so lucky?"

The crowd has grown, and I can no longer see what's going on or how many beings are coming through, but one of them roars loudly and makes my brows raise. Hopefully that one goes right the fuck back to where he came from.

Those watching begin to part as I hear a rumbly voice shout. "*Move.*"

Grouchy much? I stand and turn to leave. Drama doesn't interest me. Power does.

With my back to the portal, I start walking in the direction of my shed until an energy begins to wrap around me. One filled with warmth and longing.

No.

My head shakes, and I force myself to keep moving, quicker than before. My body obeys right until I hear *him*.

"Mate."

My eyes briefly flick toward the sky. *Why? Why now?*

When I turn around, hellbent on rejecting whoever this man is who's coming closer by the second, I find myself speechless.

As soon as my gaze locks on to his nearly black eyes, there's a tightening around my heart. A need so intense that all air leaves my lungs.

This...man, he's on his knees, chest heaving and only looking at me. The ebony strands of hair sweep across his forehead as he bows his head. "Mine."

Can he only speak one word at a time? For his sake, I hope not. Good looks will only get him so far.

His nearly black eyes flick up to meet my confused stare. There's a tugging sensation in my chest as I take in his tight jawline and taut muscles peeking out from underneath his shirt, and I itch to smooth the crease between his brows.

But I only let that feeling last briefly.

My hand waves nonchalantly. "Sorry, you've got the wrong woman."

Even as the words make me feel like vomiting, I turn away from him and head in the opposite direction.

A mate isn't in my plan. Especially not one with a fury vibrating off him in waves that could very well consume me.

CHAPTER 2

DRAKE

Weeks have passed, and every second I was forced to wait for approval to pass through this portal has only served to fuel my desire for vengeance. Vengeance so strong that I can taste the smokiness of its depths with every breath I take.

At least until *her*.

The moment my boots touch down on Earth, I'm intent on finding a witch that would be willing to go against their own kind to help me track the one that wronged me, but fate seems to have other plans.

My mate is here. Right fucking here in front of this portal.

I scan the area, blinking rapidly as my eyes painfully adjust to the brightness of this world. And then I see her.

The woman I never thought I would meet is here, and it couldn't be at a worse time. Regardless, the draw to go to her, to fall at her knees and claim her... I can't ignore it.

All need for retaliation falls to the wayside as I move forward, but the closer I get, the faster she seems to move from me. Part of me wants to chase her, yet that's not what my instincts tell me to do.

I drop to my knees, uncaring of those around me, and call out to her. "Mate."

Her back is to me, and long, nearly white-blonde hair falls down over her shoulders that stiffen as I say the singular word.

When she turns around, the burning in my chest only intensifies, and it's as if I've been struck by the stars above.

Her bright yet almost pale blue eyes appraise me, and there's a tightness forming around her cheeks as she frowns.

Does this female not understand?

"Mine." The word comes out strangled and distressed.

She needs to know what she is. *My mate.*

Except, that seems to only make things worse.

The force of a woman practically snarls before casually saying, "Sorry, you've got the wrong woman." She spins around in the opposite direction, her hair floating behind her with the intensity of her movements as she begins to walk away from me.

What in the fuck is happening?

I don't know, but I didn't spend hundreds of years locked inside my own mind only to finally break free—mostly free, anyway—and be faced with this nonsense. I'd not only been trapped by the chains that bound me, but inside the shadow world that was a prison long before that witch Kel got her claws into me.

When I finally grasped on to a semblance of freedom, thanks to our God Caius finding his own liberty, I swore it wouldn't be wasted. While my intention with that had been forged in vengeance, the same applies to the woman I've just found.

Before my mate can disappear, I'm up off my knees and chasing after her. She's moving quickly and darts behind a building, but even without access to my wolf, I don't need to see her to track her.

No, her scent—a rich vanilla mixed with a spicy cinnamon—has already been ingrained in me. A smell I won't forget for the rest of my life. One I will chase through all the worlds if I must and makes my heart explode with want so thoroughly that all the rage I've been consumed with for centuries falls to the wayside.

When I turn the corner where I last saw her, there's an alleyway, and she's just standing there, frozen against the wall in her wolf form.

Her beast is a stunning white, almost blindingly so. The purest color I've ever seen in my thousand years.

The wolf whimpers, then snarls, teeth bared and eyes narrowed.

"What is your problem, woman?" I demand, barely able to keep from yelling. She's still my mate even if she's trying to pretend otherwise and starting to piss me off.

A shimmer forms around the wolf, and she transforms from an animal to the beauty I first saw. Though, her glare is still firmly in place.

"You could see me just now?" she asks almost accusingly, as if I'm the one that did something wrong.

"It's not as if you were hiding very well," I tell her, nodding toward the open alleyway. "There's nothing to conceal you here. Especially when your wolf is that bright."

Her chest rumbles. "I don't normally have this problem."

Again, she tries to walk away from me, but this time I'm close enough to grab her.

My fingers wrap around her wrist as I tug her back toward me. Not hard enough to hurt her, but enough that her feet misstep and she tumbles into me.

The heat of her skin brushes against mine, deepening the thrum of the bond I can feel pulsing through me. "Mate."

"Will you quit calling me that?" she snaps and tries to get away again, but she's trapped between me and the brick of the alleyway.

The scowl she gives me has my lips turning upward. At least until she begins to speak again. "If you think for one second you can force yourself on me, then you better think again. Just because my concealment didn't work on you, doesn't mean I'm defenseless."

Her words are like a punch to the throat. "Force myself on you? You're my mate. Do you not feel the bond, our connection?"

She laughs in my face. "I don't know how things work in Tartarus, but in this world, a woman has the right to choose who she mates with. Fates be damned. And I don't choose you, whoever you are."

"I'm Drake Cage," I tell her, doing my best to mask the pain slashing through my chest from her harshly spoken words. "Why wouldn't you want a mate to protect you?"

Does she somehow already know that my wolf is bound by dark magic thanks to that witch? Does she think of me as not worthy?

Even though I've spent most of my life basically frozen in time and trapped inside my own mind, I could hear the world around me. Mates still existed and they were drawn to each other unlike any other kind of energy is capable of. At least back on the other side of that portal.

Is it possible that this Earth no longer possesses the same magic? Even if she finds me unworthy, I expect her to still feel *something* toward me.

She pushes at me again and this time I stumble back, unable to fight against the tightness consuming my insides and making everything burn, ten times worse than my earlier taste for revenge.

Once she's out from between my arms and no longer trapped against the wall, she gives me a onceover. "You seem capable of many things, but *I* don't need anyone. I'm doing just fine on my own. You need to accept my rejection and move on, Drake Cage."

The word "rejection" intensifies my agony, making me feel as if I've been returned to my previous nightmare, confined inside my own body, unable to control anything around me.

"No," I finally say as she's about to turn around.

"No?" Her brow raises. "So, you *do* have every intention of forcing yourself on me." Her laugh is dark and almost threatening. "I wish you luck with that."

My currently nameless mate spins on a heel and starts walking away from me, but every instinct in me refuses to let her go, while at the same time, my innate desire is to give her anything and everything she wants.

Except the one thing she's asking for.

"I'll give you whatever you want," I tell her pleadingly. "So long as you give me the chance to prove myself as your mate. Whatever reason you have to not want me, at least give me this opportunity to show you who I am before you truly decide. Until then, my answer to your rejection will remain the same."

As I speak, I can hear how pathetic I sound, but more than that, I'm desperate. Desperate for this woman. To earn her acceptance. To show her that our lives will be better spent together rather than apart.

Her lips flatten into a hard line, and her distrusting stare keeps me in place as she replies with, "Why? What do you get out of this? Are you on the run from something in your world?"

She doesn't trust me, and she's right not to, but I'll show her that she's the only being in all the worlds that doesn't have to fear me.

"You're my mate," I tell her since that's all I need to know, but apparently, that's not a good enough reason for her.

"So? You can go claim a dozen women after me like I'm sure you've done before."

Hmm, is that her actually being curious about me? Possibly, and I'm happy to take the bait.

"There may have been few before you, Mate, but there will be none after you. Not now that I've found you."

I expect at least some appreciation for my sincerely spoken words, but she chooses to laugh in my face instead. "First, stop calling me Mate, and second, I call bull-fucking-shit. You don't even know me, and lying will not win me over."

My body recoils at her accusation. "I have no reason to lie to my mate."

"I said *stop* calling me that." The growl that accompanies her words feels broken as she rubs her palms over her face.

"What should I call you then?" I ask, not giving her the space I can only assume she wishes for. She's stopped trying to run away, so I'm at least making progress.

Her fingers slide down her cheeks, and her eyes go flat along with her voice. "Nothing. You'll call me nothing, because we're done here."

It seems I've spoken too soon, but that doesn't mean she's right.

"Mate, please." My words have their desired effect, and she freezes with her back to me.

"For fuck's sake," she mutters, then faces me again. "Spencer. My name is Spencer. Does that earn me some time alone?"

Defeat is etched into her fair skin, and the vision of her unhappiness has my chest tightening another notch. As much as I intend on fighting for my—Spencer, I don't want to hurt her, either.

"Yes, I will leave you be for now," I tell her sincerely, "but I won't be far. I deserve a chance to prove myself, and whether you want to admit it or not, we are mates. Where I come from that means something and that's not anything I intend to walk away from without fighting for you."

Her shoulders sag, but I don't believe it's in relief—not after what I've just confessed. Still, she nods. "Fine. Just don't be some creep and try to watch me sleep. I will cut you without even an ounce of remorse if I find you in my...room."

"I believe that's an acceptable request," I tell her, stepping closer until I'm able to brush the back of my fingers over her reddening cheeks. "I'll be seeing you, Spencer."

She can't hide the shiver of desire that moves through her body from the contact—at least, that's what I allow myself to believe—but she does maintain her attitude.

"Unfortunately, it seems so." This time when she gives me her back, I don't chase after her.

Instead, I inhale deeply, allowing the hints of vanilla and cinnamon to further mark me, then grin widely.

This woman will be mine. I will show her that I'm worthy, and then, I will get my vengeance.

As much as I need that witch dead and my wolf back, no one will ever come before my mate. Not now, not ever.

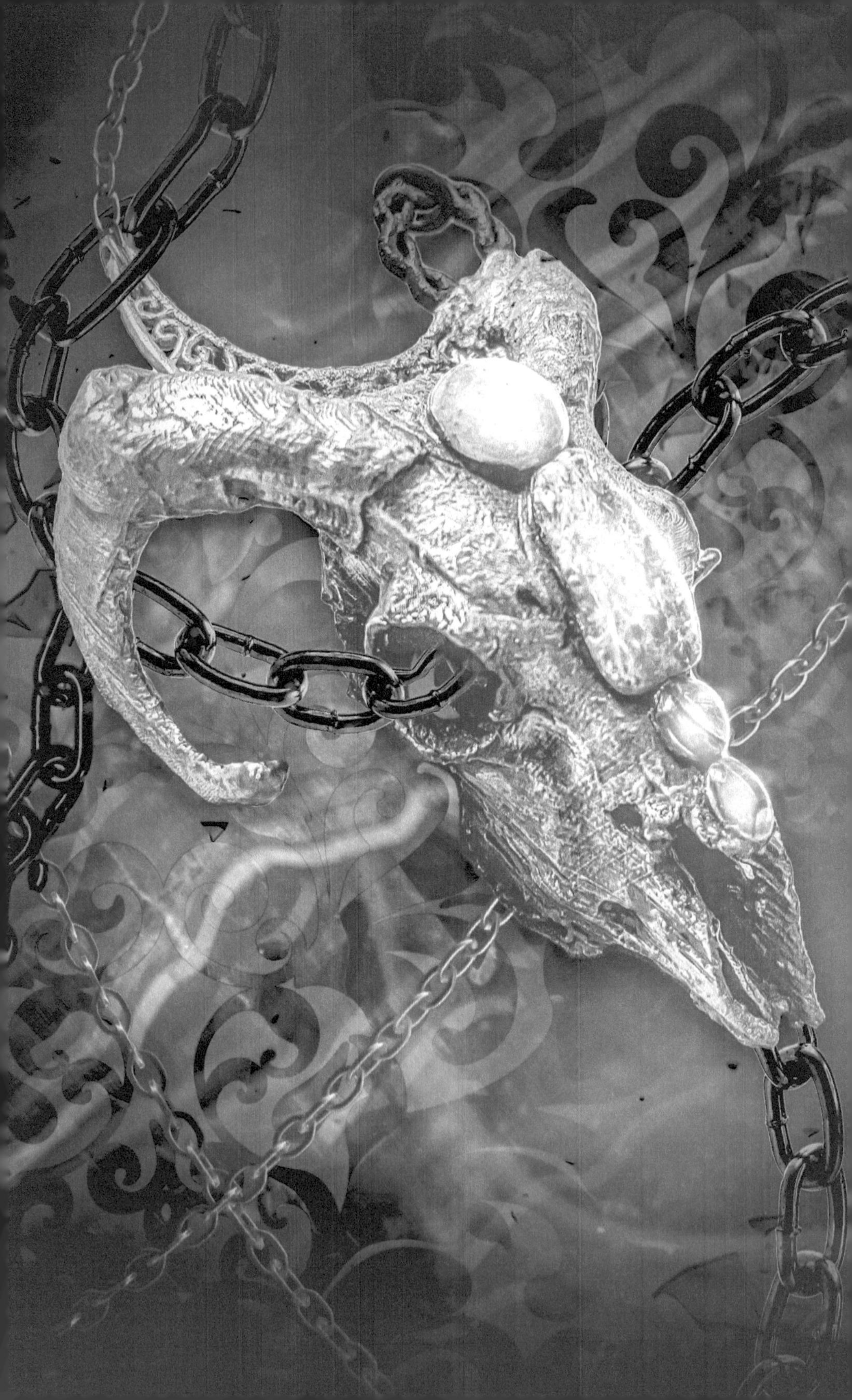

CHAPTER 3
SPENCER

No, no, no. This isn't happening. Not to me. Not now. A mate isn't what I need. Especially one seeped in that ominous energy I've been sensing from the portal. But even worse, one who can see through my camouflage.

He knew right where I was in that alleyway, and he shouldn't have been able to. I mean, maybe if he scented me thanks to the mate bond, but he could *see* me. My real wolf. He didn't see the dull brown one others usually did or the brick I should have been blended into.

That alone freaked me out, but then he remained so persistent. My rejection should have made him furious—at least, I would have assumed—but instead, he became almost desperate for my approval.

Worse, I somehow found that incredibly sexy.

Not only his pleading, but his dark eyes and the tortured-soul vibe he's rocking and the taut muscles... I can't focus on those things right now.

I've gone my whole life avoiding those who have spent too

much time dabbling in the darker side of our magical worlds, afraid they would find out about my wolf and only want to use me.

I can blend in anywhere, hide from anyone—well, I could until Drake Cage stumbled out of that damn portal—and my blood can create spells unlike any other supernatural, allowing my abilities to temporarily be given to another. At least when the witch knows what she's doing like Natalia.

Now, though, I'm being *seen,* and I don't like it.

Walking back to Kasha's, I look over my shoulder at least a dozen times. His smokey amber scent with light layers of musk have infiltrated my senses, making me think that Drake is right behind me, but every time I look, I'm alone.

By the time I turn onto my street, I'm practically running. This is absolute madness. This is what I get for not leaving when I originally said I would.

Except even thinking that if I had taken off a month ago, I wouldn't have met my mate... My chest aches from that reality and my wolf's energy is sorrowful. Though, none of that is enough to change my mind and find him.

When I walk through Kasha's yard, I have every intention of going straight to the shed and hiding there for the rest of the day, but it seems she has other plans.

The hybrid steps out her back door and nods casually. Her smile is wide, and her green eyes spark with mischief. She leans against the porch and brushes back one side of her shoulder-length copper hair. "How's it going, Spencer?"

Pausing in the grass, I take a deep inhale before turning to look at her. She's been the one that I've tried to be the nicest to considering she's letting me sort of live with her, but on days like today, when I just want to be alone, my niceness is harder to find.

"Just great," I mutter, kicking at the ground with the tip of my steel-toed boots.

She smirks. "I just got off the phone with a friend, and they told me something interesting." Her curious gaze scans the yard before coming back to me. "Are you alone?"

"Why wouldn't I be?" I ask, tension building in my chest and spreading toward my shoulders.

The shrug she offers and her growing grin don't bode well for me.

"Oh, I don't know," she muses. "Maybe because one of those shadow shifters stumbled out of that portal and kneeled before you."

Son of a bitch. I forgot he'd done that before I stormed off.

Of course that had drawn attention. Though, I don't know why anyone would have called Kasha to tell her.

"So, what if he did?" I ask tersely. "How is that anyone's business?"

She chuckles. "You might try to hate everyone, but none of us hate you, Spencer. Liv knows you live with me and that I worry about you. She gave me a heads up in case you didn't come back anytime soon."

Gods, I really am the world's biggest bitch sometimes.

Kasha steps away from the house and doesn't stop until she's standing in front of me. "Listen, I've given you your space. I didn't even question why you'd rather sleep in that shitty shed than inside the warmth of my home. But if you need help, I hope you know you can trust me. My friend Sin is the sister to Raegan. She told me a thing or two about dealing with mates from Tartarus."

Of course Kasha's connected to Raegan, the shifter who probably saved all of our lives by being mated to the God that runs things in Tartarus.

I close my eyes and take a deep breath. Trusting people

shouldn't be this hard, but when the person you love most in the world tells you that doing so could get you killed one day... Well, it's not easy, but Mom had said if I trust the wrong people, not everyone. Only it's hard to know who the right ones are sometimes. Though, something tells me Kasha isn't someone I need to keep pushing away.

Looking back at her, I give the hybrid a genuine smile. "Thank you. I appreciate the offer of help, but I think I'm okay for now. I'll let you know if that changes."

She raises a brow and smirks. "Will you really?"

Normally, probably not, but this time, I think I just might. I know nothing about shadow shifters, and she has people in her life who do. I might be stubborn at times, but I'm not stupid.

"I will," I eventually reply, and she chuckles.

"That seemed really hard for you to say, but I'll take it." Turning on a heel, Kasha goes back inside her house, and I head toward my shed.

As I walk through the yard, the heady scent of Drake still lingers, but I shake off the distraction and consider my next moves.

My heart is telling me that finding my mate isn't the end of the world, and I want to believe that, but my head has been focused for so long on getting what I need to rescue my mom and brother, then running away that anything else seems unnecessary.

On top of that, I've spent all twenty-five years of my life watching what a mate bond can do to a person. My mother has put up with emotional and physical abuse from my father for as long as I can remember. What sane person sticks around like she has?

I don't want my mind warped into thinking some stranger

walks on water and unable to make sound decisions for myself. That doesn't seem like a good time.

Except just the mere thought of Drake, picturing the intensity of his stare, the desperation in his words, the desire to...

No. Just no. Not right now. I can't go there.

When I open the door to the shed, my phone starts to ring in my pocket. I'm tempted to let it go unanswered, but there are few people in this world who have that number. Ones that don't deserve to be ignored just because I'm having a day.

I see my mother's name on the screen, and I'm not sure if my mood is about to get any better or not.

Has she *seen* something already? Her foresight has always been more of an intuition, one that seems to become more erratic as she gets older. Still, I always listen to her, and I hope she has something good for me now.

"Hey, Mom," I answer, stepping into my small space, but I don't get far when I realize it isn't my mother calling.

"Pence?" my little brother cries. "Pence, Momma needs you. He won't stop. I can't make him stop."

Peter's wailing grows louder with every word he forces out, and my heart shatters. Our piece-of-shit father is at it again, but I won't leave them alone. Not this time.

"Peter, I need you to listen to me very carefully," I tell him slowly and sternly. "Go to my room and get in the closet. Don't come out no matter what you hear until I get there, okay?"

"You're coming home?" His sniffles have tears burning in my eyes, but I don't let any of them fall.

"Yeah, bub," I tell him. "But only if you promise to hide, okay?"

I can hear my mother's screams in the background, and it's my father's lack of yelling back that scares me the most.

"Peter, go get in the closet," I tell him again as I toss my single mattress out of the way and reach for the box that I have buried beneath the floor there. "I'll come help Momma. I promise. You just stay safe."

Inside the metal storage bin under my bed, I have all my imbued coins and the different types of potions I've been collecting. Digging through my horde, I find the portal spell I need to get from Crossroads back to Fire and Fluorite within seconds instead of the days that it would take me to drive two-thousand-or-so miles through the territories.

"I will," Peter's crying voice finally says. "Just hurry."

"I'm on my way."

Ending the call, I curse the fates for doing this to my family. For giving my mother an abusive mate and for subjecting my eight-year-old brother to this nightmare. None of it is fair, and I should have killed the bastard when I had the chance. I've spent the last three years trying to get them out the right way at my mother's insistence, but that time ends now.

Reaching for my duffle bag, I shove the metal box inside first and then grab the few bits of clothes that will fit around my most important possessions.

Once I'm done, I glance up at Kasha's house, tempted to at least tell her I'm leaving, especially after the conversation we just had, but there's no time. Mom and Peter need me.

I'm about to open the portal spell when I hear soft footfalls, right before a shadow looms over me. "Are you running away from me again?"

Drake's deep tenor sends shivers down my spine. How could I have forgotten about him? Oh yeah, because my family is all that matters. Not this mate mess.

"I'll be back," I tell him, but he doesn't believe me nor should he. It would have been convenient, though.

His breath warms the back of my neck as he growls. "I don't appreciate being lied to, either."

I swallow thickly, not able to find the wit I want to respond with without fear of making a fool of myself. His closeness is messing with my head and causing an unwanted warmth to spread through my body.

"My family needs me," I plead with him. "Let me go before I have to hurt you."

Not that I think I could kick his ass fairly, but after hearing how desperate Drake was earlier, I know I could take advantage of that to get away.

"Let me help you." His reply takes me by surprise.

I turn to face him, a choice I immediately regret when our chests brush against one another, sending a tingle of something I don't care to identify through my chest. "What?"

"I heard your phone call," he says. "Your brother said your mother is in trouble. Let me help."

My eyes glare. "You were spying on me? I thought I set that boundary before. Who's the liar now?"

"You told me I couldn't watch you sleep," he says. "Nothing was mentioned about me staying close."

Cocky, sneaky fucker.

I want to set new and more specific rules, but I don't have time for this. "You can follow me, but stay the hell out of my way." My words are laced with a snarl, half because telling Drake to come eases some of my tension and half because of how much time I've now let pass.

Without wasting another second, I open the portal spell and throw the vial onto the ground. Dark blue smoke rises from the earth, and a rip in the air begins to form, growing into a swirling vortex of dark purple and silver colors until it's big enough to step through.

"What's on the other side of that?" Drake asks, but I don't have time to explain. He'll just have to find out for himself.

"Grab on to me if you really want to know." With my intentions set on the woods behind my house, I walk through and allow the magic of the portal to consume my body. At the last second, strong fingers wrap around my right shoulder and Drake's energy melds with mine.

In the seconds it takes for the portal to do its magic, I allow myself to connect with the shadow shifter. To feel the bond and wonder if things were different for me if I'd hate the thought of accepting him as much as I do now.

Though, if I'm being honest, it's not hate. It's fear. If I accept Drake, then I'm forcing my mother and brother to do the same when I've promised them all this time that it would be the three of us, forever and always.

Except that's a problem to ponder for later, because the moment we appear in the woods, I can only focus on how I'm going to stop my father.

For years, the only thing my mind could conjure was brutally ripping out his throat and tearing his body to shreds with my wolf, but my mother begged me not to.

She always told me that was because she was afraid of what would happen to me, but I also blamed the bond they shared. It still controls her to this day, making her believe staying with him is the best thing, but I'm about to change all of that.

I drop my bag on the ground and grab a stunning potion, then a knife. My sperm donor might be nearly seven feet tall and strong as hell, but I've learned that muscle isn't the only way to win a fight.

Drake hovers over me as I strap the knife around my thigh, then hold the spell in my palm. I ignore him and his curious looks. He'll just have to figure things out on his own.

Peter's innocent voice screams from inside the house. "Nooooo!"

Damn it. I told him to stay in the closet.

I start to run toward the house, ready to charge in, but come to an abrupt halt when I hear a gunshot.

My entire body starts to shake as another one goes off, followed by three more loud bangs.

No, I can't be too late. That fucker can't have killed them.

I won't accept that. Without my mother and brother, I have nothing. No family, no home, no purpose.

An abyss of defeat and agony threatens to swallow me whole, and I'm tempted to fall into the darkness. To let the pain of not hearing my baby brother's laugh at least one more time be swept away along with knowing my mother's loving arms will never hold me again, reminding me that everything happens for a reason.

Drake's warm hands squeeze my shoulders. "I'll go in there for you."

My tear-stained gaze snaps up, and I glare at the man I'm not truly angry with. "I'm going to finish this myself." My words are hurled at him with a ferocity that I'm forced to cling to for fear of drowning before I can at least finish what I came here to do.

If my mother and brother are dead, then I will avenge them. Not anyone else. Especially someone who never knew them.

I jerk out of his steady hold, ignoring how the instant he's no longer touching me, the grief feels ten times more savage. Running toward the back door, I only stop long enough to kick it in before charging forward.

Using the potion in my hand, my plan is to stun my father, then use the knife on my thigh to end his pathetic life once and for all. My wolf can have her way with him when I know he's down and not getting back up.

Racing down the hallway, I start to hear cries, soft feminine ones. They grow louder with every lengthened stride I take until the situation I'd already fabricated in my mind is replaced by something else entirely.

My mother is kneeling over her mate's body, clutching his bleeding chest as Peter stands beside her, rubbing her back, consoling her in ways he shouldn't have to at only eight years old.

They're not dead. Samuel didn't kill them.

But who took *his* death from me?

"Peter?" I say with a strangled tone, and it's not until right then that I realize more tears are streaming down my cheeks.

"Pence!" His azure eyes light up at my arrival, and when I take in his round face, there's blood splatter in his rowdy brown curls, on his skin, and ruining his light-grey sweatshirt, but it's what's on the ground next to him that hurts most.

He runs toward me, and I bend down with open arms, smiling as my chest aches almost as bad as it had outside.

"I stopped him," he tells me, his voice muffled thanks to me hugging him so tightly.

"I know, bub." The gun that had been next to his feet clued me in. One I only now remember hiding in my closet years ago.

My hold intensifies. I don't want to make Peter think he did something wrong because he didn't, but I hate that he'll have to live with this. He'll forever remember having to murder his own father. No matter how cruel of a man Samuel was, this day has changed all of us forever.

Peter wiggles out of my hold and points behind me. "Who's that?"

I don't have to turn around to know Drake is there, but instead of introducing him, I grab my brother's hand and stand up. "How about we go check on Momma?"

His lower lip juts out. "She's really sad, but also really happy."

Yeah, I imagine so. Now, it's time for her to get her emotions in check so we can burn a body and never look back.

CHAPTER 4

DRAKE

When I thought Spencer was trying to run from me, I assumed that would be the worst part of my day, but following her here, having her still keep me at arm's length, then seeing what that little boy had to do...

With my wolf still being bound, I'm able to keep my deeper rage in check, but watching how Spencer shakes with a fury that also seems to be mixed with pain, I don't know what I'm supposed to do.

I wanted to save her from this sight when she thought it was those she cared about who had died, but this still isn't good. At least, it doesn't seem so by the pinched expression on her face.

The little boy she called Peter watches me even as he's dragged away by his sister. I keep my emotions contained and nod at him, which makes him smile. Though, I'm not sure why.

The two go to their mother, and I watch as Spencer lifts her up and away from the corpse, forcing her up and into another room where I can no longer see them.

With the three of them out of sight, I decide just standing there isn't who I am, but joining them doesn't feel right, either.

Seeing the man that I know nothing about but can assume was a piece of shit right up until the moment he was killed by his own son, I decide to stay busy by disposing of the body for them.

In four long strides, I stand over the bloody mess. There are several holes in his torso and stomach, all turning his white t-shirt to crimson.

Reaching down, I grab one of his arms and begin to drag him back to the door we used to come into the house. I'm not sure where I'm going to put him, but anywhere outside has to be better than where he was.

Once I'm out the door, I toss the body onto the grass, then look for a shovel. This would be easier if I could shift and let my wolf dig the hole, but until I find that spiteful witch, I'm forced to figure things out in other ways.

While I miss being able to shift, it's been so long since I've sensed him that I almost can't remember what it's like to be a true wolf shifter. When I was locked inside my own mind, I was completely isolated even from my inner beast. That alone had me feeling insane the moment the spell broke, but the thought of killing that witch before I truly lost myself to the madness kept me motivated.

Now, it's Spencer.

I'd heard that the need to claim one's mate could make a shadow shifter mad, and while I'm desperate for her, I wonder, if by not having access to my animal half, I'm able to keep the worst of my need at bay.

I chuckle to myself. How much more desperate or crazy could I get if I wasn't cursed?

Potentially not feeling the full effects of the bond is likely a good thing when it comes to this woman, though. Something tells me Spencer wouldn't appreciate a savage beast any more than she seems to a pleading man.

Still, her preference in being left alone isn't going to happen.

I can't let her go. There has to be a way to make her see that finding her mate is a good thing and I'm going to figure out how to do that. When I told her I wouldn't force her hand, I meant it, but that doesn't mean I won't play dirty, either.

One look at her, the brief moments our skin has touched, the pain I can see hiding within the depths of her enchanting gaze... All of that made me know immediately that she's worth fighting for. Yes, fate is at play here having created this magical connection, but it's Spencer's soul that calls to me, and I'm not willing to walk away from it.

"What are you doing?" a young voice asks.

Turning around, I find Peter standing there, still wearing his bloody clothes. "I'm looking for a shovel. Do you know where I might find one?"

He nods toward his father. "Are you going to bury him?"

"That's the plan unless you have something else in mind," I say, bending down to a knee so we're nearly face-to-face.

His lips bunch together and eyes narrow slightly. "He wasn't a good man, but he was still my dad."

"So, you want to do something, but nothing too nice, right?"

Peter nods and shakes a finger. "Yeah, that."

"Well, how about we bury him, but we don't mark the grave," I suggest, then gesture toward the trees. "The grass will grow over and nobody will ever know he's there except us."

The boy stares where I'd just pointed and seems to thoroughly consider my words. "That might be good. For nobody to know he's there. I don't want to get in trouble."

My hand cups the boy's shoulder. "I wouldn't let that happen."

And I mean the words sincerely. Even if Spencer forced a rejection on me, allowing this boy to suffer for defending himself isn't something I'd stand for.

Not when I know what it feels like to be forsaken by a parent.

"You're a nice man," Peter says, a frown forming between his blue eyes. "I don't know why Pence doesn't like you."

A deep chuckle escapes me. "It's complicated."

"Adult stuff always is." He points to the corner of the house. "There should be a shovel over there somewhere."

"Thanks." I get up and head that way. When I see the garden tools piled up on the ground, I turn back to check on the boy and he's poking around his father's body. That has me grabbing the shovel and hurrying toward him, but by the time I'm back, Peter is standing up again.

"What were you doing?" I ask him, keeping my tone light.

"Taking anything that we might be able to trade," he says. "Pence is going to want to run. That's always been the plan."

Hmm. Good to know. I'll have to keep a closer eye on her.

"Do you want to pick where I dig the hole or want me to do it?" I ask, knowing that Peter deserves a chance to make this as right as possible in his mind.

His eyes go wide. "I can help?"

"Of course you can," I tell him. "I'll even show you how to use a shovel if you want."

It's been hundreds of years since I've picked one up, but I'm pretty sure I still remember.

He frowns, then looks at the ground instead of me. "I've never been allowed to touch Dad's stuff."

I bump his chin up lightly. "Well, that's the fun part about starting over. You get to make new rules. And I think you learning how to use any tool that you want should be one of them."

He nods, but there are still tears shining in his eyes. Instead of continuing to talk next to the corpse of his father, I grab his shoulder and direct him toward the trees beyond the yard. "Where should we dig?"

He looks around, seeming to inspect each one carefully before pointing between two large oaks. "Right there. In the fall, the ground is covered with leaves from the trees and it's really fun to play in. Maybe Dad will like that in his next life."

Poor fucking kid.

"You got it." I hold the shovel and gesture toward the metal spade. "See these flat spots?" He nods. "That's where you put pressure at with your foot. Watch me."

The tip of the shovel goes smoothly into the earth, and I slam my boot down on the spot I just showed him. The ground lifts as I pull the handle back at the same time and then I toss it to the side, but the dirt falls nowhere near where I was intending it to.

I guess I still have a bit to relearn as well.

"That looks kind of fun," Peter says, and I hand him the tool.

"Give it a try."

His little hands wrap around the wooden handle as he lifts the shovel up and down, almost like he's testing its weight. "I'm not—"

"What the fuck do you think you're doing?" Spencer's voice cuts through the air, sharp and furious.

Peter promptly drops the shovel and spins toward his sister. "Nothing. I'm sorry."

"You're not in trouble," I tell him softly. "I think I am."

He looks up at me and grimaces. "Good luck. I'm out of here."

The boy runs back toward the house, giving his sister a wide berth as she charges toward me. When she's within touching distance, her palms shove at my chest. "I asked you a question."

The growl in her words doesn't bode well, but I stick with honesty.

"I was disposing of the body, so you didn't have to worry about it."

"By digging him a grave and giving my baby brother the memory of digging it *himself*?" She flings the words accusingly at me. "What is wrong with you?"

I might be desperate, but I'm not an idiot and she's going to learn that one way or another. Steadying my stance, I lean over her, encroaching on her personal space as I bring my face as close as I can get to hers while still looking her in the eye.

"I was thinking that maybe giving his father a proper burial might ease some of the guilt he will undoubtedly feel later," I say, seething with quiet rage. "And to remind him that no matter how bad of a person his father was, we can still show our humanity."

"Well..." she starts but doesn't finish.

"Well what, Spencer?" I taunt, my tone still dark. "Well, maybe I'm not the worthless man you wish for me to be? That if you'd quit being so fucking stubborn that you might see I'm a worthy mate instead of judging and rejecting me without giving me a chance?"

"I didn't judge you," she says, crossing her arms and maintaining her defiance.

"But you did reject me for no reason."

Her lips thin and her eyes narrow, but I refuse to back down, even when she says, "I'm right and you know it."

I start to shake my head as she throws her hands up in the air with a huff. Spencer seems intent on running from me again, but I'm not letting her go. Not yet.

"We're not done with this conversation," I tell her as I move to block her steps. "You need to admit that you have no reason to reject me."

"I have every reason," she screams in my face. "They're right there in that house. My family needs me, and I've spent the last three years fighting to give them something better than this!"

"And you think you have to do that by yourself?" I ask, because if that's her only reason, I know all is not lost.

"I don't have to, but I want to," she says, her voice lowering back to normal. "You aren't part of the plan, Drake."

"But I'm your mate."

"And we see how well that worked out for my mom." This time she sounds defeated, and all I want to do is hold her in my arms, promising that her mother's experience isn't normal—at least not where I'm from—but I'm learning more about my mate with every word she speaks.

She doesn't need promises. She needs actions.

"Give me a chance to show you differently," I say, reaching for her hand. The moment our skin touches, an energy passes through us, and for the first time in nearly one thousand years, I hear a growl in my mind. One that is not my own.

Without thinking, I release her to rip my shirt over my head with one hand and press the other over my chest where the magical tattoo of my wolf rests. Heat rises from the black ink, and I close my eyes, but whatever brief connection I just felt to him, it's gone as swiftly as it came.

"What the hell are you doing?" Spencer asks. When I look back at her, confusion mars her perfect face.

"My wolf. I felt him."

Her eyes roll. "Do you think you deserve praise for that?"

"If you knew what I've been through, then you wouldn't have to ask that question."

The back door of the house opens and closes loudly, the noise causing both of us to glance that way.

Spencer's mother is walking toward us and her light-blue eyes, much like Spencer's, are glowing.

"Mom? What is it?" Spencer demands but doesn't move from where she's standing next to me.

I slip my shirt back on, then watch as her mother doesn't stop until she's standing in front of me and placing her hand over my chest, right where I'd just been touching. "So much pain," she murmurs softly.

Well, this is new.

Her eyes stop glowing a second later and instead of addressing me again, she pulls her hands back and turns back to Spencer. "You need to help him."

"The hell I do," she retorts. "I need to get you and Peter out of here."

Her mom grabs both of her hands and smiles. "And you will, but he comes, too, or I'm not going anywhere."

Spencer's mouth pops open and closed several times before she mutters, "You've got to be fucking kidding me."

Well, this just got even more interesting.

CHAPTER 5
SPENCER

My mother has officially gone crazy. I don't know what she sensed, but whatever it is, it doesn't... Damn it. Frustration boils deep inside me. I can't keep lying to myself. It's only been an hour since I met Drake, and I already want to touch every inch of his body.

Except that's the exact reason why I also don't want to. The power a mate bond has over a person terrifies me. My family needs me right now. The me who can keep them safe, not a version of me more concerned with a man than them.

"Mom, I know you're grieving, but you can't be serious right now. You need to listen to me. We're leaving, and Drake has nothing to do with that," I tell her, trying to hold back my frustration. She deserves better than that from me.

Mom's blue eyes narrow. "I'm still your mother. Even if you haven't always agreed with my choices, that doesn't mean I'm worthless. My instincts have protected me, and I know they'll continue to do so."

The moment "protected me" leaves her mouth, I lose the light hold I have on my temper and harshly point to the bruises on her face that are darkening in color with every minute that passes. "You call *that* being protected? You've been degraded and physically abused for years. How have you been *protected*?"

"Because you're still alive," she snaps. For the first time in my life, my sweet mother doesn't seem so sweet. "Everything I've done has been to keep you safe. You have no idea the sacrifices I've made for you and your brother. Yes, I could have run, but he would have found us. We needed all the pieces to line up, and I believe the fates were waiting for him."

She nods toward Drake, and I throw my hands in the air. "He has nothing to do with this!"

I don't want to yell at my mom, especially not when she talks about what she's sacrificed, because I know she has, but there is always another option. She just chose the easier one by staying. We could have fought back. I would have done whatever it took to keep her safe, faced any of the consequences for her.

"Spencer." Mom practically growls my name at me. "You have always seen me as the victim, believing that I had no fight in me. Maybe I was wrong in letting you see me that way, but I'm not helpless and I've always known what I was doing. I stayed with your father because I knew, without a doubt in my mind, that if I left, you would die. Do you hear me? *I knew,* and I don't regret my choices. Not the scars I carry because of them or the time I missed with you. Because you are here and safe, and you're no longer alone in this world."

Each word she speaks is thrown in my face, slashing away at me, burrowing under my skin and piercing my heart. Agony builds within my chest and by the time she's done, I want to crumble, to fall to the ground.

For years, I've blamed her for being weak, for being unable to do what needed to be done. Even just moments ago, I accused her of taking the easy way out by staying with her tormentor.

Except as she stands taller, speaks with a confidence I've rarely heard from her, and looks me right in the eyes, I can see her. For the first time in possibly my entire life, I finally *see* my mother.

The lines that shape her face, the faint scars from the fists she cared for after they made *her* bleed, every grey hair she's gained throughout the years, outshining the previous golden blonde she used to be.

She's a fucking warrior.

I throw my arms around her and hold her tightly against me. "I'm so sorry, Mom."

Her hands rub over my back. "It's okay, sweetheart. I never wanted you to know, but I think you need to know now. Especially with your mate here."

That has me pulling away and looking back, but Drake is nowhere to be seen. He had been standing right there and now...

There is a tugging sensation in my chest, directing my attention toward the house. That's only slightly creepy considering we haven't even completed the bond.

"I don't want a mate," I tell her, keeping my voice low. All the while, I just want to scream my frustrations into the void, because the words taste like acid on my tongue. "I tried to reject him, but he didn't accept."

She laughs, and her palm cups my cheek. "Of course he didn't, Spencer. Have you seen yourself? You're an incredible woman who has only ever tried to help people."

I scoff at that. She clearly hasn't been following me as closely as I thought these last few years.

"You may not believe it, my daughter," she continues, "but you're one of the kindest souls I've ever encountered in all the worlds. More importantly, your fate is not mine. You are not me, and that man you brought here is not your father. You can be happy and not alone."

I lean into her touch. "I won't be alone. I'll have you and Peter."

"Until I die and Peter finds his own way in this world," Mom says, seeming unyielding in her opinions. "And then what? I want more for you than I could have ever dreamed of. Don't let the past dictate your future."

Her words are a punch to the gut, but not in the way I expect. I want to believe her. I want to allow myself to accept Drake. After all these years, to have someone I can trust and depend on who isn't myself? The idea seems so unreal that I can't even imagine what that would feel like.

Yet, it's right there inside the house I grew up in, and I'm still standing out here, keeping a distance.

"This day is completely fu—screwed," I say defeatedly. "Can we just burn the body and get out of here? We don't need the alpha showing up if he happens to sense one of his wolves is dead."

Our alpha is kind, but almost stupid, in my opinion. My father had him wrapped around his finger, which was how I got banished so easily three years ago after stabbing my father in the chest. During one of his rages much like today, he'd threatened Peter's life because he wouldn't stop crying after having fallen out of a tree and breaking his arm. It was a line I couldn't let Samuel cross, no matter the consequences.

"Jameson is up north," Mom says about the alpha. "He was asked to sit in with another alpha while Kinsley and Grayson check out the portal you somehow haven't told me a single thing about."

The accusation in her tone isn't missed, but talking about the portal now will only lead to more talk about Drake, and I can't do that. Not yet.

"I'll find a gas can," I tell her, but she grabs my wrist and shakes her head.

"You're not the only one who saw Drake with Peter," she replies. "I think your mate was on to something. Let's bury Samuel. For Peter's sake."

I can't believe the words I'm hearing, but also, I shouldn't be surprised. He was her mate, and Peter might have been smart enough to kill the bastard, but it could be years before my baby brother truly understands what happened today. Drake and Mom are right. Peter should be able to look back on today and have no regrets.

"Fine," I say, doing my best to hide my annoyance. "Tell Drake that he can finish digging the hole then, but don't cover it up before I'm back. I'll put a cloaking spell over the body so that none of the other wolves can scent him. For all they need to know, Samuel ran away."

Her shoulders droop, but Mom at least nods as I move past her, headed toward the trees. "Where are you going?" she asks.

Without turning around, I reply, "Away."

It's time I had a moment with my wolf, without the world feeling as if it's pressing down on me.

The sun is almost setting out here, and as I walk farther from the house, I double-check the ring on my right hand, rubbing my thumb over the fire opal stone. Faint power slithers along my skin there, and I sigh contentedly. At least something is still going my way today.

Thanks to my imbued ring, I can shift with my clothes on, and they'll return to my body just as they are now as soon as I go back to my human form. I only just traded for it six months ago, and have no idea why I waited so long.

Not that I have an issue with being naked, but the inconvenience of having to either strip down with every shift or continually source new clothes was getting old.

As soon as I can sense Drake again—just the fact that I can do that now makes my stomach flip-flop—I call my wolf forward, and her energy crackles along my skin before my body feels as though it's exploding into a mixture of fur and bones that quickly snap back together, creating my second form.

She shakes out her coat, double-checking as we've grown so accustomed to that it's the dull brown we claimed as our own when I was only a pup. Well, with my mom's help.

My wolf stretches her chest and tilts her head toward the twilight sky. A deep rumble begins to build, and she lets out the most sorrowful howl that I've ever heard.

The sound has my own heart feeling as if it's been literally crushed.

But it isn't all sorrow that I sense. There's relief and hope mixed in there. The latter being the one that concerns me most.

Hope has the power to destroy us.

While we can't communicate verbally, she seems to have no problem understanding my words and my previous thought has her body stiffening and a growl reverberating from deep within.

She turns on a dime and before I know what's happening, my wolf is running back toward the house.

What do you think you're doing? I demand even though I know I won't get a response. *Stop!*

She doesn't even flinch, overpowering my command—something that doesn't happen often.

My wolf goes right for the house, but instead of going inside, she heads around the side, confusing the hell out of me.

Instead of fighting against her, I try to understand what has her acting so insane, but it isn't until she stops in front of the kitchen window and looks toward the hallway that things start to make sense.

She wants me to see what she's feeling.

How she knew that Drake would be where he is defies logic, but maybe it's just pure luck. Either way, I can't deny what she's forcing me to watch—it melts a layer of ice from around my heart.

Drake is kneeling on the ground where my father's body was, and he's using an old rag to scrub the blood from the hardwood floor. The six-and-a-half-foot-tall shifter, one who has lived in the shadows for who knows how many decades or possibly centuries, is on his hands and knees, cleaning up what I consider to be my mess.

He stops moving the brush over the ground and slowly, he looks up at me. I beg my wolf to duck, but she doesn't budge. She allows us to be caught watching, seeming to be quite proud of herself, in fact, as she lifts her head farther up.

Drake sits back on his knees, and his hands fall casually to his thick thighs, but it's his dark eyes that have me enraptured. Shadows swirl within their depths, calling me forward and begging me to allow him in, to trust him.

My wolf shivers and rumbles, thanks to the connection forming between us and this...stranger...beast of a man.

My mother's words come rushing back to me: *Don't let the past dictate your future.*

I don't know that I'm capable of that, but being locked into Drake's stare, I can almost admit that I want to try.

"Son of a biscuit!"

We hear Peter's young voice shout, and whatever trance Drake had held us in is immediately broken. My wolf runs back to the other side of the house, and we see Peter standing in the yard with the shovel at his feet and holding his chin that is dripping blood through his fingers.

Mid-run, my wolf finally relinquishes control, and I shift back to my human form without missing a beat. "What happened?" I ask as I kneel in front of my brother and start to inspect his face.

Tears fill his eyes, and he stutters. "D-d-rake told me to wait, but I th-th-thought I could do it myself. I wanted to-to-to do it."

My arms wrap around my baby brother, uncaring about the blood getting on me. "It's okay, bubby. Come with me and we'll get you all fixed up."

Drake comes skidding to a stop as I start to guide Peter toward the house where I've left my box of potions and tinctures, one of which will heal him within seconds. "I'm sorry, Spencer. I didn't realize..."

For the first time since sensing this man, I don't snap at him, nor do I want to. It's almost a relief.

"It's okay," I say to Drake. "I just need to get him inside and I can stop the bleeding."

Without hesitating, he yanks his shirt off and bunches it up, replacing my hand with the soft material. "Here you go."

Peter's tears slow, and he smiles at the imposing shifter. "Thanks."

Son of a—*biscuit.* I might be in even more trouble than I thought. At least, when it comes to Drake.

CHAPTER 6
DRAKE

Guiding Peter into the house, I can't help from noticing how Spencer keeps side-eyeing me. At first, I thought it was because she doesn't trust me with her brother, but as she stares, I realize it's not me specifically that she's focused on. It's just my chest.

Maybe she's intrigued by my tattoo that we didn't get to talk about earlier, but as she bites the inside of her cheek, I don't think so.

Spencer won't be able to fight the bond forever. Not if she's having any doubts about her previous rejection.

If there's any attraction at all on her end, the bond will undoubtedly amplify those feelings. Based on her constant glances at my muscles, I can at least be thankful the curses Kel placed on me had me frozen in time and not left withering away all these years.

My body is still that of a strong twenty-eight-year-old shifter, who spent my days strengthening my physique in hopes of one day joining Caius's guard so that I would stand a greater chance of escaping Tartarus.

"Oh, Petey," Spencer's mom calls out when we get in the house. "What did you do?"

"He was only trying to help," I answer for him. I wouldn't think after the day they've already had that the boy would get in trouble, but I'd rather be sure.

She rubs a hand over his mess of hair and takes him from Spencer. "Of course my boy was."

"I'll grab a healing tincture from the box I brought," Spencer announces, then runs off quickly.

Yeah, she doesn't seem all that thrilled with her attraction to me. Too damn bad. I'm not going anywhere.

"I'm Cara, by the way," Spencer's mother adds with a smile. "My life isn't always like this. Well, yes it was, but not any longer."

"Nice to meet you, Cara." I give her a nod and return her grin. "I'm Drake Cage."

"Yes, I've gathered." Her accompanying chuckle confuses me, but I don't get to ask what's so funny.

Spencer cuts in front of me and tends to her brother, while keeping her back to me. "You've got to be more careful, bub."

"I know. I'm sorry, Pence." His voice is quiet, but he's at least not crying any longer.

Cara steps closer to me and appraises my naked chest, but not in the way Spencer was. No, she frowns and shakes her head. "You need a new shirt. I'll be right back."

The woman goes through the kitchen and to a door past that, but quickly shuts it behind her as she slips through.

While Spencer pokes at Peter, I consider going back to cleaning up the bloody mess from the body, but I don't want to draw the boy's attention to it. Instead, I stand there with my hands in my pockets and look around at the home.

The ceilings are tall and white, helping to make it not feel as small. The furniture is all worn and stained, but everything around me is clean outside of some broken glass that also needs to be picked up.

Well, maybe not if they're all leaving.

The walls are a dull tan and free of pictures or art. Part of me wonders if that was to make sure the abusive asshole had less things to throw around.

"This is getting weird," Peter comments, breaking the silence.

"What?" Spencer responds as I watch her force his head back again.

He points at me, then his sister. "The two of you. You're making things weird. Can't you two talk to each other?"

I smirk. "That would make things better, wouldn't it?"

"I think so." Then, he winces. "Ow. Don't be mean, Pence, or I'll tell Momma."

She holds a dropper up to his chin. "I don't know what you're talking about."

The hell she doesn't.

Cara exits out of the room and once again closes the door behind her. In her hands is a black cotton shirt that she tosses to me. "This should fit, and I'm pretty sure it was never worn. Just washed."

"Thanks." I slip the clothing over my head, then wink at Peter. "Maybe she'll talk to me now."

"Probably not," he whispers back even though Spencer is still between us. "I think you really made her mad."

"One day, you'll learn—"

Spencer stands and slaps a hand over my mouth, cutting off my words. "That's enough." Then she glares back at her brother. "From both of you. Peter, go pack two bags. Whatever you can carry on your own."

The boy tiptoes between us and grins at me before he scampers off toward what I assume is his room back down the hallway.

Spencer pulls her hand away from me and turns toward her mother. "Mom, you should do the same. Is there anything out here that you want me to go through? The sooner we're gone, the better."

"Actually, I could use your help in my room," Cara says, and I take that as my cue to leave.

"I'll be outside," I add, then head for the back door.

When nobody stops me, I return to the gravesite and pick up the shovel, intent to finish the job so we can do as Spencer wants and leave this place behind.

As I start to dig the hole, I can't help thinking about what comes next. Getting my vengeance on Kel is still a priority, but I don't want to leave Spencer so soon after finding her.

Though, if I stay in Crossroads and Kel finds me...

My mate might be strong, but this witch is twisted. I don't want her somehow showing up, ruining everything.

I'll have to leave to finish the hunt I started, and if Spencer doesn't wait for me, I'll find her, too.

My teeth grind together as I continue to shovel, hating that Kel is still interfering with my life. Meeting her was the worst day of my life, and if I could go back, I would kill her at first sight.

I'd spent the first twenty-eight years of my life in Tartarus before running into Kel. Before her, I'd already been shunned by my own mother who made it very clear from the moment I was able to comprehend her words that I was unwanted. My father hadn't wanted me and, according to my mom, left her because of me. She never could let that go before disappearing around the time I turned ten.

Being alone after that had seemed safer, and it didn't take long to accept my fate. I did what I had to in order to survive, made myself a home, all while keeping to myself until *she* appeared, playing all the right cards to get my attention.

Kel claimed to have lost her memory, waking up alone and beaten one night. She'd run for days and couldn't run any longer. Or so she'd said. I'd felt sorry for her, but she'd taken my kindness for something else. For love.

She'd been relentless in her pursuits—worse than me not wanting to walk away from Spencer—showing up at my home several times a day, trying to force herself on me.

None of it worked, and after months of trying to be the nice guy, I lost my shit on her. I screamed into her face, to go away and never come back, that I didn't, and wouldn't ever, want her. Words that haunted me for years afterward given how my own mother had treated me.

Still, that hadn't given her the right to take my freedom from me. She accused me of cheating on her with another, even though we'd never been together. Hell, we hadn't even kissed.

"If I can't have you, then nobody else can either."

I remember those poisonous words like they were spoken yesterday and not over nine hundred years ago.

Right there in my yard, she'd trapped me in my own body and shielded me from sight. The few people I had made connections with would still come by, but they couldn't see me and I couldn't call out. I couldn't even move.

The only person who knew where I sat frozen was the one I had no desire to ever see again.

Kel made sure to visit with me every day. She'd put her hands on me, whisper in my ear, and at the end of every conversation, she'd ask me if I was ready to be hers.

Considering I couldn't move, I assume she felt my rage and took that as my no.

It wasn't until Caius broke through into Earth that one of the spells finally shattered. I don't know how, but I haven't questioned it a moment since.

Before I know it, I've rage-dug the hole for Spencer's father and I'm covered in dirt, but the job is done and that's all that matters.

I jump out of the six-foot-deep hole, intent to grab the body and toss him in, but Spencer is standing there, seeming as if she's been watching me for longer than I'd probably like given the unwanted trip to my past that I just took.

"Have some aggressions to take out, huh?" she muses. "I wondered if that nice guy act you've been displaying was just that. An act. I know you're the one that roared when you came through the portal. That kind of fury doesn't just go away."

She grins as if she's just caught me doing something I shouldn't be. While I'd rather her not see me angry, that's only because I believe she deserves better, not because I feel as if I need to hide who I really am.

I step toe-to-toe with her, our noses nearly touching. "Are you asking because you really want to know or because you feel as if you're better than me and are trying to make me feel less than for my actions? If it's the former, I'll gladly tell you why you might sense a layer of wrath simmering just beneath the surface."

She blinks and manages to keep her face devoid of any emotions, not even the amusement she'd just been portraying. "I only came out here to tell you..."

"What, Spencer?" I goad. "What is it that you want to say, because I'm right here and I'm not going anywhere."

Her mouth opens and closes, but no words come out. With her lips so close, I'm tempted to lean forward and taste her. Something tells me it would be worth whatever punishment she served me, but before I can make my move, she steps back.

"I'm going to go grab the cloaking spell for the body." Spencer turns on a heel and storms back inside the house, leaving me standing there watching her.

Her steps are rigid and heavy, and when she enters inside, the door slams behind her.

I'm not sure what it's going to take to win her over, but I still have time and I'm intent on making the best of it. Right after I make sure there aren't any obstacles left in our way. At least not the ones I can do something about.

Spencer's stubbornness might be a whole other story.

CHAPTER 7

SPENCER

Someone please kill me now. I think I'm going to lose my mind before the day is over, and I have no clue what to do with my rampant thoughts.

Every step I take away from Drake tugs at my heart, as if there's a tear in my chest that opens up just a little bit more every time I try to put distance between us. I'd heard the strength of a mate bond is powerful, but fuck, this is almost inconceivable.

On top of my warring emotions that I keep losing control of, my mother had to go and yell at me for being an idiot.

"Don't be a stubborn fool, Spencer. That man will burn the world to have you. If you can't see that, then you're not the woman I thought I raised."

While also informing me that a mate bond between wolves isn't out to control me. The energy of the connection is only amplifying what I truly feel, even if I'm not ready to admit it yet.

She had me with that one.

It was as if a light flicked on and I could understand what was happening around me for the first time in all too long. But then I walked outside and felt the rage rolling off Drake... No, I was nearly suffocated by it.

That had me right back at square one, believing that keeping him around isn't what is best for any of us.

Still, there's that damn tugging sensation that has my heart aching for him, and I want to strangle myself just to end the torture.

I stop in the hallway of the house and lean against the wall. Closing my eyes, I try to calm my breathing, but the moment I do, all I see are Drake's nearly black eyes. As they look back at me, I know I'm not afraid of the darkness that lies within him, it doesn't necessarily mean that he's evil like my sperm donor. But I also know that rage brings trouble, and my family has already had too much of that.

I'm not sure the connection between us that grows with every brief touch is enough to ignore why keeping him in my life could be bad.

I have little confidence that I'm going to figure this out today, so I push away from the wall and head toward the living room where I've left my bag. As I dig through the metal box of magical objects, there's a hum in the air that vibrates around me, urging me to return outside, but I don't budge from my spot until I have what I'm looking for.

Once the cloaking spell is in hand, I close the box and place it back in my bag, bringing that with me. Just because the alpha is gone from our pack right now doesn't mean nobody else will come poking around. I want to be ready to leave if they do.

When I get back outside, I take a deep inhale to prepare myself for being closer to Drake, but the action only serves to consume me with his musky scent and I shudder where I stand. Nearly a minute later, I walk further from the back door to find him standing over the grave, staring down at Samuel's body.

I peek inside once I'm close enough and grin when I find my *father* face down in the dirt. "Was that an accident or on purpose?" I ask Drake, pointing to the hole.

He shrugs. "Whatever you want it to be."

His tone has lost some of its earlier, I don't know. Luster? Persistence?

The thought of having hurt his feelings by walking away from him again makes my throat tighten and burn. I don't want him to hate me, and I don't want to feel the same about him. Maybe however this ends, it can be amicable. Though, that's only going to happen if I do as he's asked and get to know him.

"I'm sorry about before," I tell him, not really looking up. Clearly, apologies aren't my thing.

"Which before?" he asks, a bit more curiosity filling his voice. "When you walked away from me? When you rejected me? When you tried to disappear without a second thought to—"

"Can't you just consider it a blanket apology?" I interject, really wanting to add something about taking it back otherwise but manage to keep my snark to myself—mostly.

He turns toward me, and his palms cover my shoulder as his fingers squeeze tightly, seeming to be burning through the cotton of my grey tee.

I swallow and expect him to say something, but he just stares at me for what feels like an eternity.

Well, this isn't awkward at all. Where's my brother when I need him to burst in?

"Spencer," Drake finally says.

"Hmm." That's about all the reply I can muster with his hands still on me.

"You feel the bond," he states confidently. "How it grows stronger the longer and more we touch."

My head nods as I allow myself this moment to get lost in the depths of his eyes that don't actually look black now that I'm closer. They're more of a charcoal with hints of silver that appear so briefly that I could be imagining them.

"I think you're unlocking my wolf," he adds, his voice barely a whisper, but the words snap me out of whatever stupor I gave in to.

"I'm what now?" I must have missed something before because that doesn't make any sense.

"When I was in Tart—"

"I'm all packed!" Peter shouts from behind us, choosing now to interrupt. Of course.

My attention goes back to Drake, and I point a finger at him. "We're going to finish this conversation."

His hands release me, and he takes a step back. "I certainly hope so."

Turning around, I stop my brother before he can get too close. "Go help Momma with her bags and then we'll finish up here."

He pouts, but does as I ask, thankfully. I don't want him to see the body face down. He can still love our father if he wants to or choose to remember him however helps moving forward.

Opening the cloaking spell, I pour the pale pink liquid over the grave and throw the bottle in once I'm done. Drake already has the shovel in his hands and begins to cover the corpse as soon as I move out of his way.

My eyes watch as he bends forward, scoops the dirt, and tosses it back where it came from. The muscles in his back ripple from the increased efforts. Sweat drips down his forehead as he moves quicker, but he doesn't rest for a moment until he comes to an abrupt stop.

His forearm wipes over his face before he turns toward me. "Peter should finish the rest."

I almost tell him no, but I'm beginning to see that I might not know my baby brother as well as I once did, and I'm not his mother. I don't get to decide what's best for him.

"He can if he'd like," I say, then realize Peter and Mom should have been out here already. "I'm going to go check on them."

Drake catches my wrist, and I pause. His touch warms my skin beneath his fingers and spreads up my arm, straight to my chest where it starts to pool.

When I look up at him, I catch more of those silver flecks within the darkness. "Don't leave without me," he says as a plea instead of a demand, his stare observing every inch of my face.

"I won't." And for the first time since meeting him earlier today, I don't intend to run from him.

Damn it. I hope I don't regret this.

Just as I start to pull away, I hear the back door open, and Peter's complaints about how heavy the bags are.

Drake's appraisal of me is broken, and I go to help with their items. When I take my brother's suitcase, I nearly drop it, not expecting it to actually be heavy.

"What the hell did you pack, bub?" I demand, gripping the handle tighter.

Mom frowns. "Rocks."

"Rocks?" I ask and she nods before I look down at Peter. "Why?"

He merely shrugs. "They're shiny."

Right. Well, after the day we've all had, I'm not going to argue over rocks. "Anything else inside that we need to grab?"

Mom shakes her head. "Nothing of consequence."

The devastation in her voice slices at my chest. She's leaving behind the place she's called home for nearly thirty years. Memories—good and bad—lie within the walls behind us, and I hate that I've been selfish in my demands.

My mother truly has sacrificed far more than I ever realized until today.

"Do you need help, Drake?" I hear Peter ask, then fight a smile at Drake's reply.

The imposing shifter groans as he rubs his palms together. "I do. These hands aren't what they used to be, and you're just the young man to take over."

Peter drops his other bag and runs to pick up the shovel, eager to get right to work. "I promise not to bleed on the handle again."

"You'll be just fine, my boy." Mom's face softens as she watches on from several feet back, a few stray tears leaking down her cheeks.

I go to her side and wrap an arm around her, leaning my head on her shoulder. "I love you, Mom."

Her hand covers mine. "I love you more than the moon and stars."

We wait and watch together, holding on to one another unlike we've been able to do in over three years. Her warmth fills me with a strength I'd nearly forgotten I possess.

Not that of being able to take care of myself, but a reminder that strength comes from love and perseverance. Something my mother has always offered our family in spades.

As soon as the grave is finished being flattened out, Peter and Drake begin collecting leaves and branches to cover the disturbed ground. While they do that, my mom steps away from my side and bends next to the burial.

Her fingers press into the earth, and she bows her head, closing her eyes. I assume she's saying her final goodbyes to her mate, but it's not my business to ask. I let her have this moment, one she deserves and that I have no right interrupting—regardless of how much I despised Samuel.

Giving her a few minutes alone, I go farther into the trees to find Peter. "Want some help, bub?"

His arms are full of twigs with random leaves stuffed between them. "I've got it."

I catch his stare landing on Drake, and I shake my head before whispering, "Accepting help is a sign of strength, not weakness."

He slowly brings his attention back to me, a frown between his eyes. "I know."

Hmm, seems my little brother may have gotten my stubbornness, regardless of all our time apart.

"I think we have enough," Drake announces, and the relief on Peter's face is undeniable as he runs toward the grave with his haul.

Mom is standing up again when I go back, and she watches as Peter disguises the upturned dirt.

"Got it," he announces proudly as he puts the last stick into place. He, too, bends down like our mother, but unlike her, he doesn't keep his thoughts to himself. "I hope you can be happy now, Dad. We're going to be just fine with Pence. She'll keep us safe."

Emotions burn at my throat, but I don't shed a tear. I refuse to cry at this man's gravesite. Not even if the tears wouldn't be for him.

Instead, I distract myself with getting another portal spell, then realize I have no clue where we're going to go. I have two extra people with me now. Two of the most important people in my life. I can't just take them anywhere.

Mom's hand cups my elbow, and she quietly says, "Take me to your home."

I look over at her, my lips downturned. "I don't have one."

Her responding smile only furthers my confusion. "Yes, you

do. In Crossroads. That's where we're supposed to be right now." She looks at Peter and Drake, then back at me. "All of us."

There isn't a part of me that wants to deny her, so I don't bother. "Crossroads it is, then."

Her eyes spark with love, and I return her smile as I get the portal opened.

Drake and Peter come closer, each one reaching for me. Peter and Mom both have one of my hands as I step forward, but it's Drake's hold on my shoulder that I feel the most, that weighs as if the world is balancing right there between the two of us.

Maybe not the entire world, but quite possibly mine.

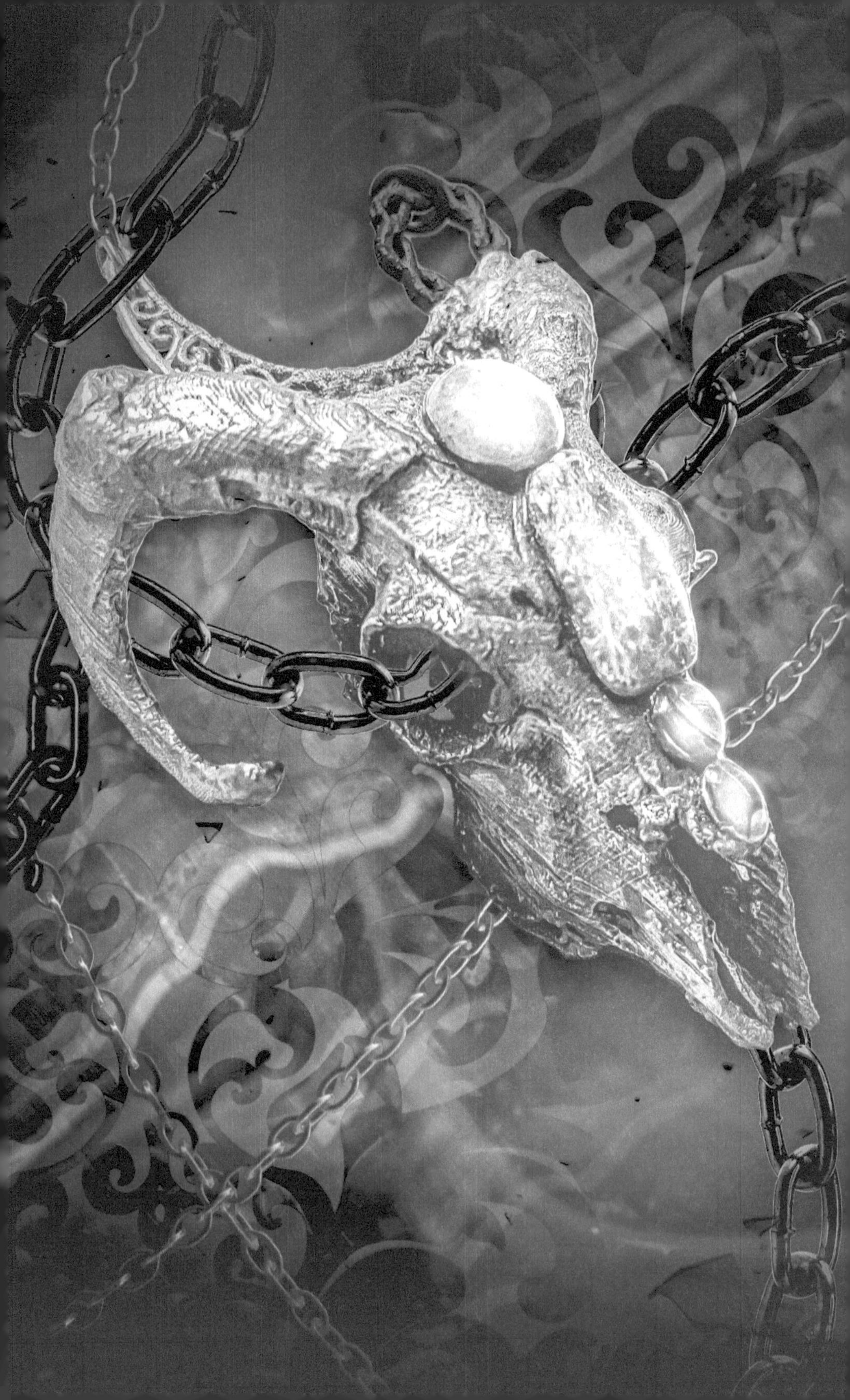

CHAPTER 8
DRAKE

Arriving back in Crossroads immediately has me on edge again. The energy of Tartarus is ever present in this town. Not heavy enough to feel weighed down by, but there's a lingering sensation that makes my skin prickle even this far from the portal as we arrive back at the house I followed Spencer to earlier.

Her mom looks up at the modest home beside us, smiling. "This is where you've been living?"

Spencer's lips turn down. "No. I'm in this one. Though, I'll have to fix that today, because it only fits one single mattress."

We all turn to find the shed I thought was where she just kept some of her things.

"*That's* where you've been living?" her mother asks before I can, and we both seem equally eager for the answer.

"It's temporary," Spencer replies, avoiding eye contact and heading inside. "I had plans to build a home before we were all together again."

My mate doesn't say it, but she's embarrassed. A fact that I want to do something about, but I don't know her well enough to do so yet.

"I think it's cool," Peter announces, following his sister. "Your own hideout. I've always wanted one."

"Right," Spencer mutters, bending down and digging through her bag.

I glance back at the grey house behind me and peer at the windows, but I don't sense anyone inside. "Who lives there?" I ask.

Spencer doesn't answer me, and it's the deepening frown on her mother's face that keeps me from pressing for an answer and addressing Cara instead. "What's wrong?"

She seems to snap out of whatever moment she'd been lost in as she smiles up at me. "Oh, nothing at all."

Spencer finally turns back to the rest of us but talks directly to her mother. "I need you and Peter to stay in this shed. I'm going to place a cloaking spell around it once I shut the door, and then I need to go see someone. When I get back, we're going to get out of here. If there's anywhere you've ever wanted to go, think hard about it, because we need to move."

"Why?" I demand, the annoyance that she doesn't seem to also be speaking to me gets the better of me.

Spencer finally looks up at me and shakes her head. "Because this isn't my home."

She ushers her family into the shed with few words shared between them, then pours the cloaking spell around the exterior of the wooden structure.

When she tries to brush past me, I reach for her arm, halting her movements. "Where are you going?"

"I need to go see a witch about some trade items," she tells me, and I don't know why, but the moment she looks up at me, I can no longer control my actions.

Heat builds where my palm is wrapped around her forearm. From there, it spreads up my arm and toward my chest. The moment the energy begins to pulse through my veins, I lose all conscious thought.

I step forward, closing the space between the two of us, and my other hand reaches up to cup Spencer's cheek. She flinches but doesn't back away, and before I can think too hard about my actions, my lips are pressed against hers.

Her mouth is soft against mine, melding to me unlike anything I've ever experienced. The desire to taste her grows stronger by the lingering seconds, ones that seem to pass so slowly, it's almost as if time stands still.

My tongue slips between the crease of her mouth, and an explosion of power ignites within me, burning at my chest until I'm certain that I might explode, but before that can happen, Spencer's fist becomes well acquainted with my jaw.

"What the fuck?" she practically growls.

What the fuck, indeed.

I rub the tips of my fingers over my heart where my wolf is caged. The actual heat I feel there causes a crease to deepen between my brows.

Spencer's voice lowers, and she steps closer to me, but this time I don't dare touch her. "Don't you ever fucking do that again."

My mouth twitches as I fight a smile. Oh, I definitely will be, but next time, she'll be desperate for my kiss.

"What's wrong, Spencer?" I taunt, no longer holding back my grin. "Have I just reminded that cold heart of yours what it's like to feel?"

"I *feel* plenty," she spews, but loses some of her earlier venom as she adds, "Just not for you."

My eyes openly move over her face, then quickly down her

body before going back to her hardened stare. "You can keep lying to yourself, but we both know you could have stopped that kiss before I even touched your lips."

She opens her mouth, but no words come out. Instead, she shoves me, and when I move to follow, she swivels back around, causing me to slam into her.

My hands instinctively grab her arms to stop her from falling over, and the sneer she sends my way has me shaking my head. "You're the one that stopped abruptly."

She pushes me back as she rights herself. "I was going to tell you that I'm... Never mind. I can't do this right now. I have other things to worry about first."

Spencer tries to walk away from me again, but this time I side-step her and move into her path. "What were you going to say?"

Her piercing blue eyes bore into me, and my heart swells just from the single look, even if she's still trying to hide her emotions from me.

"I was going to tell you that I'm sorry for," her hand waves between us, "whatever this tension is. I don't want to fight with you. I just want to keep my family safe. And the more we argue, the further I get from those goals. Maybe it's better if we just part ways now."

She wants to be done with me? Yeah, I don't believe that for a second, not with the way her voice cracks at the end. She's fighting a battle with herself over this bond, but I'm not willing to sit by and let the wrong choice win. There have been moments throughout the day when I've seen her question her stubbornness, a look in her eyes that doesn't match the tone of her words, and that's all the hope I need to continue with my persistence.

"Keep telling yourself that, Little Dove." I bump the underside of her chin with two fingers.

Her head jerks away from my touch as she huffs, seeming to

fight a glimmer of a smile. "You're insufferable and, as I've already said, my name is *Spencer*. Not mate or little...Dove."

The way she chokes on that last word makes me grin.

"Oh, I'm fully aware," I say as she walks away, giving me her back and a view I quite enjoy of her ass in the worn jeans that sculpt her lower half.

Spencer might not be full of peace, but she is my hope for something more than the hate I've been filled with for centuries.

My hope and light, thanks to her alabaster skin and her nearly white hair that flows behind her like the wings of the bird I've just deemed her.

CHAPTER 9
SPENCER

One moment I want to give this man a chance—at least enough to understand him—and the next I want to scream in his face, doing whatever I can to get him to walk away now.

Mostly because he's right.

I saw his intent to kiss me coming from a mile away. Worse, I anticipated it, craved the touch of this man, wondered if... My head shakes. Damn it, what is wrong with me?

My wolf hums inside me, reminding me that there isn't anything *wrong*. It's this bond. One I don't want to want.

If he'd just be a raging asshole, everything would be so much easier.

With Drake following right behind me, I make my way to Spells. I need to see Natalia and make my final deal with the witch.

"Where are we going?" Drake asks, matching my pace, but staying just a step behind me.

"*I'm* going to see a witch. Like I said before."

He chuckles. “Are you always so pent up and rude, or are you trying extra hard just for me?”

His question makes me misstep, but I catch my footing before I can stumble.

Stupid, insightful male.

“This is who I am,” I say, and the lie threatens to strangle me. I certainly don’t want to be this person. “If you don’t like it, you’re welcome to turn around and walk away.”

Drake leans forward and whispers in my ear, “If I did that, you’d hate every step of distance I took. Even if you’re too stubborn to admit it out loud.”

For the rest of the walk to Spells, I remain silent. Have I gone past the point of ridiculousness? Quite possibly, but this was all thrusted on me moments before my little brother had to kill our father. Emotions are high, and I’m floundering within their beating waves, doing my best to survive. It doesn’t help that I’ve been taught to keep people at a distance for my own protection all my life. I can’t help that being defensive is my go-to when I feel backed into a corner, alone, overwhelmed, all of the above.

When I open the door to Natalia’s shop, the songbird lets out its normal tune, but for once, doesn’t cause me to wince.

“How enchanting,” Drake muses as he glances up at the bird. Of course, he likes the damn sound.

Natalia waltzes into the front of the shop, her eyes bright with magic as if she’d just been in the middle of a spell. “Spencer, twice in one day.” Her stare flicks briefly to Drake. “And you’ve brought a friend. I’m not sure whether to feel lucky or to be concerned.”

“We need to make our last trade, Natalia,” I say, ignoring her musings. “I’m leaving Crossroads.”

The fall of her shoulders matches the down turning of her lips. “I hoped we’d have more time.”

Yeah, so did I.

"Well, things changed," I reach for a notepad and pen on the counter. "I need all of these things, and you can take whatever you need from me as payment. Just remember, I know how much all this is worth."

Natalia has never been greedy in our deals, but I can't help throwing out the warning. Except when I'm done making my list, it isn't me she's staring at any longer, it's Drake.

As I slide the paper toward her, she finally gives me her attention, but not completely as she skims my demands. "I don't have all this on hand, and it's a lot of magic that I'll need to use to conjure today."

She's bargaining. I guess I thought too soon.

"What do you want, Natalia?" I growl, letting my sour mood bleed through my words. "Today isn't the day to play games with me."

The witch points at Drake, who has remained tense behind me. "He's from Tartarus. I want his blood, too. Could be interesting."

"He's not—"

"I'll do it."

My head whips back around to Drake. "This isn't your problem."

He leans in closer, making me freeze in place. "You are my mate. I *will* help you."

His gruff tone leaves no room for argument, and to be honest, I don't want to argue. My family needs this stuff to help us disappear, and if Drake wants to help, I'm done fighting him.

I have to be for my own sanity. Though, in what ways remains to be seen.

"Fine," I say, then turn back to Natalia. "When can you have everything ready?"

"It's already late, but I can get this ready by morning," she replies, still eyeing Drake. "I want his part of the trade as upfront payment. You know, in case you skip town before the exchange has been made."

My teeth grind together. I'm tempted to tell her no, but I'm not stupid. I realize that in this situation, I need Natalia more than she does me. There's no convincing her otherwise after having admitted that this is our last deal.

And of course, Drake doesn't seem to mind.

He steps beside me and holds his arm over the counter before glancing at me. "Can I trust you to tell me when she has enough?"

For a brief moment, as we stare into each other's gazes, I want to reach up and press my hand to his heart, to promise him that he's not in any danger. Except that's not what I do.

I merely nod and force my gaze away from him, consumed with the emotions swirling inside me. The less I mentally resist Drake's presence, the more relentless they become.

This man. I knew the moment I heard his roar coming through the portal that he was going to be trouble. I just didn't realize how profoundly I would be affected by him.

For years, I've kept myself safe, had a plan, and stayed on a certain path as much as I've been able to while living as a Houseless supernatural.

Now, it's been less than twelve hours since Drake Cage stumbled into my life, and I have no clue where I'm headed to next.

My mother's earlier words continue to whisper through my mind. *I believe the fates were waiting for him.*

They hold a truth I can't deny, even though I've tried to more than once since she spoke them.

While Drake gives his blood, he's paying more attention to Natalia than me for once, and I allow myself to take in his tall form. His cheeks and chin are covered with a dark stubble. Faint scars in the shape of thin lines appear on his skin every so often while his pulse beats three times as fast as the rise and fall of his muscled chest.

My heart swells and tenses all at once. Tiny fragments beg me to care for this man, but the shattered pieces inside me no longer fit together. Not after being beaten by my own blood, for having to hide who I truly am, for being banished from my only home and forced to do things I never dreamed of in order to survive.

I shiver as past memories threaten to come back, and the action draws Drake's attention. He catches me staring, but I don't turn away. Instead, I allow myself a moment to pretend nothing is wrong. That he's just a normal shifter and accepting him could be as easy as breathing.

He blinks first, a furrow forming between his dark brows, and that's all it takes for me to return to reality.

Well, my reality. The one I've created to keep myself safe since being on my own.

"Are you okay?" he asks softly, but instead of answering him, I turn toward Natalia.

"That's enough."

The witch reaches for a jar and swipes some oil over his wrist as she speaks. "I know, Spencer. I won't break your trust, even if it's our last trade."

She never has, and she deserves better than my shitty attitude. "Thank you. For everything. Text me when you're done and I'll be here, no matter the time."

She smiles wide and picks Drake's blood up from the counter. "See you soon."

Drake is right behind me as we head for the front door, following so closely I can feel the natural heat that seems to radiate from him.

I'm tempted to ask for space, but I keep my mouth closed as

we get outside. Though, I come to an abrupt halt when I realize the songbird didn't sound the second that I opened the door.

Interesting, but doesn't really matter. Soon, that pesky creature will be a distant memory when we leave this place behind.

Drake is stopped right behind me. "Do you sense something?"

"No," I reply, keeping my tone as light as I'm capable of. "I just want to get back to the house."

He stops at my side, and I can see his smirk. "Then, *let's* go."

His persistence is going to be the death of me, but I have to admit, things could be worse as far as Drake is concerned.

Without realizing what I'm doing, I grab Drake's wrist to lead him down the alleyway behind Spells. I could have just let him follow, but instinct has me reaching for him, and it's several seconds later that I pull my hand back, settling it in front of me.

He continues to follow without commenting or questioning the different path we're taking, but I can sense his tension and I snort. Maybe he's wondering if I'm taking him to a dark corner to dispose of his body.

I'm a lot of things, but a murderer isn't one of them. I choose to think of myself as a survivor instead. When I've had to kill in the past, it hasn't been because I've wanted to, that's for damn sure.

We pass a stretch of old buildings and approach a few rundown structures. This way, there are no streetlights, and I normally keep to the more populated areas, but this is the quicker way back to Kasha's.

The moon is at least exposed and not covered by clouds. It's full and shining brightly, lighting the path we're taking. Before we're halfway to the house, Drake grabs my wrist and halts my forward momentum.

"What are we doing, Spencer?" he asks, and I'm oddly disappointed that he didn't use "Dove." Though, I don't let myself ponder why that might be.

When we're facing each other, I almost ask him if he means what we're doing right this moment or if he's referencing the elephant in the room also known as our mate bond. One look into his pleading eyes and I have my answer.

The mixed emotions inside me don't seem so conflicted here alone with him under the night sky, so much so that I have to look away from him. The intensity of our connection fills me in a way nothing else ever has, and I don't know what I'm supposed to do or say.

Except the imposing wolf shifter doesn't allow me even the slightest reprieve from his presence. He lifts my chin with his fingers, forcing me to look at him as he says, "You can tell me anything."

Those five words pierce through my skin and right into my heart, making my stomach churn with the weight of their truth.

Gods, what is wrong with me? I'd be a fool to deny this man, to pretend that everything he's shown me and made me feel are anything other than sincere and filled with pure intentions.

It hasn't even been a full day, but I know if I don't say my next words, I'm only harming myself. I'm so damn tired of fighting.

"I take back my rejection." The moment I finish the sentence, a rush of energy pours over me, pushing down on my shoulders and nearly taking me to my knees. Hell, I might have fallen right at his feet if he didn't grab me, pulling me against his chest.

Drake breathes me in as I'm consumed, little by little, by his tight embrace. "Oh, Little Dove. You have no idea what you've just done."

His words are spoken with a rumble in his chest that a lesser woman might be afraid of, but not me. I lean into his touch and hope like hell that his strength is going to be the very thing that saves the lives of those I love most in the world.

"There's something that I need to do first," he says, surprising me with his dark tone. After all his persistence, I expected him to be more thrilled about my newest revelation.

"What could be more important than your mate?" My walls are instantly back up, believing I've somehow been duped as he starts to shake his head, attempting to hold me again.

"No," I snap, breaking free from his touch. "You don't get to practically beg for my acceptance and then tell me I have to wait once I give in."

I'm close to walking away before I do something I might regret, but the anguish pulsing off Drake keeps me in place and forces me to pay closer attention. I took my rejection back for a reason. Overreacting now isn't going to help anyone.

"You don't know what I've been through for the last thousand years," he says with a hurt in his voice that lashes out at my own chest.

Holy shit, he's old, but I don't focus on that tidbit of information for long. Especially not when he doesn't even appear to be in his thirties, but more than that, the need to apologize to him is nearly overwhelming.

"You're right," I say sincerely. "I'm sorry for not giving you a chance to explain yourself or for continuing our earlier conversation. Neither of us asked for this, but that doesn't mean we can't work together to figure things out. What is this something that you need to do?"

As I finish speaking, I don't hear anything Drake might be saying next. I'm held hostage by the renewed flood of emotions within me. Feelings I can assume a normal shifter might have been consumed with the moment they first laid eyes on their mate, but life dealt me a different hand. Mine had required me to be anything other than soft, to not care for anyone other than my mother and brother.

With every new breath I take, the bond between Drake and me begins to turn into something tangible, something I don't know that I can handle, but that I no longer want to let go of. Especially when I finally hear a fraction of what he's saying.

"...she kept me trapped and tortured me for over nine hundred years."

Knowing that someone hurt my mate, tormented him even—now that makes me a little murderous. Something I don't expect, but also don't hate.

"Who hurt you?" I demand with a conviction that seems to take us both by surprise, and the moment he ensnares me in his gaze, I hope like hell that I've just made the best decision in my life and not the worst one.

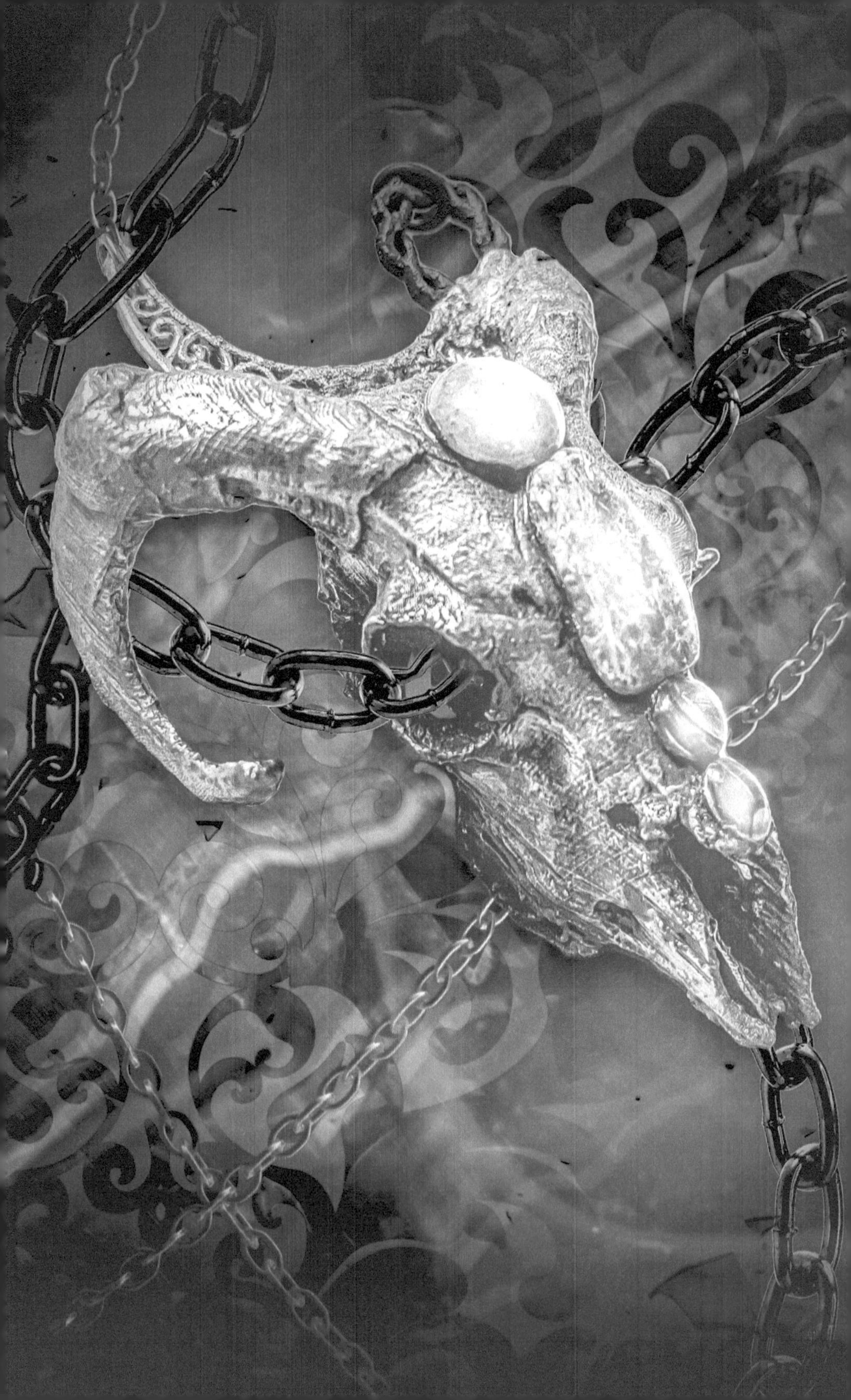

CHAPTER 10

DRAKE

The moment Spencer took back her rejection, it was as if I could finally breathe for the first time in my life. At least for a few seconds, then I remembered the witch that will continue to stand in my way of true happiness until I've ended her life.

I hadn't expected Spencer to take back her rejection so soon. Obviously, I'd hoped, but for the words to actually leave her mouth when I was still certain she'd remain stubborn—that's something else entirely.

"I've mentioned briefly about my bound wolf, but I haven't told you how he became that way," I tell her, standing just outside a grassy area behind the buildings on our right.

"What do you mean?" she asks, head tilted and eyes narrowed. "Bound how?"

She must have been more distracted than I realized when I was just speaking.

"I turned down a witch named Kel, and she apparently wasn't pleased with being told no," I say. "She put a curse on me that kept me trapped inside my own mind for nearly one thousand years. It didn't break until Caius broke through to Earth, but she must have used two different spells because my wolf is still chained inside me."

I lift my shirt over my head to show her the actual chains surrounding my wolf tattoo. One that hadn't been there before I met Kel. Though, the moment it's exposed I realize it's changed.

The chains that are drawn around my snarling wolf have begun to unravel. Not entirely, but he's not as bound as he used to be.

Shit, even a few of the links are cracking. My fingers press over the black ink, and the same warmth I felt earlier returns, but I still don't sense my inner beast.

Spencer steps forward, her hand raised. "*This* is your wolf?"

"A representation of him, yes." I reach for her and bring her palm closer, curious if physical contact from our mate is what has made the changes I'm seeing, or if it's just being so far from Kel.

Spencer's hand carefully settles over my chest, and her fingers splay out over the tattoo. Less than a second later, a glow from beneath her touch begins to grow. It's faint, but I know I'm not just seeing things because Spencer gasps, pressing harder against me.

"Am I doing that?" she asks, her voice barely a whisper.

"I wasn't sure before, but I believe so," I say just as reverently. "You're breaking my wolf free."

"Where is this Kel now?" she asks. Gone is the admiration she just spoke with, replaced with a rage I myself have lived with for far too long.

When her eyes move from my tattoo to my face, I can also see the flicker of wrath within their depths. A hint of jealousy that elates a part of me, knowing this woman is beginning to care for me with such intensity.

"I don't know, but I followed her scent to the portal and confirmed with the guards that she came through," I say. "Wherever she is, I'll find her and make sure she can't ever hurt you."

Spencer laughs, but it's not a joyous sound. "Hurt me? That's not even a thought that crossed my mind. When was the last time you saw her? Do you have a picture of her or something of hers that we can track?"

The way her words come out with a growl has me enthralled. I never thought a woman could fascinate me as Spencer has, but for the first time in my existence, I'm beguiled. I want to know everything there is to learn about my mate. Every nuance, every curve on her body, the things that make her lips tilt upward, and those that do the opposite.

Except her tapping foot tells me that those things will have to wait.

"The last time I saw Kel was in Tartarus," I say, answering her first question. "She had moved into my house and kept me frozen in place outside. I saw her leave one day, and it was over a month before the part of her spell that kept my body contained broke. I can only assume that was when she went to Earth. I followed after, but it took me weeks to get across the islands to the castle, and then I had to wait to be interviewed before being allowed in."

"No wonder you were so pissed off when you came through that portal." She smirks, and the look has a smile growing on my face as I cup her cheek.

"But you took all that rage away the moment I saw you." My breathing becomes ragged, and I'm tempted to kiss her again, but her next words take away my opportunity.

"Well, it hasn't taken away mine," she says with a growl. "We need to find her and set your wolf free." She pauses, her eyes roaming over my still exposed tattoo as she frowns. "He shouldn't be trapped."

The way she says the words with such conviction and allows her stare to linger over the black ink, I start to wonder. "Can you sense him?"

Briefly, her lips flatten. "Maybe? There are flickers of something that I thought was just the bond, but when I touched the marks there, I not only felt the heat of the energy between us, but there was also a coldness, a hollowness that threatens to..."

She looks away and doesn't finish her sentence. I can only guess what she might be thinking, but I don't ask her to elaborate. She's already given me more today than I expected for weeks to come.

"I will find her and make sure she can't hurt you or your family," I promise. "Nobody will hurt you because of me, Spencer. *Nobody*."

Her head lifts, and she meets my steady gaze. "*We* will find that witch. I'm going with you."

"What about your mother and brother?" I ask, hoping they'll be enough reason to keep her away from this mess. I don't want Spencer anywhere near Kel. Not when I'm unsure what the witch may be capable of here on Earth.

"I've been safe here for months," Spencer says confidently. "I can ask Kasha or Natalia to keep an eye on them. They'll be fine as long as the witch doesn't come here, tracking your scent."

"And if she does and we're nowhere near your family?" I ask. It's a reality I've already thought about myself when it comes to Spencer and has given me pause on leaving at all.

Vengeance isn't worth having if I lose everything else in the process.

Spencer seems to consider my words while also being distracted by the wolf on my chest. I slip my shirt back on and hold her cheeks within my hands, forcing her eyes to focus on me. "We don't know each other, but if you believe nothing else, then know that I can handle Kel on my own. Stay here, protect your family, and wait for me."

Her head shakes within my palms, and she jerks out of my hold. "No. I mean, you're right, we don't know each other, which is why you're also wrong. I didn't just let you in to be left behind." Her hand gestures between the two of us. "Your rage, it's like my own, building with every passing second. I won't stand by and do nothing. You didn't let me deal with my father on my own. This witch is nothing different."

I hate to admit that she's right, but she is, and if I'm being honest with myself, I don't want to leave her behind. Not when I've only just found her.

Nearly a thousand years of living alone in my own head, trapped in my body as Kel convinced everyone I had a broken mind, a shifter who couldn't control his inner beast, making sure no one went looking for me. Not a single person I'd gotten to know over the years had questioned her, thanks to the magic she wielded. As the years turned to centuries, my home was no longer mine, but Kel's, and nobody ever spoke of me again.

"Okay," I say. While I know she may think it's for her benefit, I'm fully aware that my decision is selfish. "We'll stick together. Whether that's here or out there."

She pauses, almost as if she doesn't believe me, but finally nods. "Good. Now, let's go check on my family."

Her hand flinches, almost as if she's going to reach out for me, but then decides not to. When she turns and gives me her back, I chuckle to myself. At least this interaction felt more like two steps forward and only one back.

Lengthening my stride, I'm at her side before she can get far. I lean in toward her and brush her hair out of the way before whispering into her ear. "You're mine, Little Dove."

There's a hitch in her breath, but that's the only sign she gives that my words have their desired effect. Outside of that, her speed picks up and I keep pace with her.

We get to another street, and across from it, I notice an arch that stands probably over five hundred feet into the skyline. It seems to serve no purpose, cracked and covered in dead vines, but I'm sure at one point, people marveled at its size.

"What the hell?" Spencer mutters, bringing my attention to right in front of us instead of lingering at our surroundings.

Two beings stand before us. One man, another wolf shifter, and a woman whose identity I can't seem to suss out, but she's some sort of shifter. I think.

She stares at Spencer with turquoise eyes that are shadowed by dark blue hair falling around her face. "You're interesting," she says first, speaking to my mate.

Spencer smirks and crosses her arms. "I could say the same about you."

"Yes, you could." The woman winks and stands a little straighter. "I didn't come here for you, but now that I have. Her eyes close briefly and the man with her stiffens at her side, wrapping an arm around her and whispering in her ear so low that even my wolf hearing can't hear his words clearly.

When I reach for Spencer, ready to get out of here, she's already walking toward the strangers. Instantly, I'm on alert and sizing up the man. He's tall, but still several inches shorter than me. His blue eyes flick between me and my mate as he rubs his jaw, a ring with a red stone at the center glinting under the moonlight above.

"Spencer," I warn her, but she isn't listening to me.

She seems to wait for the woman to reopen her eyes, and when they greet each other, Spencer tilts her head. "What are you?"

"Again, I could ask you the same thing," the woman says with a chuckle. "I'm Lia. This is my mate, Markus. We were just checking out the area after..."

"Curious about the portal?" Spencer asks, keeping her tone light.

"Something like that," Lia replies. "The two of you are headed somewhere."

The way she says the words so confidently has me on edge. "Just out for a walk."

I don't mean to snarl, but after all Spencer has said, I don't know who we can trust here, and the man Markus is too tense for my liking.

"Come any closer and I will tear your head from your shoulders," he practically growls at me, then turns his attention to Spencer. "Both of you."

Lia moves and stands in front of her mate, temporarily giving us her back. They seem to be having a silent conversation, and I use that as an opportunity to grab Spencer's arms. "Let's get out of here."

"Hmm, I'm curious," she tells me before I drag her anywhere. "Let's hear what she has to say."

"How do you know she has anything to say?" I ask, keeping my eyes locked on the couple.

Spencer shrugs and watches alongside me. Finally, the unknown woman gives us her attention again. "You're headed somewhere," she repeats. "You'll want to go North, but not too far. Maybe just a couple hours and then wait there before coming back. You'll need," she counts on her fingers, "three portal spells. Don't travel through normal means. You'll only find more trouble."

We both open our mouths to speak, but she cuts in with another laugh. "Oh, and Spencer? Try trusting those around you. Not everyone in the world is out to kill you. Once you quit running, you just might find that you've attracted all the right people into your life. Not just the wrong ones as you've been assuming."

"Who the hell are you?" Spencer demands, finally with the appropriate amount of suspicion. She steps forward, stance wide and arms loose at her sides.

"Don't fret. I assure you, I'm a friend," Lia replies with a wide smile I can almost believe is sincere. "But I know you're really asking *what* I am. I'm just another unique shifter who prefers not to be known. Something you're all too familiar with."

I expect Spencer to pop off with something rude or defensive, but instead, she surprises me for the second time tonight. Though, Lia's words have me even more intrigued. What about my mate is so unique that I haven't figured out yet?

"Thanks for the heads up," Spencer says. "What are you really looking for? Maybe I can help you find it."

Lia and Markus share another look, but this time, they're both grinning. "We're good on our own," the latter replies.

They turn and walk away without so much as another glance, giving us their backs as if we're not a threat.

"Today has been fucking crazy," Spencer says with a heavy sigh. I almost disagree with her, because I know one day, when I look back on this time, I won't remember most of this bullshit.

I'll only remember Spencer.

CHAPTER 11

SPENCER

I'm beyond ready for bed, but I know my day isn't even close to over. I need to check on Mom and Peter, then chat with Kasha. Asking her to take care of my family isn't something I foresaw myself doing, but she's offered to help enough that it's time I took her up on the offer.

Between the story Drake shared with me and what Lia, the unknown shifter, just said, I know we need to go after this witch. I can't exactly say why I trust Lia, but there was something in her eyes that gave my skin goosebumps and instantly put me at ease. As if she was a long-lost friend and could do no harm. Not only me, but my wolf as well.

While normally that would have made me run in the opposite direction, today has been full of things I couldn't have predicted. I'm trying to accept that sometimes it's better to just let things happen instead of trying to command them.

I have spent too many months—years, really—keeping everyone at bay because of what I've been told. It's time I stop listening to others and learn how to trust my gut. Not that I think my mother was wrong in warning me about others knowing about my wolf, but I'm starting to see I used her words as a crutch.

That time is over.

"Are you sure you want to take back the rejection?" Drake asks when we're only a block from Kasha's, taking me by surprise.

My head whips up toward him. "What? Why do you ask that?"

He shrugs and shoves his hands in his pockets. "You haven't really said much since we walked away from those shifters. Just wondering if you're having second thoughts."

My head shakes before he's even done speaking, and the desire to soothe any doubts that I've put in his head nearly overwhelms me. "Sorry, just a lot on my mind. I don't regret taking it back earlier, and I'm still sorry for my harshly spoken words."

He stops and reaches for my hand. "I took you by surprise. I understand why you tried to run."

"Yet, you're not sorry for refusing to let me get away," I say with a chuckle, very tempted to find out what kissing him will be like when I'm fully accepting of his touch.

"Not even a—"

We both turn as a burst of magic appears behind us, and it's almost adorable how he tries to move in front of me as if I need protection. While sweet, he's going to need to learn that he can be my mate, but I'm my own heroine.

Plus, this new arrival isn't a threat.

"Natalia," I say with slight suspicion. "I thought we wouldn't see you until morning."

Her stare is wide and bright as she glances around, then throws a velvet bag at Drake. "You need to leave here and never come back."

"What the fuck are you talking about?" I demand. I've never

seen her all twitchy and with her head on a swivel before, and I don't particularly like it.

"His blood," she whispers. "He's been marked, and I won't have that kind of dark magic in my home. Not anywhere in Crossroads." She looks at him again and glares. "*Maudit.*"

The witch says the singular word with a French accent I've also never heard her use.

"What does that mean?" I ask, glancing between Natalia and Drake because he doesn't seem all that surprised by her reaction to him.

"He is cursed," she says reverently. "Destruction will follow him before great death, and I won't have that here. Not when we've spent years making Crossroads the safe haven so many of us need." She unclips another bag from her side and tosses it at me. "Here is what you've asked for. I don't need anything else from you. Just get him the hell out of our town."

Natalia disappears before I can ask any other questions, so I'm left hoping Drake is going to be more forthcoming.

"What the hell is she talking about?" I ask him the moment we're alone.

His mouth downturns. "I don't know exactly, but I'm also not surprised. Kel kept me contained for years just because she could. She could have killed me, but the thrill she got out of torturing told me all I needed to know about her."

"So, you have no idea how you've been marked and why Natalia thinks you're the epitome of destruction?" This isn't making any sense, but I also want to have patience with Drake. Taking into account the little he has told me already, this isn't his fault. He came here trying to fix things before I got in his way.

His fingers rub over his shirt, right above where I know his tattoo to be. "This could be the mark she's talking about. I always just assumed it was a symbol used to keep my wolf chained, but maybe I've been wrong. The destruction piece makes no sense at all."

"Obviously the destruction is going to be us tearing that witch bitch to shreds," I say with a huff. "We need to get back to my family. All of this just became a lot more complicated, and I need to know they're safe."

I start to walk away, and he grabs my wrist, halting my movements as heat runs up my arm. "I won't let anything happen to them or you. You know that, right?"

My first thought is to tell him no, because I don't know him, but I also don't think he's lying. I believe that Drake would do whatever he can to protect me. Except I've seen shit I can't unsee. We don't always get to control what happens, no matter how much we want to.

"Let's just hurry." When I turn away from him, a sour taste fills my mouth, and my chest tightens. Damn it. What the hell is wrong with me?

That's a question I don't have to think long about for the answer.

The mate bond.

The longer I'm with Drake, the more I allow myself to care about what happens to him, the stronger the pulsing sensation within me becomes. My wolf even seems to be waiting for the moment I fully give in and fuck his brains out, but I need to get my head clearer before I let that happen.

I might have taken back my rejection, but I'm not going to walk into a lifetime commitment blindly or lock him into having a mate who leans heavily toward crazy.

When we walk into the backyard and I see the shed door open, my heart stops and any other thoughts are a distant memory. Where the hell are they?

My feet are running before I've even fully processed what I'm seeing. All the air is sucked from my lungs as I nearly yank the door off its rusty hinges to confirm what my head already assumed: the shed is empty of the two most important people in this world to me.

"Mom? Peter?" I yell their names as if that will magically conjure them, but I can't even scent them. They're not here.

Panic is quickly replaced by fury, and all I can see is red when I step into the shed to grab my bag that I never unpacked earlier.

A hand wraps around my shoulder and the arm attached to it becomes well acquainted with my fist as I break the contact, but before I can land the second hit, I realize I'm not alone. The threat isn't here with me.

"Shit," I mutter to Drake who hasn't backed up an inch and doesn't appear to have even considered defending himself from me. "I'm sorry. I forgot.

"You can forget a hundred more times," he says, face filled with concern, "and I'll still be right here with you."

Is he really this damn nice? He can't be. Not *all* the time. Maybe that's my problem with him. He needs to be more of an asshole for me to like him more. Did I really just think that? Gods, I really am fucked up.

"Pence?" Peter's young voice calls out from the house, and I practically shove Drake out of my way to see my brother.

He's standing in the doorway of Kasha's house that I've never even entered myself. He's changed into clean clothes, possibly even showered, and is holding a steaming cup of hot chocolate if I'm smelling it correctly.

"Your friend is so nice," he says with a wide grin. "She made me cocoa and Mom something else I'm not allowed to have."

Kasha has never given me a reason to distrust her. Hell, I was even going to ask her to do just as she seems to have already done, but I can't seem to stop my guard from going up anyway. The hybrid invited my family into her house when she shouldn't have even known they were in the shed. *That* I'm not okay with, regardless of her intentions.

"Peter, come here," I command, then glare at the shadow that appears behind him.

Kasha steps out in front of my brother and rolls her eyes. "I've always thought you were a bit ridiculous, but this is over the top. I won't harm your family, Spencer."

I step forward, but Drake stops me, whispering in my ear. "Take a deep breath. It's been a long day. What matters most is that they're safe and not actually missing."

Closing my eyes, I lean into his warmth without meaning to, but the moment my back touches his chest, I can breathe a little easier. Drake is right. I know he is, and I want to stop being so damn paranoid, but no matter how much I want to, changing a lifetime of distrusting the whole world in a day isn't possible.

"Spencer Lane, get inside this house," my mother's voice calls from farther away.

When I finally blink, Kasha is still there on the porch. My first instinct is to glare at her, but I know she probably only did what she thought was right. At least, I hope so. If not, the upside of all this is that I'm about to let out a lot of the aggressions I've been keeping at bay today.

For now, I'm going to have to go inside that house and pretend that none of this bothers me until it actually doesn't or something else changes. Otherwise, I risk making an enemy out of Kasha. Considering I already have a witch to contend with now, I don't need the fae-wolf on my bad side, too.

"Thank you," I tell Drake as I look over my shoulder at him.

"Everything is going to be fine, Little Dove," he promises with a sexy grin.

I do my best to agree with him, but until I know that my

family is truly safe and that this witch Kel can't do any more damage to my mate, I'm not sure I'll be able to believe his words.

With only a slight reluctance, I go up the wooden steps to Kasha's back door and she moves out of my way. Peter instantly pulls on my hand and drags me into the house. "I don't know why you've been staying out there. Even the couch in here is more comfortable than the flat thing out there."

Yeah, I bet, but being comfortable hasn't been my focus these last few years. Though, I don't tell him that.

"Can I have a drink of your cocoa, bubby?" I ask, wanting to make sure there isn't anything in the drink that I should be worried about.

He hands me the white mug, and as the porcelain touches my lips, Kasha steps in behind me. "You really think I'd poison a child? You're more paranoid than even I could have guessed."

More guilt weighs down on me, because I know she's right.

Taking a quick sip, I hand the cup back to my brother. "Where's Mom?"

"In here," she answers, and I move past the kitchen, through a short hallway, and into a living room.

My mom sits on the couch with a crystal glass filled with dark red liquid I can assume is some sort of wine. Her face where there had been deep bruises forming when I'd left her is now completely free of any signs of the injuries that I know she sustained earlier. More importantly, but also concerningly, there's a smile on her face.

"Mom," I say with hesitation. "Are you okay?"

She pats the cream cushion next to her. "Better than okay. Come sit."

I glance behind me, and I don't see Drake. I can sense him in the house, but I'm surprised he didn't follow me. Peter, too.

Interesting.

Mom hands me a glass, and her grin falls a little. “I think we’re overdue for some real talk.”

Great. Just how I wanted to spend the rest of my evening.

Still, I don’t tell my mother no. I might not have always agreed with her decisions, but I love her more than my own life. I’m pretty sure there isn’t anything in this world that I could deny her, which is also one of the reasons I stopped fighting Drake.

Sitting down next to her, I take the offered glass, but I don’t taste it. Alcohol is probably the last thing I need right now.

My mind is already screwed up enough on its own.

CHAPTER 12

SPENCER

Sitting next to my mother feels almost surreal. I've been working toward having her back in my life for so long that it's hard to believe the moment is finally here. Though, she doesn't seem to be in the same awe as me.

"You've disappointed me, Spencer," she says first, and I choke on air.

I guess she's done pulling her verbal punches with me.

"Excuse me?"

She looks around the small living room, then back at me. "Why have you denied yourself these things? Why have you chosen to separate yourself from every other soul on this earth? All that seems to have done is cause you harm, and I don't understand why you'd do that to yourself."

I laugh harshly and can't stop my voice from turning sharp. "Because that's what *you* taught me. To never be myself, not to *show* myself, not to trust others."

Tears shine in her eyes as she shakes her head. "I didn't intend for those things to go hand in hand or to extend outside of our pack. When I told you not to trust people, I didn't mean that you shouldn't *ever* do so. I just didn't want you to give your trust too easily to the wrong people. By hiding yourself and never allowing your true wolf to be seen, it was only to protect you, but I can see now how that notion has only hurt you."

Mom clears her throat and wipes at her wet cheeks as she takes another drink before continuing. I could say something, but the more I'm around her, the more my heart hurts for the last twenty-something years that I've lived with this pain, these secrets.

"I never got the chance to show you the right way to live," she says. "We were always so focused on being careful that you never did get to the fun parts of life and I'm sorry for that. More sorry than I think I'll ever be able to show you, but it's not too late to make changes, to teach you now."

"To teach me what?" I ask, my voice cracking because I don't want to be angry with her. I don't want to hold on to all the negativity that I've been gripping like a lifeline and using as a shield.

"How to let people love you the right way."

I open my mouth to speak, but she holds her hand up. "I know you've loved me and your brother all these years, and you've been living for us, but that's not the same as letting us love you. We haven't done that in the way you needed. Peter because he's too young and me because I was waiting for... Well, that doesn't matter. What does is you understanding that it's better to take a chance than live in fear. Though, seeing you now and knowing you've found your mate, I have a hard time regretting *all* my choices, because they've led us right to this moment. One that isn't all bad."

My shoulders start to shake from the weight I've carried over them for as long as I can remember. I hear my mother's words, I understand them, and hell, I've even been trying to tell myself some of the same things already tonight, but that doesn't mean the pain of my past has disappeared.

Mom wraps her arms around me, encasing me in her love just as a rumble builds inside my chest from my wolf, her personal way of attempting to soothe me.

The love from the two closest beings in my life consumes me, smothering all the hurt and helping me heal. Not entirely, but enough that I hope I can get my emotions in check.

"You shouldn't regret any of your choices, Mom," I finally tell her. "I know you did your best with the cards we were dealt, and I don't hold anything against you."

She pulls back and holds my face between her warm hands. "Oh, my sweet Spencer. That's part of the problem. You should be angry with me. You should yell or cry or whatever it is you need to let it all out once and for all. More than that, you should have other people in your life that you can count on besides thinking that me and your brother are all you have. I've only spoken with Kasha briefly, but I can already tell that you shouldn't be sleeping outside like an animal."

For the first time in much too long, I snort and genuinely laugh. "I am an animal."

She shoves at my shoulder, but also cracks a smile. "You know what I mean."

That I do, and between my own epiphanies, the earlier words of the unknown woman Lia, and this conversation with my mom —hell, even meeting Drake—maybe there's a chance that I can change without losing myself in the process.

Normally, I'd dig in my heels even further, just like I had when I chose to sleep in the shed, but I know I need to be done with that part of my life. Maybe it's because I'm just so fucking tired of it all or maybe it's just today, but I fall back onto the couch with a heavy sigh.

"I'm done." My head leans against the cushions, and I close my eyes, taking a deep inhale. I need this moment to myself, to reflect on the day, my heart, my mind, all of it.

The couch shifts, and I listen to my mother's footfalls as she silently exits the living room. I don't pay attention to where she goes. I stay right where I am with my eyes still closed.

My wolf is quiet but present, and I lean into her strength that has become my own in the years since I was old enough to understand that I would never be alone, not truly.

Am I really going to be someone's mate? Allow the need to protect him to come before everything else?

Instead of a direct answer, I hear Lia's words repeat inside my head.

Once you quit running, you just might find that you've attracted all the right people into your life.

There have been brief moments over the last couple of months being in Crossroads that I've considered staying right here, bringing my mother and brother here and building a home within this town instead of hiding away from the world.

Have I already stopped running and didn't realize it? And if I have, are those who I've disregarded as annoying or as having ulterior motives the ones I should have been trusting all along?

I've always had one foot out the door even when I've been stationary, but after today, I'm over it. There's a possibility in the morning that I'll go back to being the distrusting shifter I've been for years, but as the essence of Drake beats inside my cold heart, warming it from the inside out, I don't want to go back to that dark and lonely place I've been hiding in.

Today, my world was turned upside down. I can keep fighting against literally everyone in my life, or for the first time ever, I can put trust in someone other than myself and start really fighting for the people I care about most.

I realize now that I've been telling myself that I've been doing everything I can to save my family, but really, I couldn't stand the thought of living alone for the rest of my life.

I needed them more than they ever needed me.

Minutes pass, and I stay right where I am on the couch, unmoving with my eyes still closed. The sounds of Peter's laughter begin to fade, as do the voices of the other adults in the house until there is only silence.

I begin to think that I'm on the verge of falling asleep right where I sit, but as time continues to tick by, I find myself in a state of suspended being that I've never experienced before.

I'm free of all my worries. There's nothing I need to fix or acquire. There's nobody waiting on me. There's just me and my peace.

Yet, I'm not alone.

It takes more concentration to sort out who's with me, but the more I search for the presence of others waiting for me just beyond the wall of my own mind, the brighter their lights become.

Mom and Peter appear to me first, likely because they're most familiar to me, but Drake is an immediate third. The second his essence is recognized, his glow intensifies in my mind even more than my own family. I want to reject that notion, but I stop myself. The more I just let things be instead of trying to control them, the calmer my heart is.

Next—and this surprises me—is Kasha. Her light is dim, but she's there, waiting. She's followed by Natalia and even Corvin, the alpha whose pack I've rejected more times than he deserves. His kindness is something I've shunned like a disease, but I'm starting to see that I've been wrong.

I don't know what any of this means or how I even got to this state of being, but now that I'm here, I don't ever want to leave.

This is the happiness I've been fighting for, and if I open my eyes, I'm afraid it will all slip away.

The shape of a wolf appears next, her light as white as my own wolf's natural fur. It isn't until she's closer and I can see her eyes through the brightness that I realize it *is* my wolf.

What are you doing here? I ask, the calmness in my voice not sounding at all like the woman I've been for too long now.

Our fight is far from over, but this peace you feel? We can have that and so much more, she replies with reverence, though her mouth never moves. Hearing her voice, a softer version of my own, makes my heart race. She's never spoken to me with words, only growls and through my own intuition, which I very well could have been getting wrong for some time now.

She continues, not acknowledging my shock. *Just because you've resisted doesn't mean you've lost. Keep your heart open, Spencer. Listen to those around you and we'll be home before you even realize it.*

I try to ask her how this is possible, but as I think the words, no sounds reiterate them and the space I've only just found begins to fade away.

The harder I try to grasp it, the quicker the light dims until it's gone completely and I'm back on the couch, alone in the living room of a hybrid I don't really know. Though, my interest in changing that has increased tenfold.

Voices from the kitchen filter back into my thoughts, and I catch Drake say "Kel." That's all it takes to have me standing up, but I move too fast and the room spins.

I reach out for the couch to steady me, and my stomach churns, forcing me to close my eyes. The action immediately calms me, and I hear the faint echo of my wolf's rumblings.

Think before I act.

That's not anything she's just said, but it's also not something

I often do. I'm always triggered to deflect and run, right into or away from things. Maybe it's time I pause first.

With that notion at the forefront of my mind, I walk calmly into the kitchen, no longer feeling weak. In fact, I'm the complete opposite. My heart beats with a renewed purpose, my breathing is deeper, and my eyes are seeing things in a whole new way.

Hell, even my skin seems brighter than ever before, just like the glow I was seeing of those I've been trying to push away.

When I enter the small kitchen, I glance to the right. There at the wooden dinner table are Drake, my mother, and Kasha.

"Where's Peter?" I ask, glancing around and even under the table. He is only eight.

"I sent him to bed," Mom says. "Kasha gave him the room she's had set up for you."

I don't miss her pointed tone, but I also don't acknowledge it. Though, I do something that seems to take them each by surprise.

"Thank you, Kasha," I tell her sincerely. "He needs a safe place to lie his head tonight. Now, what have I missed?"

Each of them, even Drake, blink at me, but don't respond right away. I take a seat next to my mate, allowing my knee to brush against his under the table and grin when I hear his sharp intake of breath.

Maybe letting people in won't be pure insanity. Maybe I can also have some fun in the process.

CHAPTER 13
DRAKE

I don't know what happened to Spencer while she was in that living room, but it's almost as if a completely different person has sat next to me.

My gaze keeps traveling her way as the others speak about nothing of interest to me. Every time she catches me, she meets my stare with a smirk, one that seems to hold a secret that I'm dying to know.

"So," Cara says, looking pointedly at her daughter, "Drake told us about your run-in with Lia and Markus."

Spencer shrugs. "Nothing different than what I'm used to getting from you."

"He also mentioned Natalia showing up right before you got back here," Cara pushes, and part of me wonders if she's trying to bring her daughter down from whatever cloud she's floating on now. Though, Spencer doesn't seem to let the topics get to her like I would expect after having spent the day driving her mad.

"And we're going to deal with her," Spencer says confidently. "But the witch doesn't actually have the power to kick us out of

Crossroads. We'll let her calm down and go see her in the morning as planned. Whatever crawled up her ass is only because something scared her, and while we know we need to leave, we're not doing so because of Natalia's commands."

"Whatever crawled up her ass..." There's the Spencer I've seen most of the day. I was beginning to worry that after everything that's happened today, we'd broken her, but maybe not.

Five minutes ago, I agreed with Spencer's mother, but seeing my mate now, I'm not sure acting right away is the best course of action. I start to say as much, but I'm interrupted.

Kasha swirls the glass in front her as she casually looks up. "Whenever you go, I hope you know that your family will be safer in my home than in that shed or anywhere else you might try to stash them."

"Speaking of." Spencer's eyes narrow. "How did you know they were in there?"

Cara frowns and lifts a hand. "Peter might have been trying to clean up and opened the door without thinking, breaking the concealment spell."

"Well, at least that tells me there isn't anything wrong with the spells Natalia has been giving me," Spencer says, relaxing back into her seat before turning back toward Kasha. "What do you want for letting them stay here?"

The fae-wolf flattens her lips and glares at my mate. "When will you start trusting people, Spencer? I don't need something in exchange for doing what's right."

"Fair point," she replies, drumming her fingers over the tabletop. "Fine. They can stay in the house, but if anything happens to them, even if it's just an *almost* happens, I will hold you personally responsible. I don't care what kind of powerful hybrid you are. Nothing can protect you from me if they're not kept safe."

Everyone, including myself, tenses around the table. It's not hard to feel just how right Spencer is. Kasha might be a hybrid, but from what I sense, she leans heavier toward her fae side. There's an undeniable power that she exudes, and threatening her probably isn't the best idea, but that doesn't seem to change anything.

"I would expect nothing less from you." Kasha smirks, then finishes off her drink. "Cara, you'll have to share the room with Peter or take the couch. I'm going to head to bed." She gives me and Spencer her attention as she stands. "The two of you can do as you, um, need. Just don't destroy my property in the process."

Her words make no sense to me, but the heat I suddenly feel emanating from Spencer and the scent of her arousal pieces everything together rather quickly.

Well, that's uncomfortable to have said right in front of her mother. Almost more than realizing it's been nearly a millennium since I've had sex, yet they're talking about it so casually.

Before anyone else can comment on what may or may not happen between Spencer and me, Cara gets up as well and dramatically fakes a yawn.

"It's been a long day for me," she says, staring more at the table than us. "I'm going to lie down with Peter. You know, in case he has any nightmares."

The possibility of that is high, but even if he does dream about shooting his father, I have no doubt that boy is going to be just fine.

As soon as we're alone, I expect things to become awkward, but Spencer starts to laugh, covering her mouth as her whole body begins to shake.

I really need to figure out what the hell happened to her tonight. Starting with the moment she took back the rejection.

Not that I'm complaining—I'm rather fond of this less

stressed version of Spencer—but I also want to be sure she's not having a mental breakdown after all that has transpired.

"Spence?" I say softly, grabbing her leg under the table. "Are you okay?"

She nods, wiping tears from her cheeks. "I don't know if I've ever been better." Then, her hands reach for me, and she brings my face closer to hers. "I'm going to kiss you now."

Not only her words, but her actions put me in a temporary state of shock. I don't move for a long second, even as her lips press against mine, igniting the bond between us and making my heart race.

It isn't until one of her hands slides around the back of my head, gripping tightly to my hair that I finally awaken.

A rumble builds in my chest, and I open my mouth, deepening the kiss. She tastes even sweeter than she smells, and the need to touch her everywhere is overwhelming. One of my hands slowly moves up her arm, and the other instinctively goes to her chest, flattening over her racing heart.

The rapid thrumming beneath her shirt calls to me like the most powerful siren song to ever exist. This woman is mine. I knew that the first moment I realized she existed, but kissing and touching her as I am, not feeling any restraint on her end, I know there's no going back.

If she were to change her mind again, I'm positive I would merely cease to exist after that.

"I know it's not much," she says between kisses, "but the mattress in the shed isn't *that* bad."

Not that I would even consider turning her down, but I need to know why she's suddenly ready to go all-in with being mates. That might make me stupid, but I've spent centuries being tortured. I won't have her regretting this decision tomorrow and hate myself for it the rest of our lives.

Pulling back, I take a steadying breath as I stare into her light blue eyes. "Spencer, wait."

Her fingers start to tug at my shirt, but I grab her wrists.

"This might make me the biggest fool in all the worlds, but I'd like to talk to you first."

Her head tilts to the side as she finally pauses her movements. "This is not how I saw this going."

"You and me both," I mutter, already mentally kicking myself in the ass for what I'm *not* doing. "What happened tonight? What's changed your mind about me?"

"Getting right to the point. Seems like that's everyone's choice this evening." She smirks, leaning back in her chair. "I'm not entirely sure if I'm being honest, but I do know one thing: I'm done fighting against everyone in my life."

Instantly, my chest aches and I reach for her. "It wasn't my intention to cause you more grief."

She shakes her head and offers me a half-grin. "You might have been the least worst part of my day."

I think she's attempting to make me feel better in her own way, so I try not to take offense that I'm still considered a "worst part" in any form, least or not.

She continues, "I've spent my entire life believing in one thing: that I can't trust anyone or be myself. That who I am, what I'm capable of, isn't something to be shared with the rest of the world, not even my own father."

The more I learn about the woman, the more I understand why she wanted nothing to do with me. Still, I can't regret not letting her walk away.

"Do you wish he would have known who you really were?" I ask her quietly as she seems lost in thought.

She blinks, then shakes her head. "He was evil long before I was born, but I do wish for my mother that things had been different. I can't imagine being tied to someone you were forced to love, but also feared so thoroughly."

Her fingers twist in her lap as she goes back to my original question. "When I was sitting on the couch, alone with my thoughts, I realized that letting go of my desire for control was exactly what I needed. The moment I agreed in my mind to just let things be what they're going to be, I'd never felt freer. Maybe it's because I feel exhausted, but when I let my walls down..." She pauses and shivers. "It changed everything."

I want to ask what she saw, but the reverence in her voice makes me believe the answer might be better kept with her. That maybe in time, she'll show me instead of telling me with words. Much like she does now when she grabs both of my hands.

"I'm sorry I rejected you," she admits with another laugh. "I don't apologize much, and I don't open up to people, but for the first time in my life, I just want to let go of the tight hold I've kept on my own life and see what happens."

I squeeze her fingers before releasing her to stand. She starts to glower, but the moment I pick her up from the chair, her smile returns. "What do you think you're doing?"

"Taking my dove to her room, so I can watch her fly," I whisper in her ear as I hold her close and let my teeth scrape over her skin there.

If Spencer wants me, then she's going to get all of me.

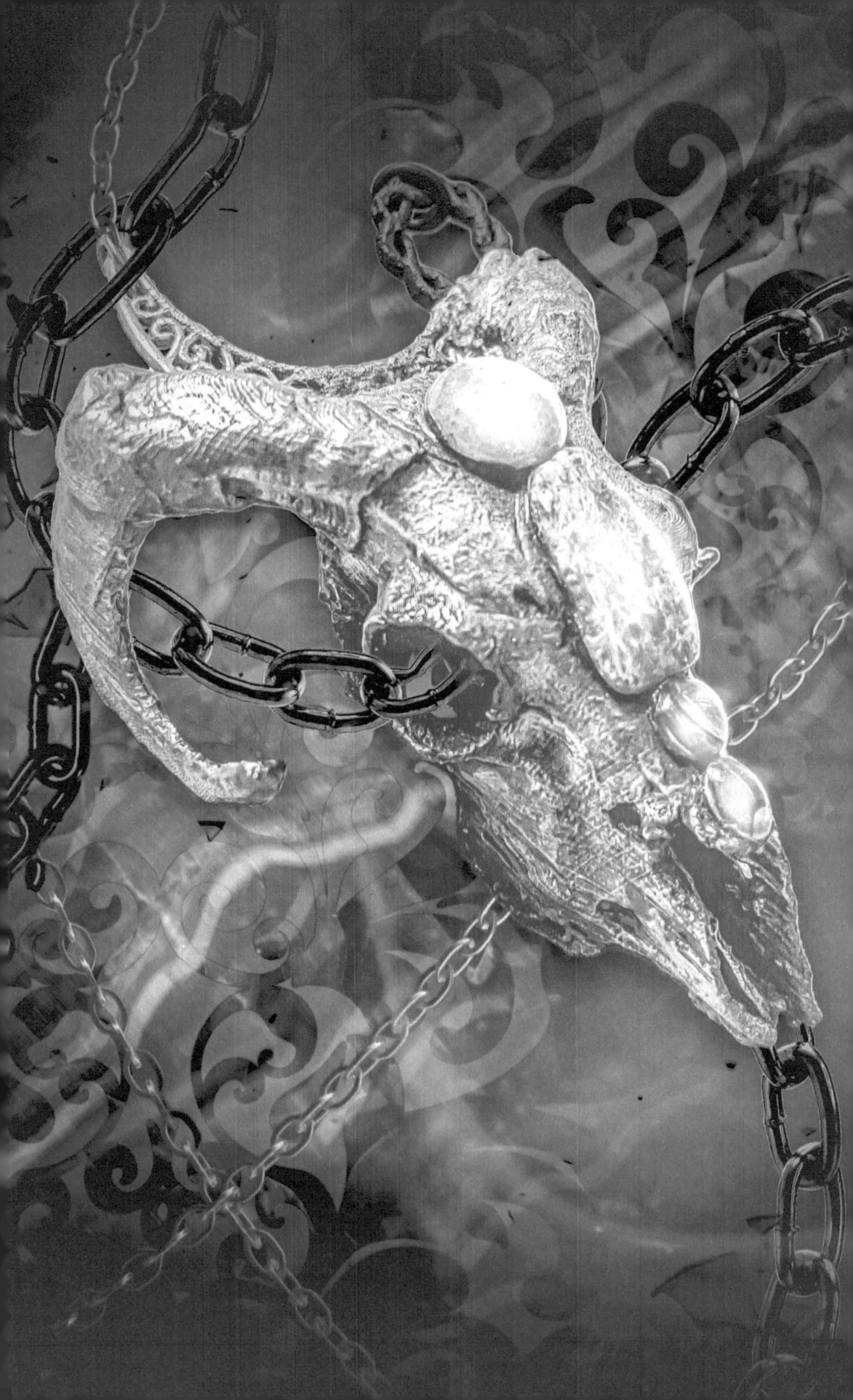

CHAPTER 14
SPENCER

Every other second, I expect the old me to rear her ugly head and take back everything I felt in the living room, but that doesn't happen. Not as Drake carries me outside to the shed, not when I place another cloaking spell around the small space for privacy, or even when we begin to strip each other of our clothes.

Instead, the more time that passes, the more relief I feel at no longer feeling the need to push everyone away, and the more I want to pull everyone closer.

Well, at least Drake and that's exactly what I do without an ounce of hesitation.

My borrowed shed isn't big, and his imposing form makes the space seem even smaller, but that doesn't stop either of us. With my mattress back in its normal spot in the corner, we practically fall on top of the lumpy surface, our legs tangled together.

He lands on the bottom with a grimace on his face. "How long have you been sleeping on this thing?"

I shrug. "Just a couple months."

"I'm going to find us a house," he says with a growl. "One with a real bed. You deserve better than," his eyes look around, a bit of sadness in them, "this."

He's right, and I've been working toward "better," but looking back now, I think I was always going to be in my own way.

Leaning forward, my nails scrape against his chest and I kiss him, but before things can get heated again, my right hand begins to burn.

"What the fuck?" I mutter, sitting up and trying not to be equally distracted by his hard cock beneath my ass.

Drake's chest is glowing and, right before my eyes, the chains around his wolf are moving. I point and raise my brow. "Is that normal?"

"No, definitely not," he says as his fingers tighten around my hips. Before I can say anything else, he flips our positions and has me on my back. "But that's a problem to worry about later."

Or maybe it's not a problem at all. I know Natalia said that Drake is marked for destruction, but there isn't anything evil that I sense inside him. She had to have gotten it wrong, and the curse he has, maybe it can be broken by finding one's fated mate.

Before my mind can get too far off track, Drake grabs the back of my neck firmly, lifting my head closer to his. His dark eyes contain more of those silver sparks that I noticed earlier, and he licks his lips as if he's prepared to devour me for his last meal.

"You're mine, Little Dove."

Four words have never sounded so sensual, but the fact that they don't make me want to run as I did earlier is the biggest win of the day.

My wolf rumbles inside me, her agreement clear as I sense her presence rising to the surface. She's as eager to claim our mate as I've suddenly become.

I don't know how I've gotten to this moment after the fucked-up day I've had, but the relief inside me is too great to ignore. Maybe the fates aren't so idiotic after all.

Only time will tell. For now, I'm done fighting. I have to be.

Drake's hand cups my face and there's a look of reverence in his gaze that melts the last pieces of ice I've kept around my heart. My head nods ever so slightly and he lifts up just enough to reach between us. He grabs his cock and rubs the head over my clit, making my entire body jolt with need.

As I start to reach forward, he puts me out of my joyous misery and thrusts inside me. My mouth pops open with an audible gasp and I'm clinging to his arms as he somehow keeps going deeper and deeper.

The moment he's fully seated within me, an energy builds inside my chest, expanding with every beat of my heart and heating the rest of my body. Drake, on the other hand, seems to be frozen in place. His eyes are closed, and his jaw is tense, but he doesn't seem to be in pain. At least I don't think so.

I lift my hand, and when I touch his face, he shakes his head.

"What's wrong?" I ask, suddenly feeling as if maybe sex so soon wasn't the smartest decision I've made lately.

His chest rumbles, and he starts to move, but barely.

My stare catches movement on his chest, and the longer I stare at his tattoo, the more I realize it's moving in real time. His wolf is shaking, and the chains around him have fissures forming within the metal, but none of the remaining restraints are breaking.

"Your wolf," I whisper, my hand hovering just above the mark, but not touching it.

The scorching temperatures emanating from that part of his body remind me that I was already burned by the mark once. We should probably stop in case this isn't a good thing or some sort of beacon to the bitch that cursed him, but when I try to roll out from under Drake, his eyes finally open. "No. She won't take this from me, too."

The pain in his voice slashes at my heart as if I've been physically stabbed. I barely know this man, but the more I let him in, the more he tells me, the more I'm ready to murder on his behalf.

As I look into his heady gaze, his eyes are nearly black, and the silver flickers I saw before are nowhere to be seen, but there's an intensity etched within his stare that I can't deny. Drake needs me. Maybe more than either of us understands.

The thought causes a disturbance within me, but it's not fear for the unknown or being tied to this man that shakes my foundation at its core. It's the fact that the longer we remain pressed together like this, the more his pain begins to bleed into me.

"I've got you," I say, keeping my gaze locked on his face.

He blinks slowly, and when he reopens his eyes, a bit of the tension he's been holding there seems to ease. He starts to move above me again, rocking his hips. With each forward surge, the air feels as if it's stolen right from my lungs.

The energy that had been building at my chest returns, swirling frantically inside me. The stronger the power gets, the faster Drake's movements become.

"The bond," he forces out with a strangled tone. "Can't... control..."

A sensation of need blasts through me, coming directly from Drake, and there's a feralness about him as his fingers grip my hair, holding the strands so tight that tears prick at the sides of my eyes.

His growls become louder, and I notice his canines extending as if his wolf is breaking through, but nothing more happens beyond that.

"You can let go," I tell him when he seems to be holding back, his muscles remaining coiled beneath his taut skin as he moves with precision above me.

His head shakes. "I'll hurt you."

This time I grin. "I'm not fragile. I promise you."

Sweat breaks out along his forehead, and he lets out a guttural roar as he tilts his head back. When he stares at me again, I can't stop from smirking.

There were several moments earlier today that I thought this man was soft and possibly a little pathetic for practically begging me to accept him, but staring at him now, seeing the beast he truly is, I start to understand that there's a lot more to Drake Cage than I'd initially given him credit for.

His hand wraps around my throat, not so tightly that I can't breathe, but with enough pressure that I'm aware of every breath I take. He slams into me, eyes focusing entirely on my body.

My legs wrap around his waist as I take every bit of him, over and over again. My body shakes, and there's little to nothing I can do other than hold on, but that's more than enough.

Drake leans forward, increasing the pressure and grabbing my chin roughly. I think he's going to say something else, but instead, he closes the bit of distance between us and kisses me with a ferocity I should have expected.

His tongue demands entry into my mouth and owns everything it touches. He tastes every corner, and I can barely think, but at the same time, I've never felt more empowered.

I grip his arms tighter and soon find myself matching his thrusts with my own vigor. Our bond is growing with every passing minute, and the stronger our connection becomes, the more powerful my own wolf feels.

An energy unlike anything I've experienced before starts to warm my own skin. I ignore the sensation in favor of focusing on the way Drake is not only fucking my body into oblivion, but also owning my mouth like it was created just for him.

Yet, the more time that passes, the stronger my own sensations become. My insides tighten almost painfully, and I'm certain I'm about to come, but before that can happen, Drake breaks our kiss and slows his pace.

His eyes—that are once again sparking with silver—drag over me, but I don't feel the least bit self-conscious. In fact, the longer he seems to inspect every inch of my naked skin, the harder it is to breathe, and the more I squirm beneath his currently halted movements.

"You're glowing," he says with a smirk.

At first, I think he's trying to compliment me, but then I realize the shed is brighter than it should be, and I actually *am* glowing.

My skin is almost translucent, and my hair has officially turned white instead of the platinum blonde it normally is.

"Stunning," he whispers before leaning closer and holding me with more control than he had just minutes ago.

"Don't be gentle," I tell him in case he thinks this new development is something to be careful with. I've never felt more formidable, and I need him to finish me off before I combust—literally.

"Your wish is my command." A rumble echoes from him again, and I release any lingering tension that was building up, thinking I'd lost the beastly side of him.

He grabs my legs, bringing them forward until I'm nearly bent in half and my ankles are resting against his shoulder. My fingers can barely reach him, and I start to complain, but then his hips surge forward and all breath escapes my lungs once again.

The glow around my skin doesn't cease and the shivers racing through me only grow with intensity as Drake pushes closer and places his hand over my chest.

His touch sends a vibration through me from his own shaking, and the connection of the bond feels as if it's tightening around my chest. My heart is pounding wildly, doubling in time with every thrust.

My hands wrap around Drake's wrist, and I pull him closer, ignoring the protesting from my legs being contorted. I need to touch him and hold him and taste him.

With unfocused eyes, I manage to grab hold of his face even though I was aiming for his neck and drag him closer. His lips are a hair's breadth away from mine when he slips a hand between us and rubs a finger over my clit.

Instead of kissing him as I intended, I cry out, my body giving into the release that's been building. As an orgasm rips through me, and right before I lose the hold on my mate, I feel the quakes of his own release.

Just as I think it's over, that we're officially bonded, my chest expands and my back arches. The glow around me intensifies, and in the next second, Drake is pulling me up. I wrap my legs around him, still keeping our connected position as he helps me sit up.

Tremors move through the both of us so strong that I can't tell which ones are from me and which are his. I grab his face and kiss him, needing this closeness to take away the weight of the bond that presses in on me.

It's not painful in a way that makes me want to run from it. Instead, I want to dive right into the fire and let the flames consume me.

Drake doesn't disappoint, either. He kisses me until every thought leaves my muddled mind and all I can feel and hear is him.

I have no clue how much time passes, but the intensity of the bond snapping into place finally releases us and Drake leans against the wall behind us. I keep my legs around his waist and lay my head on his chest, listening to the sound of his slowing heartbeat.

His fingertips move lightly over my back, making shapes I can't translate, but it's the pulsing of the bond within me that holds most of my attention.

"You're not glowing anymore," Drake says, his featherlight touches now moving over my shoulder before going down my arm.

"That wasn't the only unexpected thing." I lean back and glance at his wolf tattoo. I place my palm over the black ink. It's still warm, but not burning like before. "Can you feel your wolf now?"

A darkness falls over his face, and regret fills me for asking the question even though I have no clue why.

"That's something we need to talk about."

The way his voice darkens ruins whatever high I've been riding and, suddenly, all I want to do is murder that bitch witch.

CHAPTER 15
DRAKE

The moment I tell Spencer that we need to talk, I feel her walls start to come back up. Not just by the physical way she pushes me away and stands to get dressed, but there's a dampening in our new bond connection. As if she's closing me out, taking away the one thing I will cherish above all else for the rest of my life.

Still, there's something she needs to know before anything else. Something I didn't know until our bond began solidifying.

I follow her movements and dress, but the moment she pulls her shirt over her head, I grab her shoulders and force her to look at me. "Spencer."

"What?" There's a darkness within her tone that reminds me a little too much of myself.

"When I said we needed to talk, nothing I want us to discuss changes the fact that you're my mate and there's nothing I wouldn't do for you." My eyes watch her face the entire time I speak, but she's pulling farther and farther away from me by the second. "I mean that."

She tears out of my hold and gives me her back. Her shoulders are rising and falling rapidly as she seems to be struggling for control.

I step closer again but don't touch her as I whisper, "Don't push me away again. Tell me what's wrong."

Her hands shake at her side, and the harshness of her voice breaks my heart. "All I can think about is killing Kel. The longer I stand here, the worse..."

She can't finish her sentence, but she doesn't need to. I close my eyes and focus on the newly formed connection between us. The pulsing light I sensed before that ties us together is now tinged with a darkness that I never wanted Spencer to know of. At least not on such a personal level. Yet, it seems the rage I carried with me from Tartarus is quickly consuming her.

Closing off my emotions from the bond is the last thing that I thought I would do soon, but I won't destroy my mate. Even if that means I can't fully have her yet.

With my gaze focused on the back of Spencer's head, I put up a mental wall between us. The more fortified the separation becomes, the easier she begins to breathe. My heart breaks while I force myself to smile as she turns around.

"What did you do?" Her fingers rub circles over her temples.

"You were feeling my rage," I tell her honestly. "I took it back."

The lie burns through my body, scorching my insides, but I won't tell her that I've blocked her out unless I have to. She'll demand that I stop, and I won't hurt her with my past.

Maybe this is exactly what Natalia was speaking of when she said that I was destruction. I try not to think too hard on that, because if my fate is destroying Spencer, I'd sooner die than let that happen.

She rolls her shoulders and shakes her arms out. "How are you so calm when you have all that fury lying just beneath the surface? I couldn't even last two minutes with it."

Her arms wrap around my waist when I step closer to hold her. If I can't feel the beat of her inside me any longer, then I at least need physical contact.

"The pain is something I've learned how to live with," I tell her, doing my best to hide the worst of my frustrations.

Spencer pulls back to look at me. "You said before that we need to talk about your wolf. What about him?"

I don't want to keep anything else from my mate, and my thoughts from earlier no longer seem all that important. I start to tell her we can discuss this later, but she shakes her head and glares.

"Nope. You had something to say and you're going to do so now," she says assuredly, her face no longer tainted with my darkness. "Tell me what's on your mind."

A smile forms on my face. Her commanding tone makes me want to strip her naked again, but I shove the imagery to the back of my mind. I want my mate to know me, and she needs to be prepared in case I lose control.

"When I froze earlier, it was for two reasons," I start to explain. "The first and most important was because for the first time since scenting you, I truly understood what the bond between us meant to me. I'd heard that for those like me—shifters seeped in the shadows from Tartarus—meeting our mates can make one feral, but I didn't experience that with you at first. I had desperation, but the wildness wasn't there. I think it might be because of the spell still attached to my wolf and the moment you gave yourself to me, you freed him. Not completely, but temporarily enough for me to truly grasp the intensity of how much I need you."

She holds me tighter, her face softening. "How so?"

"I needed your touch so fiercely that I thought I would die without holding you," I tell her honestly. "Being inside you, feeling our bond expand and take root, watching your walls come down, all of that brought out the best and worst in me. I knew right then that you are all I need in this world, that everything else could disappear besides you and I would still be fine."

Her hand reaches up, and I lean my cheek into her gentle touch as she says, "But? Something else happened. You were hurting and that doesn't line up with what you're saying now."

At least she isn't pulling away, knowing that there's more, because she's right. My curse is even worse than I understood before meeting Spencer.

"Kel didn't just trap me inside my body," I tell her. "She linked herself to me. She knows I'm bonded with you now."

The moment the words leave my mouth, I wish I could take them back, but Spencer needs to know even if the truth hurts us both.

"How?" she practically growls, her shoulders stiffening beneath my touch and a deep crease forming between her narrowing eyes.

I double-check the wall I've erected is still up and I'm not making matters worse for her. The block is still present between the worst of my rage and Spencer. Though, it's not hard for me to remember that she was angry when I first met her. I'm sure whatever epiphanies she's experienced today can't have completely changed that, nor can I control all of her emotions.

"I assume she's somehow tied herself to me using whatever curse she placed on me," I say, because all we can do is guess at this point. "But the one thing I am certain about is that any spell can be broken by the death of its creator. Whatever Kel did to me, it will be undone when I kill her."

"Not if I get my claws around her throat first." Spencer snarls, but this time, her rage feels more controlled and not all-encompassing like it was just moments ago. "But what did you mean that she's linked to you? Can you *feel* her?"

The way her eyes turn to slits tells me that her wolf is lurking just beneath the surface and the way I answer this question needs to be done carefully.

"I can't feel her," I say honestly. "I merely sensed her energy when our bond first started to solidify. She's angry, and I have a feeling that means she's going to come after us sooner rather than later."

"Not if we go after her first." Spencer picks up my boots and tosses them at me. "Get your shoes on. We're going to see Natalia again."

My brow scrunches. "She made it pretty clear that she isn't going to help us."

"And I'm going to make it *pretty clear* that she doesn't have a choice."

When I first met Spencer, I had no doubts about her strength. She's a fighter through and through. But seeing her eyes glow with the force of her fury tells me she's been holding back—or maybe my wall isn't working as well as I hope. Either way, this is going to be interesting.

By the time I have my boots on, Spencer is waiting at the door with a dagger sheathed at her hip and some sort of spell in her hand.

"Are you going to use the witch's own magic against her?" I ask as we exit the shed.

"Natalia isn't the only witch I've done business with." She looks up at the bright moon sitting high in the sky and grins before glancing over at me. "Do shadow shifters go into heat?"

I nod, a little confused with the rapid change in subject. "Why?"

"I didn't think about it earlier, but tonight is a full moon," she explains. "I have two weeks until my first heat cycle now that we've met. Guess that gives us a deadline because, from my understanding, now that I've met you, I'll be pretty much useless for anything other than sex for two days once my heat starts."

The lower half of my body can only think about the fun that will be, but the more logical part of me knows we will either need a powerful cloaking spell or Kel will need to be dead by then.

My hope is for the latter.

"Good to know," I tell Spencer, then gesture toward the house. "Should we let them know we're leaving?"

She shakes her head and frowns. "It's been a shitty enough day for my mom and Peter already. They should sleep. I have my phone on me if they need to reach us."

I take her word for it since it's her family and she's not wrong about the day. I just hope the boy isn't having nightmares.

We leave Kasha's property and walk toward the center of town. It's the middle of the night, but there are still people out and about. Though, nobody pays us any attention, which I find odd given the rumblings I heard while waiting to pass through the portal. Others that had already come back talked about how they were the center of attention. Most didn't like that and came back to Tartarus quickly, while others had seemed to take advantage.

When we get nearer to the portal, there's a draw to go closer toward the swirling vortex, but the desire isn't anything I can't ignore. If I have my way, I'll never step foot in that dark world again. Though, if Spencer finds herself curious about my old home, I just might have to make an exception.

She gives me a onceover, a crease between her eyes, but doesn't say anything.

"What's wrong?" I glance around us, but don't sense anything abnormal.

"Nobody is paying attention to you."

And here I thought that was a good thing.

"Would you rather they were?" I ask, hoping I already know the answer to that.

Her lips flatten as she pokes at me, blinking and looking closely at my skin. "I wonder..."

She keeps staring at me like she expects to see something, yet nothing about me has changed. At least, not that I can tell.

Spencer shakes her head. "Never mind."

I want to press her further, but I can see the witch's shop from here and I'm instantly on guard. Coming to Natalia seems like a bad idea, but Spencer has known her longer and I'm not going to stand in my mate's way when she wants to do something. I don't intend to, anyway.

We enter the shop, and tension builds inside me as my eyes move constantly, a part of me expecting there to be a trap waiting for us. The place is quiet, not even the songbird above the door making a noise.

I grab Spencer's hand. "We should go."

"Fuck that." She snickers. "This witch doesn't scare me."

"I should," Natalia's voice calls out, seeming to come from nowhere yet everywhere all at the same time.

There's no movement within the shop. I can't even scent the witch, which is a problem that makes me worry more about my mate than it does myself, even though I'm the one Natalia wants gone.

"You shouldn't have come here," Natalia adds, still keeping herself hidden.

"And you shouldn't have pissed me off earlier," Spencer replies with a rumble. "We had a deal and you're breaking your end of it."

"I did no such thing," the witch replies. "I gave you what you asked for, even when I didn't get full payment. Now, it's time for you to leave."

Spencer's arms cross. "No. I want to know what has you so scared. Whatever you think you found with my mate's blood, you need to take a second look and tell us everything."

Natalia's shimmering ebony hair appears first, followed quickly by the rest of her until she's standing right in front of Spencer. "You don't tell me what to do, wolf. I've put up with your attitude because it served me at the time, but you have no idea what I'm capable of."

Spencer doesn't back down even for a second. "I have some idea, which is why I'm not going anywhere. Drake was cursed by a witch, and we know curses can be broken. Given you've just admitted how powerful you are, you're going to break it and tell us where we can find Kel so we can kill her."

I thought the plan would be to kill Kel so that her death would break the curse, but if there's something Natalia can do, that works as well.

The witch wraps her hand around Spencer's throat, and in the next second, I have her pinned against the farthest wall from my mate, snarling in her face. "Touch her again and I will rip your head from your shoulders."

Natalia merely smirks. "You're physically strong, but your wolf is still trapped. You'll do no such thing. Now, release me."

Before I can consider complying with her command, she presses one finger against my chest and sends me flying back across the room.

I land on my ass at Spencer's feet and find her grinning at me.

"Well, this just might be more fun than I could have predicted," she says, and I realize our versions of *fun* are vastly different.

CHAPTER 16

SPENCER

There's always been an underlying wrath within me having grown up as I did, but whatever I absorbed from Drake earlier is giving me whiplash. One moment I want to burn the world and in the next, I'm within touching distance from the tranquility I had earlier.

Regardless, my goals aren't changing. I know what I want, and Natalia is going to help whether she wants to or not. I don't get to run away this time and neither does she.

"Are you done with your magic games?" I ask her as Drake gets up and stands next to me. "I'd like to finish what we started earlier."

"That's not happening," Natalia replies with a sneer. "I already told you. I'm not messing with the dark magic inside him. Not tonight, not ever. That isn't the business I'm in, and you already know this, so don't waste either of our time."

Yeah, I'm fully aware of that, which was one of the reasons that I came to her in the first place. But this time, I'm going to demand an exception.

"Did you think that all these months of sharing my secret with you that I haven't had a way to protect myself if I needed to?" I ask the witch casually. "That would be rather stupid of me, wouldn't it?"

This finally gives her pause. "What are you talking about?"

"I'm *talking* about the fact that I've watched your building." I stalk closer to her. "I know who your most frequent clients are. I know that you very rarely put cloaking spells up and that even on occasion, when you have important supernaturals in here that prefer to remain anonymous, you forget to conceal your conversations. But the most important part you've failed to consider is the ramifications of using *my* blood in so many of your spells."

She's smirking and lets out a light cackle. "That only puts you in the crossfire if you tell anyone whatever it is you think you know."

Standing right in front of her now, I lean in close and whisper, "No, that just means I can find every single person using magic with my blood."

Her eyes go wide, but not in shock, in fear. "You wouldn't hurt them."

"My mate is in trouble, and that puts my family at risk," I reply smoothly. "Do you really think there is anything I *wouldn't* do to ensure their safety?"

I'm full of shit, but Natalia doesn't know that. Guilt gnaws at me. I don't like lying or threatening innocent people. Especially after seeing her light within my mind earlier, I want to consider her someone we can trust, but not at the expense of Drake. We need her to help him, and if Natalia needs to believe I'm still a heartless bitch a while longer, that's a risk I'm willing to take.

She swallows thickly. "What do you want?"

Just as I presumed when I came up with my blackmail, Natalia cares too much for the people she helps. She left herself vulnerable. The only difference between when the idea occurred to me all those weeks ago to use that vulnerability against her is that now I feel guilty doing so and I didn't before. Still, that doesn't change anything. I have to keep up with the ruse.

"That's much better." I pat her shoulder, then turn toward Drake to find him watching me closely. I can't tell what he's thinking, but he probably now believes that I'm the worst person in the world for threatening innocent supernaturals. At least I can tell him later that I'm only bluffing.

"Why don't we get comfortable?" I suggest, inviting myself into her backroom. I've only been in this part of the shop a few times. The first time was when I was deciding to do business with her. I felt the need to inspect every inch of the place and be certain she wasn't up to any kind of shit I didn't want to be involved in. The other times were on my more paranoid days, when I needed to be absolutely sure we were alone while she took my blood.

Drake stays right by my side, and Natalia trails behind closely. I can practically taste the sour venom she currently has for me, but I can't allow myself to care. There's too much on the line.

Behind the curtain, there are walls of completed potions, ingredients for more complicated spells, and random supplies that don't hold my interest. The space is darker than normal, but it's also the middle of the night so I shouldn't be surprised.

I take a seat on the black leather couch and Drake stands next to me, staying silent. As I stretch my legs out and cross one over the other, I smile at Natalia who also chooses to stand. "So, how about you tell us why you really freaked the fuck out earlier and how we can break the curse on my mate before going after Kel ourselves?"

Her russet eyes glare at me. "You're truly screwed up in the head."

"Try telling me something I don't already know." Playing the part of a sadistic killer is almost too easy.

But it's too late to back out now. I need to see this through. I can apologize to her later when Kel is dead and no longer a problem, because the fact that Drake said he could sense her isn't something I intend to let last long.

I might not have wanted Drake at first, but now that I have him? Nobody else will touch what's mine.

Natalia nods toward him. "His blood contains old and sinister magic that hasn't been seen in this world for centuries. So long, in fact, that most believe these witches were nothing more than a fable used to scare us into maintaining a pure bloodline."

She pauses, idly rearranging the bottles on the shelf next to her before she continues. "There was a coven millenniums ago. Their leaders were mated to demons, ones hellbent on power. Stories say, they recruited the worst of the worst, finding ways to increase their lineage magic until they were unstoppable. Our elders say the coven was killed off, but I'm starting to believe otherwise." Natalia glances at Drake. "The darkness in your blood? Whatever curse she's placed on your wolf is likely the only reason you've survived this long with that much dark magic pulsing through your veins."

"How do you know this for sure?" Drake asks, his voice gruff.

Instead of answering him first, she glances at me. "When I mix your blood with my magic, the crimson turns white before becoming almost translucent. That's the purest kind of power I've ever mixed with my own." While this revelation is new to me, I don't get to say anything before she looks at Drake again. "When I did the same to your blood, it turned black and then began to smoke. Not even the dark witches still on this Earth can make their blood truly go black. Not like this. I knew right then what I was dealing with, even though it should be impossible."

Drake grabs my shoulder and frowns. "She could be right. Tartarus is thousands of years old. Kel might have been sent there at the creation instead of born in the world like I was. I never wanted to know her well enough to ask that kind of question before she spelled me."

"So, what?" I ask, looking between the two of them. "She's one witch left from a coven that no longer exists. That doesn't mean she's unkillable. Quit trying to scare us, Natalia. Break the curse and tell us how your ancestors killed her coven before."

Natalia frowns and shakes her head. "She could have been banished for a reason, like because she couldn't be killed. We have no clue, and I'm not willing to risk my life to find out."

I'm up on my feet in the next second and glaring at her as my chest rumbles. "But you'll risk the lives of everyone you've helped by refusing me?"

She steps toward me, but I don't back down. Even though I'm bluffing, I'm not scared of her or her power. I never have been, and I sure as shit don't intend to start now.

"Quit threatening people, Spencer," she says calmly. "Lying doesn't look good on you. You might have gotten to me before, but I wouldn't have done business with you for so long if you had that kind of evil inside you."

Damn this smart witch.

My mind scrambles to think of another way to force her hand, but before I find something to throw back at her, she surprises me once again.

"I didn't say I wasn't going to help you," she snaps back. "I said I wouldn't risk my life. If you two want to be idiots and go after her, then I won't stop you, but you won't return to my shop again until she's dead. If you do," she looks back at me, face devoid of all emotion, "I will help this other witch find you."

I'm pretty sure that's as good of an offer as we're going to get, so I nod. "Fine. We have a deal, then."

Natalia goes back to digging through her shit on the shelves, I assume to find items that we wouldn't know to ask for that might help us survive killing the darkest of dark witches from the sounds of it. Even assuming that, when I turn back to Drake, I'm not afraid.

He spent hundreds of years trapped inside his own mind and body, basically frozen in time. While my situation of running and gathering for the last three years can't exactly compare, I'm ready for this to be done for the both of us.

This entire day has awoken a part of me I'm not sure I ever knew existed. For the first time in maybe ever, I want all the things I thought I could never have. I want a real home that isn't filled with fear. I want friends I can count on. I want—my stare stays on Drake—*him*.

Change happens fast, and being done trying to control everything around me is a peace unlike anything I've known.

We will find Kel, kill her, and end whatever nightmare she might be out there right now trying to conjure.

"Are you sure this is what you want?" Drake asks me quietly.

I grin up at him and nod. "The moment I accepted that there was no point in fighting the pull toward you, it was decided. I don't do anything half-assed, and I won't live the rest of our lives wondering what's around the next corner. Nobody should live that way."

Saying that now makes me realize how dumb my plan was before. Building a cabin in the woods and hiding my family there would have been doing just that, but it was the only option I could think of while still respecting my mother's wishes to not kill my father.

Though, that's no longer a problem.

Natalia makes an odd noise, garnering my and Drake's attention. When we both look her way, she's holding a towel and dusting off an old bottle as she turns around. "There you are."

"What's that?" I ask.

The glass is etched but I can't make out the finer details from across the room. The top isn't the normal cork style I often see. It's made from silver and worn down so much that there are only faint lines from whatever design was once there.

"Something that will help," she says confidently. "Like I said before, I've only heard the stories of these witches. By knowing how powerful her spell is through Drake's blood, I can guess that this Kel was higher up in the coven. Maybe not a leader, but possibly so. Either way, you're going to need old and new magic to combat whatever she has become in Tartarus. This is the start of that."

She hands Drake the possibly ancient potion but doesn't release it once he holds his hand out. Instead, she grips on to him and stares intently. "You will only get one shot at breaking the curse. If anything goes wrong, I can almost guarantee your death, and I make no promises this will work."

Her sharp gaze cuts to me as she takes the potion back. "You will make a magical vow right here and right now that if this fails, if Drake dies, you cannot retaliate against me or anyone else because of what you're making me do."

My chest rumbles, and I want to punch that cocky look right off her face, but I know she's not doing anything that I wouldn't do to ensure the safety of those she cares about. Though, hearing her say that Drake could die, I'm not sure how I feel about risking his life.

Looking back up at him, I shrug. "Maybe running wouldn't be so bad."

The thought makes me want to vomit after envisioning what

life could be like with a mate, in a real home, making a life for myself that I never thought I could have.

He's so tense that his head shake is barely perceptive. "I can't live like this forever, Spencer. And I won't subject you to a life with only half a mate. You're better off without me than keeping me like this."

The anguish in his voice breaks me and reignites my desire for murder all at once. I hear him, but I can hardly feel him. I didn't notice it earlier, not until he said that I would be living with half of a mate.

He's hiding his pain and rage from me. There's no denying that now, but that only serves to make me want to fix everything for him even more than before.

I turn back to Natalia, confident that fate can't be so cruel as to tease me with a mate like Drake only to take him from me.

Whatever the risk, he's going to be okay and there's no believing otherwise.

He's not destruction. He's mine. *All* mine.

"Whatever you need to do to break the curse on my mate, get it ready," I tell Natalia. "You're going to free his wolf, and then you're going to help us with the spell to kill this bitch once and for all."

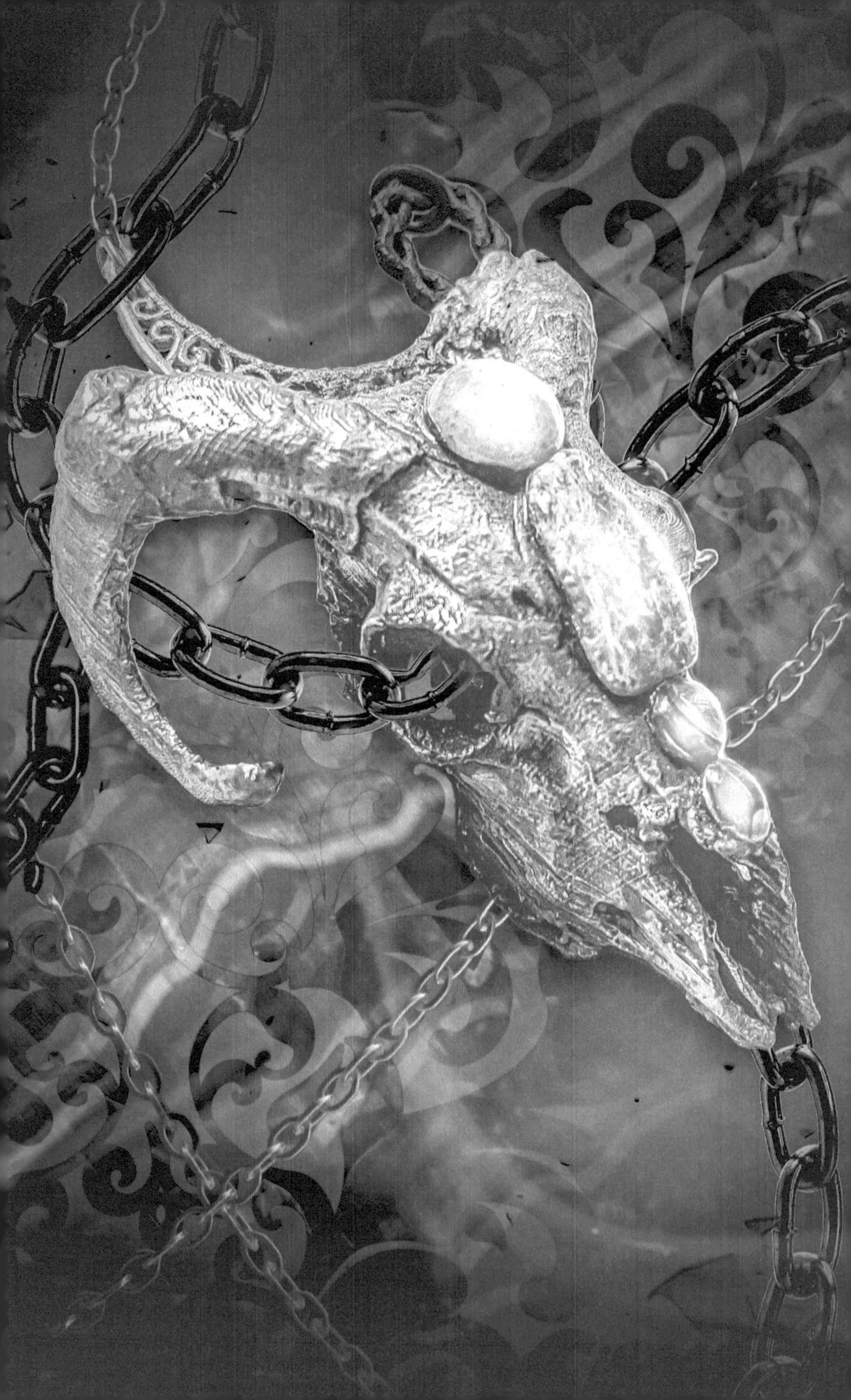

CHAPTER 17

SPENCER

Natalia sighs, and her lips flatten. "Well, this isn't going how I expected or even hoped."

I chuckle. "Did you expect me to give up just because of your little warning?"

She shrugs. "Pretty much."

I guess I can't blame her for that. That's what I would have done before. At least, I would have considered that option more heavily, but not anymore.

Drake was right earlier when he said I deserved better. But not just with my living conditions, with everything in life, and I'm going to start demanding just that out of the universe.

My mate grabs hold of my elbow, turning me back toward him. His eyes are on me, swirling with emotions I can't understand when he's blocking me out.

I hold his cheeks in my palms and smile. "I can handle all of you. You don't need to hide yourself from me."

He shakes within my hold. "What my rage did to you earlier, I can't let that happen again."

"You didn't give me a chance to figure it out on my own," I tell him. "I know what will happen now. While I appreciate you trying to protect me, I can handle this and so much more. Next time, give me the chance to show you."

He drops his forehead to mine. "I'm sorry, My Dove. I didn't know what else to do. I don't want you living with what I have. It's not fair."

I push up onto my toes and lightly press my lips against his. "Fairness doesn't matter when we're mates. Part of the purpose of the bond is so that we can share each other's burdens, not hide who or what we are."

This time he grins. "Who are you and what have you done with the Spencer I met outside the portal?"

My laugh is deep and rumbly. "She's still here, I promise you that, but I realize life isn't as black and white as I was trying to force it to be."

"As fun as it is to be a third wheel in your newly formed mateship," Natalia drones, "I apparently have work to do, and unlike the two of you, I'd rather not have an audience."

I've crossed lines tonight, threatening her past a point that I'm honestly surprised she's still willing to help us. Knowing that, I don't comment on her attitude, because it's not undeserved.

"We'll leave, but nothing changes," I tell her. "You offered to break the curse on Drake's wolf, and we understand the risks. How long do you need to make this happen?"

Her hardened stare begins to soften, and she shakes her head with a heavy sigh. "You're lucky I know how pure your energy is."

I'm not sure how I'm supposed to respond to that, so I don't, waiting for her to answer my previous question.

"Give me all of tomorrow and the following night," she says. "That will allow me enough time to break down Drake's blood and possibly learn more about Kel. The more I know about her magic, the easier it will be to *not* kill him."

Drake growls from next to me, but I've known Natalia long enough to understand that she doesn't talk about killing my mate flippantly. If he were to die, the witch wouldn't take that lightly, even if she might try to pretend otherwise.

"We'll be back the following morning, then," I say as I lace my fingers through Drake's.

Natalia holds up a hand, her gaze appraising Drake with undisguised scrutiny. "Wait a minute. Why did she spell you in the first place?"

"Because she's a fucking psycho," he spits out with disgust.

The witch clicks her tongue. "Try again, without all that pent-up rage."

My chest tightens and the need to comfort Drake nearly overwhelms me until I find myself stepping closer to him and placing a hand on his arm. No words are spoken out loud, but the moment I touch him, his gaze is on mine.

I'm frozen in place as if he's seeing into my soul and there's nothing that I can do but stand here and let him have a look around.

The thought frightens me, but only for a split second. The longer we're focused on one another, the more a sense of relief I feel, as if I'm truly being seen for the first time in my life.

A minute or two goes by and he finally nods, then gives Natalia his attention again. "I met Kel in Tartarus. She kept crossing paths with me and trying to strike up conversations. I casually brushed her off, but she started insisting that we should be together. When I snapped at her one day, she decided that if she couldn't have me, then nobody could. I spent over nine hundred years frozen in my current state, unchanging but aware of my surroundings, while she basically took over my home and life."

Natalia crosses her arms and taps her foot on the ground as she seems to mull over the information. "That's helpful. I'll need more blood from both of you, assuming you didn't bring back the vial I returned, and then I'll get to work, but I mean it. Don't return before the following days' morning or you'll risk ruining my process. My shop will be closed while I concentrate on this spell."

That makes me feel mildly better. Though, I didn't have any doubts before that she would take this seriously. If I did, we wouldn't be here.

"Will you be able to tell if Kel is close?" I ask since she'll have traces of the witch's magic.

She nods, relieving some of my tension caused by the fear I have of putting my family in danger. "I'll set up a perimeter spell that will warn me of any dark magic linked to that in the blood of your mate. It should give you enough time to act, but if that happens, you're on your own."

Fair enough.

"Then, I believe we have a deal," I tell her, stepping forward to offer my blood first. "Take what you need."

I'm in a hurry to get back to the house and make sure nothing is off there. I'll need to have a chat with Kasha about protecting her home with as much magic as I can offer on top of whatever the hybrid is capable of. If Kel is as powerful as Natalia has been saying, then I have to assume she can track Drake, which means she'll know where he's been.

Though, if the witch bitch comes for him or my family before we find her, she'll have one hell of a fight on her hands, even if we're not entirely ready.

The next morning, after only sleeping for a few hours, I wake to the sound of Peter's laughter. For a brief moment, I allow myself to forget we're all still in danger and just smile, because it's been too long since I've awoken like this.

Drake is lying next to me, staring at me with a deep crease between his brows.

My body tenses, and I sit up quickly in bed. "What's wrong?"

"Your phone has a message on it," he says gruffly.

I tilt my head, wondering who could upset him that would have my number, but I can't think of a single soul.

Reaching for the device, I see several messages and frown.

Natalia: I actually need the two of you to come by today. Unlocking his wolf can't wait.

Natalia: Don't ignore me. I'm trying to help you.

Natalia: You won't like it if I have to come to you.

Natalia: You're such a pain in my ass.

"Huh." I set the phone down, then stretch, but Drake still isn't pleased.

He grabs my shoulders and forces me to sit up. "That's all you have to say. 'Huh.' I tried waking you several times, but you wouldn't budge. We need to go find out why her plans have changed."

The last message was sent only ten minutes ago. Not that I don't have a sense of urgency for this situation, but I know Natalia. She's not going to leave the safety of her shop when she's working on something so important, and I'm not in a hurry to find out if my mate is going to die today. Though, I don't tell him that.

Still, I don't want to cause Drake any more stress. I pick up my phone again to text her back, letting her know we'll be there within the half hour and her reply is immediate.

Natalia: Hurry your furry ass up.

Fucking witch. While I intend to do as she's demanding, there's something else I need to do first and that's check on my family before having a little chat with Kasha. I need to know if what we've learned changes her mind about protecting my family.

Getting up, I reach for his hand and offer him a grin. "Just a quick check in with the others and then we'll head to Spells."

As we dress, I realize nothing feels different between us. My head and heart know this man is my mate, but the pulling sensation, the desire to touch him... None of that is present.

"You're still blocking me out," I state, keeping my frustration from my voice. He frowns and reaches for me, but I step back. "Tell me why first."

"I already did." He sighs. "I don't want to hurt you."

My head shakes, and I can't hold back the echoing growl coming from my chest. "And I made it clear that you didn't give me a chance to show you I can handle whatever hurt you're hiding."

This time, when he comes for me, I don't back away. Drake holds both of my hands and bends until we're eye level. "Give me until after Natalia frees my wolf at least."

He's asking for a compromise, and I don't want to yield, but he can't keep the pain out of his eyes. I'm learning that when they're all black, it doesn't just mean he's furious. My mate is also hurting.

Leaning forward, I kiss him, lingering for several extra seconds. "Okay."

He seems surprised by my agreement but doesn't comment. A

loud thud echoes from outside the shed and then I hear Peter's voice.

"Sorry, Pence," he shouts, making me grin.

Drake follows me outside where we find Mom and Peter in the yard, playing catch with a lime-green ball that seems to have seen better days. Even still, they're both grinning and seem to be having a blast. Not what I expect the day after that jackass died, but who am I to say how they should process murder?

Peter waves. "Want to play?"

I give him a big smile. "I'd love to, but I need to do something this morning. When I'm back, we'll have some fun, okay?"

"Sure!" He goes back to tossing the ball in his hand until Mom nods, but before she does, her head cocks sideways. I wonder if she's seeing something we need to know about. When she doesn't say anything, I don't overthink the situation and head inside, hoping Kasha is around so we can talk.

I've spent months telling her that the shed is enough for me and now, without notice, I'm going to ask her to keep the two people I love most in the world safe from a threat we know very little about.

Nothing to worry about at all.

Drake and I enter through the back door at the kitchen and she's sitting at the table, drinking a cup of coffee, her face grim. "I was hoping you would come see me."

Great. I was *hoping* my worry would be for nothing, but maybe not.

"What's wrong?" I ask, not sitting, but standing tense behind one of the chairs with Drake beside me.

"We need to talk," she starts, tracing circles around the rim of her steaming mug. "And you can't be angry with what I say next."

I *harumph* because my previous disappointment is suddenly

being eclipsed by the way she's starting this conversation. "What did you do?"

Kasha nods at the backyard. "I used magic on your mother and brother."

The rumble in my chest is so loud that it echoes through the kitchen. "You did *what*?"

She stays seated, seeming unfazed by my wrath. "Based on what I learned last night, you have a lot going on, but your family needs you. Except you need to be there for them in other ways, at least for right now. So, I solved a problem for you. I made it so that they remember what happened, but they don't have an emotional response to the...incident."

My mouth opens, and I'm certain the fae-wolf is about to wish she never existed, except that's not what happens.

Rationality kicks in just before I verbally rip into her. "Did something happen last night?"

She nods. "Peter woke up screaming, and your mother couldn't stop crying as she tried to console him. I had to do something, and I was pretty sure you weren't home or at least didn't want to be interrupted. I couldn't let them suffer."

What comes out next seems to shock everyone in the room. "Thank you. You made the right choice."

Kasha blinks several times before chuckling. "You're welcome. Though, I expected more of a fight. I even doubled my caffeine intake to deal with you this early in the day."

I nod my head toward Drake. "This is your fault," I tease. "You're making me soft, and you've only been here a day."

He merely shrugs and takes a seat first. "I'm a murderous shadow shifter. Whatever changes you've made are on you."

He's full of shit. He's the biggest cinnamon roll I've ever met. One that melted the *icing* around my heart quicker than I could have ever thought possible.

While I also blame the magic of the mate bond, there's no denying that Drake holds a goodness within himself that appeals me to him even with him blocking our bond.

He might have come out of that portal raging, but he had every right to be. The fact that he changed his plans—foregoing his vengeance temporarily—the moment he saw me is all I need to know for now.

Giving Kasha my full attention again, I take her in, observing her bright blue eyes and her genuine smile as she sips her coffee. I can easily admit that Drake's kindness isn't the first I've succumbed to, regardless of all the warnings my mother had given me growing up.

"Considering you made sure they're mentally okay, I hope that means you don't have a problem still protecting my family once I tell you that the witch who cursed Drake isn't just any old hag. She's possibly one of the original dark witches and several millenniums old." I drop the bomb of information casually, but I don't expect her response to be just the same.

Her eyes begin to glow, and she grins. "Magic has never scared me, in any form. That's not changing today."

Huh. I maybe should have been getting to know Kasha these last few months instead of keeping her at arm's length. She just might be more badass than I've been giving her credit for.

"There will be no place safer for them than my home," she adds, sitting a little taller in her chair, a prideful glint in her eyes. "I can assure you."

For the first time in maybe ever, I accept her promise without feeling the need to question or threaten her. When I do, a light around her intensifies so briefly, I can't tell if the flicker was only in my mind or her showing off or a reminder from my little mental shakedown last night.

"We need to head to Spells, but we won't be long," I tell her as

Drake stands from the table, reminding me that his eagerness to be free is just as important as anything else.

Kasha grins behind her mug. "Have fun with the witch."

Yeah, that's not going to happen. At least not until I know my mate isn't going to die today.

CHAPTER 18

DRAKE

Since the moment I saw the message on Spencer's phone about unlocking my wolf, I haven't been able to think of anything else. For over nine hundred years, I've been forced to live without my other half. The first couple hundred were the worst, and I shudder at their memory.

Fury that doesn't even come close to touching what I have now. If Kel had merely caged my wolf and left me as I was, I could have murdered half of Tartarus. Hell, I wanted to.

My only saving grace was the fact that I couldn't move.

Even now, thinking back on those darkest days, my chest tightens and my fingers curl into fists, desperate to beat in someone's face.

I should be thrilled knowing that by day's end, I'll be reunited with my wolf. Yet, for some reason, all I can focus on is the bad that has happened since losing him.

All the time that was stolen from me, the life I could have had, the few people in my life that I thought might have given a shit about me.

"Drake?" Spencer's voice breaks through my fiery haze, but it's her touch that startles me most.

Her fingers are ice cold against my heated skin. Not only that, but the glow from my tattoo is back, bright enough that it's shining through my shirt.

"We don't have to do this if you're not ready or unsure about the consequences," she says quietly, nodding toward Spells.

How the hell are we here already? I don't remember any of the walk from Kasha's to here. Not even a flicker of the crowds I'm sure we passed.

What the fuck is wrong with me?

"I know Natalia is—" Spencer starts to say, but I shake my head.

"It's not the witch. It's just..."

"A lot," Spencer finishes for me and I nod. She grimaces, then adds, "I hate to admit this because I don't like believing that Kel is truly linked to you, but what if she knows that you're about to set your wolf free and break the rest of her curse? What if she's fucking with you right now while she still can?"

That thought hadn't even occurred to me. I realize Spencer sees me mostly as the desperate man who wouldn't let her go, but I've lived with this underlying wrath for centuries. It took countless years to control the darker parts of me, and that isn't a side I want my mate to know.

Except she also needs to be aware that I'm not as perfect as she seems to think.

"If Kel is screwing with me, she's only pulling on my true emotions," I say honestly. "I was born into a prison world, built for darkness. Controlling my inner beast was something I had to learn to do on my own after being abandoned by my father before I was even born and then again by my mother when I was ten. My anger problems only grew from there. I'd thought I was getting a hold on them after nearly two decades on my own. Then, *she* showed up."

Looking back now, it was as if Kel had known every button of mine to push. The ones to make me sympathize with her, befriend her, and even how to be furious with the witch. Everything except how to make me fall in love with her.

Hell, I wasn't even attracted to her. Not once had I even considered fucking her. A fact that I'm sure pissed her off nearly as much as my rejection.

Spencer's hand covers my chest. "I didn't know about your parents. I'm sorry."

Her words soften some of the hardness around my heart that has grown throughout the morning. "It's in the past now. Let's just get this done."

Her brows pinch together. "Are you sure?"

No, I'm not, not in the slightest, but I've let this go on for too long now. It's time to take control of my life again.

Holding Spencer's face between my hands, I quickly kiss her and force a smile to my face that I know will bring her a semblance of peace. "I'm positive. Let's go inside."

She nods as her eyes search my face. I'm not sure what they see or even if she buys my bullshit, but either way, she reaches for the door to Spells and pulls it open.

We turn to go inside, but Natalia is already there. "Oh, good. You're here. Follow me."

The witch heads toward the alleyway we took last night, but Spencer doesn't move. "Where are you going?"

Natalia turns back, looks at me, then Spencer before chuckling. "Did you really think that I was going to unleash a wild animal in *my* shop? That would make me the stupidest witch in existence."

She makes a point, but there's still another concern. "What

about the dark energy from the curse?" I ask. "Letting that out into the world probably isn't any better."

She makes a clicking noise with her tongue and keeps walking as she replies, "It's like you two don't trust me. I have this handled."

Her confidence seems strong, but still, my earlier rage lingers just beneath the surface. The only thing keeping me in check is Spencer's hand wrapped around mine.

She keeps casting glances at me but doesn't say anything. I know she's worried, and I'd be lying if I said I'm not as well. Still, I need to do this.

I need to know if there is a chance that I can have my life back even if we never find Kel.

While I've made the assumption this whole time that she's going to come after me, it hasn't been far from my mind that maybe she chose to run from me.

Now, she could have been running back to Earth to see if her family is still alive and had every intention of coming back—that's what I believe most—but she also could have been done with her prison and my stubbornness.

Still, there won't be a day that passes for the rest of my life that I won't wonder when she might reappear if we don't end this. I don't want to spend my life with Spencer that way. She deserves better than that and so do I.

We get to the park, and I realize we had passed by it last night, but I hadn't paid any attention. There are thick trees spread out, green grass overgrown by at least a foot, and broken benches. Not somewhere I assume too many people visit any longer.

Natalia stops about thirty feet into the grass and points to a tree, then at Spencer. "You'll wait over there. Drake, stand in front of me before I put up the barrier spell."

"You're not separating us," Spencer says with a deep rumble.

I put my hand on her shoulder and offer her another forced smile. “Listen to her, Dove. I need to know you’re not at risk of being hurt or I’ll fight the spell.”

Which would then cause me even more pain, but I don’t add that part for Spencer. She’s smart enough to figure that on her own.

Her fingers grip my shirt, and she yanks me forward. “You better be okay. I didn’t decide to like you only for you to die the next day. Got it?”

I grin widely. “Yes, Mate.”

She kisses me with a ferocity that I’m happy to return, but as soon as my hands grab her hips, a bolt of shock runs through my spine.

“Not that this isn’t sweet, but this is a time-sensitive spell,” Natalia says, looking everywhere but at us.

Spencer backs up and lets out a heavy breath. “You’re going to be fine.”

I’m certain she says the words more for herself than me, but I agree with her anyway. “This will be over soon.”

At least I hope so.

I stand in front of Natalia, and she pulls a vial out of the inner pocket of her black jacket. Throwing it on the ground, a shimmering fog appears, rising about ten feet above us before spreading out and creating a thirty-foot diameter.

Spencer is standing close by, watching, but I don’t look back at her. I don’t want her to see the fear in my eyes. The parts I’ve been trying to hide from her since the moment she woke up.

It’s not just my rage getting the better of me, it’s the fact that I haven’t forgotten Natalia said I could die from this spell.

To have my life end after last night’s glimpse of the joy I could share with my mate for the rest of our lives… I can’t stand the thought of losing that.

"This is going to hurt," Natalia says, sympathy heavily lacing her words. "You can survive this, Drake, but you're going to need to fight. Kel has had her magical claws in you longer than any other spell I've broken before. I'm going to have to burn you from the inside out to remove her presence and set your wolf free. Are you ready for that?"

Without hesitating, I nod. "I can handle whatever you need to do."

She frowns and glances back at Spencer before looking at me again. "I've blocked out the sounds from the outside world and she can't hear us, either. You might be able to handle the pain you're about to endure, but something tells me that your mate is another story. Just know, you're not going to be able to hear her throughout the process. It's just me and you."

Considering I've hated witches since the moment I met Kel, I feel oddly at peace as soon as she says that. Maybe it's not having to worry about Spencer's screams or scaring her with my own or even just acceptance that this is happening regardless of what the outcome is going to be. At least my hell will finally be over.

Whatever the reason, I close my eyes, focus on the image of my wolf, even if I can't feel him right now, and let my body relax. "Do whatever you have to."

Natalia says nothing else, and I keep my eyes closed, pushing away as much of the fear and wrath as I can.

I won't die today. I can't.

A warm hand covers my chest where the tattoo is. There's a pulsing sensation that starts to thrum in time with my heart, and the spot gets hotter by the second.

Natalia removes her touch, but the heat only intensifies, and my heart rate increases tenfold. Every muscle in my body tenses and my teeth clench together so tightly, I expect them to shatter by the time this is over.

The witch wasn't kidding when she said she was going to have to *burn* the curse out of me.

My veins are on fire and my lungs feel as though they're filled with smoke. I want to open my eyes and make sure I'm not truly on fire, but I don't dare change my position.

A war is waging within my body, and I can't relent even the slightest.

Only the battle to maintain control is growing more fragile by the second.

If I were to look, I'm nearly certain that my skin is melting off right now, starting right at the tattoo. Sweat drips from my forehead, down my face, and continues over my chest and arms, so heavily that it might as well be raining on me.

I try to suck in a breath of fresh air, but it's as if I've just swallowed a handful of pine needles. My throat screams in protest of the air I so desperately need but can't seem to grasp.

"Quit fighting, Drake," Natalia's voice demands. "Release what's inside you or you're going to die."

I don't realize I'm fighting anything. I'm just trying to stay focused, but then it occurs to me that I'm fighting the pain when I'm probably supposed to succumb to the inferno growing within me.

Spencer's face flickers in and out of my thoughts, and I don't want to hurt her by showing how much this actually fucking hurts, but Natalia is right.

I can't keep this contained any longer.

Dropping to my knees, I lean forward, digging my fingers into the earth beneath me, and throw my head back. My roar comes from deep within and the longer I make the guttural sound, the less the fire burns.

"Again, Drake!" the witch yells above my screams.

My rumbles are so loud that the ground under me begins to

shake along with the rest of me, and my bones are aching from the weight of the curse that clings to every inch of me.

I couldn't pinpoint the darkness before, but with the lightness of Natalia's spell, the shadows stand out starkly within my mind, making me want to vomit.

"You're almost there," Natalia says calmer. "Just focus on what your heart wants."

Instantly, I see the peaceful face of Spencer sleeping beside me. I may have only had one night with her, but there's no doubt in my mind that my heart will never need anything ever again besides her.

My mate's eyes flutter open in my mind, and when she smiles up at me, the world melts away. There's no more agony within me, there's only her.

Until I realize that's only my imagination.

The fire within me changes, the burning stops and is replaced by an itching along my skin that reaches my bones until I feel like I'm coming out of my skin.

"Shift!" Natalia commands, and the memories of my wolf return to me.

This isn't pain, this is *power*.

My wolf. He's here and not just a flicker of my inner beast. The full force of his energy is wrapping around me and pushing outward. I can't hold back any longer, and when I let him come forward, it's as if my body explodes to the point of never being able to come back together again.

Screams echo around me, but I can't tell where they're coming from. The world is black, and I can't feel anything other than pure anguish. No part of me is whole anymore. I can't even feel the connection to Spencer that I've been blocking out.

Fuck! Spencer.

Panic takes the last of the breath I manage to inhale, and

another deep roar leaves from somewhere within my body that I still can't quite feel until there's something lashing out at me, sending shockwaves through me.

My sensations slowly come back to me, and when I can open my eyes again, I'm still on all fours, but this time, there are paws beneath me instead of my arms and legs.

I search for my mate, both in person and inside me. As soon as my wolf's eyes land on hers, we see tears streaking down her cheeks and her fists are resting against the shimmering shield meant to keep her safe.

Taking a deep breath, I draw on the bond I know is somewhere, yet hiding from me.

You shouldn't have done that, a woman's voice I won't soon forget echoes through my mind. *I'm going to find that little bitch of yours, and I'm going to force you to watch as I cut her body to pieces, inch by inch.*

You won't lay a hand on her, I snarl back to Kel. Killing her can't happen soon enough.

She cackles, and the sound makes me want to vomit. *I'll do whatever I damn well please. You have no idea who I am.*

I know you're the creation of a demon, I snap back. *An impure witch who should have died along with the rest of her coven.*

There's a brief quietness, and it's almost as if I can feel her slithering around my mind. *You're going to regret ever saying that.*

And then there's nothing.

Kel's presence is gone and, in the next beat, it's replaced by the thrum of the bond I have with Spencer.

My wolf's growls grow louder, and his teeth snap. He needs blood, and not just any blood. That fucking witch's.

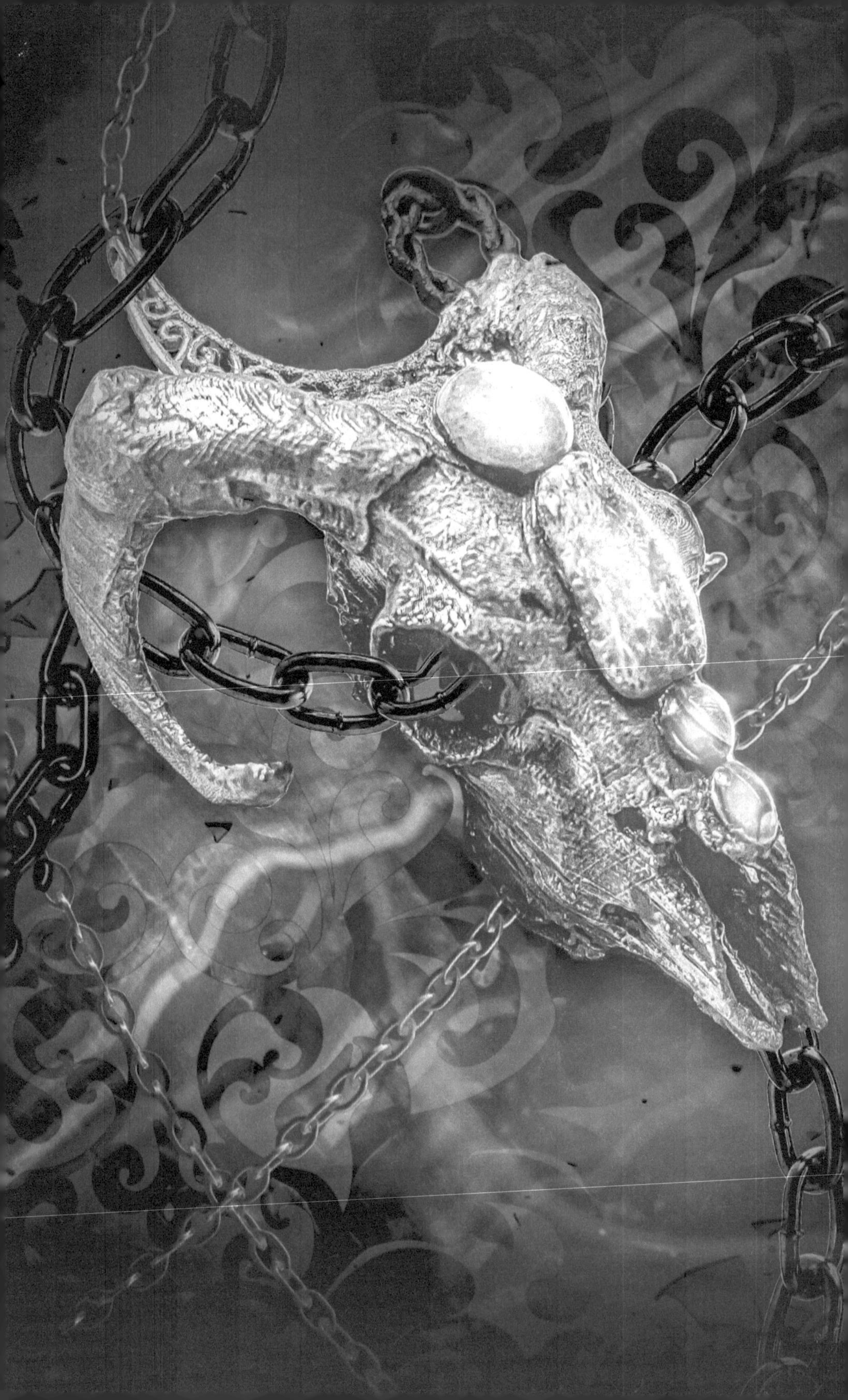

CHAPTER 19
SPENCER

What in the fucking fuck was that? My heart is still racing, and every part of me trembles with mixed emotions—mostly fear with heavy doses of fury weaved through.

Watching Drake be consumed with agony hurt me more than I expected. All I wanted to do was jump through that barrier Natalia set up and relieve him of whatever he was going through. Then, when his body began shaking to the point he started to disappear right before my eyes, I lost my damned mind.

I thought, for too many seconds, that I'd lost him. He was gone. I couldn't feel our bond or sense any part of my mate within me.

Try as I might, that fucking shield wouldn't break and I couldn't get to him. All I could do was stand there screaming for Drake and threatening Natalia's life over and over.

By the time my voice goes hoarse, the shadow that had consumed my mate finally materializes into a large wolf. A dark, shadowy beast with glowing orange eyes, sharp teeth, and a growl that makes goosebumps travel over my skin.

The barrier is still up, but I press my palm against the shimmering surface, holding the gaze of Drake's animal. My own wolf is right there with me, begging to be set free, but I keep her back. This is my moment. She can have hers later.

The steady beat of my bond with Drake is back, thrumming strong within my chest and spreading through the rest of my body. The wall he'd been keeping up isn't there, and his rage comes flooding back to me, but this time I swallow the smokiness of his grief and keep control of myself.

The curse is gone, but my mate is still hurting.

Finally, the shield falls, and I practically fall forward in my haste to get to him. The wolf is still snarling, but he doesn't frighten me —not the odd color of his eyes or the salivating around his jowls.

I stand before him, his wolf's head at my chest, and hold out a hand. "You're okay," I promise. Though, I'm not entirely sure that's true.

He nudges forward and my fingers slide through the nearly black fur, gripping tighter than I mean to, but I can't help myself. For too many moments, I thought I'd lost him.

I thought I killed him by bringing him to Natalia.

Now, his rumbles soothe the jagged edges of my nearly shattered heart, and I want to curl up next to him, never to move again.

Our connection expands throughout my body, calming the rest of me as I continue to stroke his head and stare into his eyes. The longer we stand there like this, the less of a glow there is.

He pushes closer to me, and I wrap my arms around his thick neck, bending over to hold him closer. "I thought I lost you," I whisper into his coarse coat.

The wolf's growls deepen. I'm not entirely sure how to interpret the response, but I can assume he probably thought the same thing.

"I've contained the curse, and he should be free of the worst of it, but—"

My head swivels around, and my snarl cuts off Natalia's poorly timed words. "*Be free of the worst of it...* What the hell does that mean? I thought you were breaking the curse."

She doesn't even blink at my rage. "I said I could break his wolf free. There was nothing else promised, Spencer. He's more powerful now than he ever would have been without what I did here today. At a great risk to myself. You should be thanking me that I was even able to do this."

Her tone is flat and straightforward, but I still want to rip her face off. Though, I know that's not because I'm furious with the witch. At least, not this one.

"Thank you," I finally say, standing up straighter to face her but still keeping a hold on Drake's wolf. "Not that I don't appreciate what you've done here, but do you have anything else for us?"

She holds up a bottle of black liquid and shakes it lightly. "Tomorrow morning is still when I hope to be done. I just realized that the amount of Kel's magic in Drake's blood wasn't enough for me to create anything defensive for you to use. I needed something more potent, and I had a theory."

My eyes bulge and jaw tightens. "All this was on a theory? Not something you knew for sure?"

Natalia just shrugs. "Isn't all magic just a theory?"

No, I'm pretty sure it's not, but the witch walks away before I can say anything else. That's probably a good thing. Although we likely couldn't take down Kel without Natalia's help, there's a chance, with how frayed my emotions are, that I would say something I couldn't take back if she hadn't walked away.

Drake's wolf shivers next to me and scratches at the ground. When I look back at him, he's staring at the trees further into the park.

"Do you need to run?" I ask, then shake my head. "That's a stupid question. You've been locked up for centuries. Of course, you need to run."

I grab both sides of his head and press my face closer to his. "Stay close. We can't get too far away yet."

There's no telling what's going through his wolf's mind. I'm honestly surprised he hasn't run yet, but then I feel a tugging on our bond, and it occurs to me that I'm keeping him here.

I couldn't imagine what would have happened to him if the curse had been broken and he hadn't found me.

Alright, Wolf, I say to my own inner animal. *You get your time with him, but not long. We need to get back to the house. We have no idea what breaking the curse did in the way of alerting Kel of what we're up to.*

She grumbles in reply, pushing forward until my skin begins to itch.

I step away from Drake, and the small amount of space between us makes him whimper, but I don't take long to shift. Or more accurately, my wolf doesn't let me slow her down.

The transformation is mildly painful thanks to the urgency of the change, but once we're on all fours with the bond beating wildly within our heart, nothing else matters.

Drake's wolf tilts his head back and lets out the loudest of howls. The sound is like a siren song to mine, calling us forward.

The wolves touch their foreheads together, then begin to lick and sniff each other around their necks. The actions are sweet and like a balm to the last of my shattered nerves.

Everything is going to be just fine. One way or another, we're going to come out of this okay.

Drake's wolf nips at mine and causes her to growl. The sound is playful, but also a warning that she isn't to be fucked with. Like human, like animal.

He doesn't seem to be deterred and goes for her again, but this time we dart out of the way, and his teeth close on air.

He wants to play, I tell my wolf. *Show him where to run.*

By the time I've even finished speaking, her claws are digging into the earth and she's sprinting forward.

The midnight-colored wolf is right on our heels, his rumble sending shivers through my own wolf. His stride is longer, but we have more practice, so it's easy to keep the lead as we race through the park. Wind rips around us, stirring up all kinds of scents, but the only one that matters is the musky amber smell coming from right next to us.

My wolf lets out her own howl filled with joy and anticipation as we start to circle the park. It's not a huge space to stretch our legs, but enough to work for the moment. Later tonight, we can venture out again for a longer run.

Together, our wolves continue to chase one another through the park, moving in and out of the trees, jumping over long-forgotten play structures, and overall, enjoying the hell out of themselves.

Finally, though, it's time to stop. Half because I still haven't heard Drake's voice since he freed his wolf and half because my family isn't far from my mind.

I know Kasha said she would protect them, and I have no doubts she's powerful, but that doesn't mean my worry for their safety is any less.

My wolf relinquishes control, and I shift back to my human

form first. When I look back at Drake, his wolf is still staring at me. "What's wrong?" I ask even though I know he can't reply.

The wolf steps forward, his head lowered and stalking toward me. Well, this is different.

His tongue swipes over his sharp canines and there's a deep rumble from within his chest as he gets closer.

I'm tempted to move or bring my wolf forward, but I'm too curious about what Drake's animal is up to.

I hold my hand out when he's close enough and he rubs his snout across my palm. "You're safe here," I tell him. "Nobody will trap you again."

His growl nearly has me jumping back, but I stay steady, knowing he needs my support right now.

Leaning forward, I run my fingers through his dark coat again and breathe him in. Just as I open my mouth to say something else encouraging, the fucking wolf bites me right on the shoulder.

"What the hell?" I screech as I jump back.

Without meaning to, I punch the beast in the face. "Bad wolf!"

Except he doesn't seem at all ashamed of what he's done. I swear he's grinning at me as he lowers on his haunches to sit.

My hand covers the bite and comes back with blood when I pull away. Not a lot—he didn't bite deep—but still. There's going to be a...

"You marked me," I say, unable to hold back my chuckle. "You sneaky wolf. I'd say sorry for punching you, but you know damn well you deserved that."

His head lolls to the side, and I realize that his eyes have changed from the glowing orange to a bright amber. Much better than before.

Finally, he trots back and shifts. Only I forgot one important thing: Drake doesn't have a magically imbued ring or amulet to prevent his clothes from disappearing during the transformation.

A very naked, but also grinning Drake stands before me. "That was intense."

"And your cock is hanging out for everyone to see." I point toward his crotch. "Maybe you stay in wolf form until we can get you some clothes, yeah?"

He glances down and shrugs. "Not like most people haven't seen one before."

"Except I don't need anyone else seeing yours." I can't stop from growling as I speak, which only serves to make his smile grow wider.

"It's okay, Mate. You're mine and I'm yours," he promises. "No matter what anyone else sees, I only *see* you."

The distance between us is quickly swallowed up when we both lunge for one another. It doesn't matter that we're in public and anyone could be watching. The need to touch and kiss him is too strong to ignore any longer.

His hands grasp my face as he pulls me impossibly close, his lips on mine, tasting me with a vigor I happily match.

"I thought I lost you," I murmur between kisses.

"Nobody can take me from you that easily."

Gods, I hope not.

I've only known the man mere days, but I can't picture a life without him in it any longer.

My hands cover his chest, and the feel of his heart beating beneath my palm calms the last of my nerves. My eyes suddenly do a double take. "Your wolf tattoo. It's gone. Like all the way gone."

He glances down but doesn't seem the least bit worried. "It wasn't there before Kel, so it makes sense that it's not there now. I'm taking that as a good thing."

I sense a hesitation from him through our bond, but when he

doesn't add anything further, I let the oddity go. It's been an eventful morning, and we need to take this as a win.

I kiss him once more, then step farther away. "Shift and we'll head back to talk."

This time, he doesn't make a joke, and any worry-filled rage I'd momentarily pushed down is right back at the surface.

Something tells me we're not even close to being free of Kel even if Drake has his wolf back, but that's going to change and soon. I'll make damn sure of that.

CHAPTER 20

DRAKE

Heading back to the house, we first make a stop at a clothing store where Spencer buys me some clothes. I stay in my wolf form, waiting to change until I'm in the backyard of Kasha's place.

Everyone is inside as I go into the shed and dress quickly. When I come back out, Spencer is looking up as if she's inspecting the sky.

"What's wrong?" I ask her, adjusting the waist of the jeans that are one size too small.

She keeps her gaze up for another second before facing me. "Just wondering if we'll know when Kel shows up."

My chest tightens at the mention of the witch. I have to tell Spencer what happened after I first shifted, but I don't regret the extra time we were able to spend together in our wolf forms.

I trace my fingers over the two puncture marks on her shoulder from my beast. "Didn't that one shifter say we should head North? I wouldn't worry about her coming here."

"Lia. I almost forgot about that little interaction." Spencer sighs, then grabs my hand. "Later today, we can go back to town with the coins I've traded for so you can get some proper clothes and a ring like mine. I have plenty of magic to trade that isn't just from Natalia."

My hand intertwines with Spencer's as I nod toward the house. "Let's go check on Cara and Peter, then we can figure out the rest."

A crease forms between her brows. "You wanted to tell me something."

"It can wait until later," I say honestly. "Nothing is going to change right now."

At least I hope so.

I didn't much care for our run-in with the unknown shifters last night, but with my wolf back, I'm thinking a bit more clearly.

Lia had mentioned us heading north, and as soon as Natalia has what will hopefully help us, that's exactly what I intend to do.

Whatever plans Kel has, I can't let them come here.

"Pence!" Peter calls out from the house. "You're back."

She bends down as the little boy runs toward her. She scoops him and hugs him tightly. "I am. Now, tell me all about your morning."

He wiggles out of her hold but grabs her hand. "We're making grilled cheese for lunch. Kasha let me help flip them. Come eat with us."

As if on cue, my stomach growls, making everyone laugh as I say, "I think my stomach accepts."

I follow the two of them inside, and a heaviness weighs down on me when I see Kasha at the stove, Cara setting the table, and allow Peter's excitement to consume me.

This is what a home should be like, and it's nothing I've ever had, but looking at Spencer, I know I'll do and give whatever I have to in order to make that happen for us.

Not only because I crave this future with her, but because we both deserve peace and happiness.

After lunch, we played a game of something called "Go Wolf." It wasn't hard to catch on. All I had to do was try and match as many of my cards to those in someone else's hand. If I guessed wrong, and they didn't have the card I needed, they'd tell me to "Go Wolf."

The statement makes no sense but made Peter giggle every time someone said it.

Now, we're headed back to town. Only we don't go the way we've been using the last couple of times. Spencer leads the way through a few more residential streets and stops at another house before turning toward me.

"There is another witch that lives here," she explains. "I don't know her like I do Natalia, but I've heard she makes rings for shifters like the one I have." She holds up her hand and wiggles her middle finger with the silver band and white stone that has flickers of a fiery orange through it.

"And that's why you weren't naked like I was?" I ask, just making sure I understand why we're here.

"Yep." Her eyes drift toward my pants. "Now, nobody else will need to see your goods except for me."

That makes me chuckle. Jealousy is adorable on my mate.

"Whatever you think is best," I tell her as we step toward the walkway of the house. Before we get very far, Natalia materializes in front of us on the sidewalk.

"Are you seriously going to another witch for something after all I'm doing for you?" Her tone is laced with equal parts disappointment and shock. "I can't believe you, Spencer."

My mate's brows raise high on her forehead. "I thought I was being considerate by not putting more on your plate. You know, because I do understand how much you're doing for us."

That has the witch calming down, but not by much. She crosses her arms with a huff. "What do you need?"

Spencer nudges me with her elbow. "He needs a ring to make sure he doesn't keep losing his clothes when he shifts."

Natalia snickers. "Wasn't really a problem before, huh?" I snarl and she holds a hand up. "Too soon for jokes. Got it. Well, I have some premade on my shelves. I just need to soak in his blood, which any witch would need to do, and if I were you, I wouldn't be giving anything of the sort away to just anyone."

She makes a good point, one Spencer seems to comprehend quickly. "I didn't think about that."

"And that's why I've been tracking him." Natalia gestures toward me. "Well, part of the reason. I knew you'd want to be able to find him in case his wolf went feral and took off without you."

I hadn't even questioned how she knew we were here, but I guess I should have.

"My wolf is in perfect control, thanks to Spencer," I tell the witch, so she doesn't try any other magic shit with me *just in case.*

An odd noise leaves the back of her throat. "Right. Now, come with me."

She grabs both of our hands and, without any other warning or explanation, teleports us back to her shop.

Rematerializing takes my breath away and I have to bend forward, resting my arms on the counter in front of me before I can feel my lungs working the way they should.

"Don't do that again," I say with a growl.

"Don't cheat on me with lesser witches."

This witch is getting a little too comfortable with us now that she knows we need her more than she needs us.

Spencer recovers quicker than I do and places her hand on my back. "She means well."

"And that's the only reason my wolf hasn't bitten her head off."

While I meant what I said about my inner animal being in control of his rage, that doesn't mean he isn't murderous within my mind right now.

Without Spencer, there wouldn't be anyone safe from our destruction until we had our vengeance, but thanks to the mate bond, she has become our focus. Knowing that our mate wants to do this the safest way possible, utilizing the help of Natalia to lessen the risks, is the only reason he didn't flee earlier.

Biting her helped to calm him as well. Her sweet vanilla tinged with a spicy cinnamon aroma now has a layer of my smokey amber scent weaved through it. I would have preferred to have her consent in the marking, but seeing as she doesn't seem to mind, I try not to either.

"Let's get you two sorted and out of my shop," Natalia muses as she breezes through the curtains that block off the back of her shop.

Spencer and I stay in the front, but we're not left waiting long. The witch is back in under a minute and sets a black ring with an orange stone in the middle on the counter. "Seems fitting, don't you think?"

I honestly don't care about the ring, but since Spencer is so eager for me to have it, I nod. "It will work."

Natalia holds out her hand. "I need more blood."

This time I growl. "Haven't you had enough?"

"Enough to unlock your wolf, keep you alive, and continue working on something powerful enough to kill Kel, yes," she says. "But I need every drop I already have. You want this ring, which I wasn't counting on, then I need more blood."

I give her my wrist when Spencer doesn't object. Though, she does surprise me when she apologizes.

"I know this is a lot," she says, standing next to me as Natalia cuts into my wrist.

"It's fine." I offer a smile, hating that she's feeling any guilt and knowing it's because of me.

She shakes her head. "It's not fine. Not at all."

Her words are sharper, and I want to console my mate, but not here. Not with an audience.

Natalia finishes and heals the cut before taking my blood and the ring with her toward the back room again. "Give me five minutes."

I glance at the curtain, then at Spencer before lowering my voice. "Are you sure you trust her? I know she helped with my wolf, but going after Kel with magic we didn't create ourselves could be dangerous."

She doesn't hesitate in her answer. "I trust Natalia. I didn't realize how much until recently, but she hasn't let me down yet and I don't believe she will with this."

One of the things I've grown to admire most about Spencer besides her love for her family is how sensible she seems. Once she decides something, she believes in that with her whole heart. There isn't an in-between with her. People are either all-in in her life or they're an outsider. It's a trait I respect and hope to learn from.

"I do have something else for you to do while I'm working on this spell, Spencer," Natalia calls from the back room.

My mate raises a brow at me as she yells back. “What’s that?”

The witch doesn’t reply, and Spencer shakes her head. “I’m going to see what she’s talking about.”

As she pushes the curtain aside, Natalia appears, eyes bright as she tosses the ring at me. “All done. The sunstone is linked to your blood and will keep you from being naked when you don’t want to be.”

“And what am I supposed to be working on?” Spencer asks, her foot tapping on the floor of the shop.

Natalia steps back, flicking the braid her dark strands are held in behind her. “I’ve been testing some things with your blood, and I believe you’ve been holding back. Not purposely, but I have a theory.”

Spencer’s teeth ground together, but she takes a deep breath before responding. “Another one? What have you done with my blood?”

“Nothing sinister, I assure you,” the witch says, “but I’ve come to realize that your camouflage ability extends beyond changing your wolf. That was part of my previous theory as well.”

“What does that mean?” I ask when Spencer seems torn between tearing Natalia’s face off and hearing her out.

The witch smirks. “I doubled down in my efforts after you left last night and sped up some of my tests while the spell I’m concocting brews. Most of my theories proved accurate, and you’re going to need to figure them out for yourselves if you have a chance in hell of taking down Kel. She’s already gathering her own power and asking about Crossroads.”

“How do you know?” I ask, hoping like hell that doesn’t mean she’s close by.

Natalia hands Spencer a vial of a clear liquid but looks at me. “I might not leave my shop much, but I have plenty of friends in places most would least suspect.”

I guess we were going to have to take her word for it. Well, maybe. Spencer might be changing her thoughts about trusting Natalia after this conversation.

"What did you do with my blood?" my mate says sternly, stepping forward and pressing her palms on the counter, the only thing separating the two women.

Natalia stands her ground and looks Spencer right in the eye. "Remember what you know, Spencer. I'm not the enemy, and I've been testing things with your blood for months now. I've never once crossed a line I shouldn't, and I haven't now. You know this. Until you remember that, I'm not telling you anything else."

"If I didn't already, I'd have already leapt over this counter and ripped your throat out," Spencer says, only slightly calmer than a moment ago. "Tell me what you did."

"Fine. You want things to be that way, then." Natalia pulls a vial from her back pocket, then tosses it toward Spencer. "If you drink that, it will enhance your abilities and we can do live tests on my theories, but until you truly calm down, I don't recommend taking it."

Spencer raises the vial and inspects the clear liquid. "What the hell are you talking about? What are these abilities that you think I have?"

"I *know* you have the capability of camouflaging as you like to call it," Natalia says, "but your wolf isn't the only way you can do that. You can attract people to you, and you can also seem as if you don't exist to others. There's a pureness within your albino wolf that draws on the greatness of others, along with protecting you from those with ill intentions."

Well, that's new and something I've never heard of.

"What the hell are you talking about?" Spencer asks, eyes narrowed. "I spent the first twenty years of my life being plenty noticed by the evil that lived in my house."

"Was he noticing you or were you making yourself known?" Natalia counters and, when Spencer fails to answer, it seems my mate has been rendered speechless.

Things just got even more interesting, and possibly not in a good way.

CHAPTER 21
SPENCER

Natalia's question leaves me speechless. I might even be in a bit of shock with that revelation. My head begins to pound, and my heart races as I think back to all the fights that occurred in our home growing up. Worse, the more physical ones that transpired when I became more than just a pathetic pup.

Every single memory begins with me charging forward to stop my sperm donor from laying into my mother or keeping Peter out of harm's way. Never once had I been the initial target.

Holy shit.

Something specific Lia said last night comes back to me as I try to level out my breathing...*you just might find that you've attracted all the right people into your life.*

I've *attracted* them. Had the unknown shifter used that word on purpose? Does she know what I am or what I can do? Suddenly, I want to go track her down and ask a few more questions.

"So, I understand what all that means on a surface level," I finally say, "but something tells me you're not just pointing out the obvious here."

The witch leans forward on the counter and smiles. "You're starting to figure me out."

"More accurately, I'm realizing that the moment you stopped needing me more than I needed you, you decided to have fun with my life." Not that I think she's being sinister about any of this, but the more the scales tip in Natalia's favor, the more changes I can see in her.

Her grin remains. "Just be thankful I don't intend to take too much advantage of that. Now, for your abilities." She points to the vial still in my hand. "Drink that when you're ready. It should enlighten you to the point that you'll sense the varying levels of your energy. Your human form, your wolf form, and the magic that makes you who you are. Focus on the thrum of your power and, if you're truly ready, the rest will make sense when it's time."

Her words don't give me a lot of confidence as far as what I'm going to learn, but before I can ask any other questions, she dismisses us.

"Now, get out of my shop." Natalia points to the front door. "I have work to do, lives to save, and spells to perfect."

She isn't wrong about that.

"We'll see you first thing in the morning, then," I say as I take Drake's hand and head for the exit.

He squeezes my fingers as we leave Spells but waits until we're in the alleyway again before speaking. "Are you going to drink whatever is in that vial?"

Yeah, something tells me he might not be thrilled about this plan of Natalia's.

I hold the clear liquid up, inspecting it for anything unusual, but there's nothing to see besides the obvious.

"What she said makes sense," I tell him, pocketing the vial.

"Even Lia said that I attract the right people in my life. Makes me curious, you know?"

His stare focuses on mine, and he reaches up to roll a section of my hair between his fingers. "I do and I won't tell you not to do this, just like you didn't tell me not to unlock my wolf when I could have died, but I won't lie. Her spells make me nervous."

What he's not outright saying is that he hasn't had a great experience with witches in the past and trusting one so explicitly now feels wrong, but he doesn't need to come right out with those words for me to take them into consideration.

"How about I show the vial to Kasha?" I suggest. "She isn't a witch, but she's still familiar with magic. Maybe she can give us more insight than Natalia was willing to."

His shoulders drop, and the beginnings of a smile start to appear on his face. "That might be best."

I don't fault him for his suspicion. While I do trust Natalia, we've asked a lot of her and she's never before mentioned this about me. Considering how long she's been playing with my blood, getting a second opinion can't hurt.

"Want to try your ring out?" I ask with excitement. "We could shift and run back to the house. Normally I walk, but I also haven't been getting out as much as usual these last few days. I can't imagine your wolf would be upset by the short run."

Drake's chest rumbles, making us both chuckle. "No, I don't think he would be." He glances at the black ring now placed on his right pointer finger. "Do I need to do anything special, or it just works on its own?"

"Mostly, it works on its own, but I still instinctively think about my clothes when I shift," I say with a shrug. "I'd rather put forth more effort than have something go wrong."

"Right." His jaw tenses, and he looks away from me.

I step closer, forcing him to meet my stare. "What's wrong?"

"I was just picturing you being naked in public." He shakes his head. "I understand why you didn't like me being that way before."

His admission makes me laugh. "Well, it's a good thing we don't have to worry about that any longer." I grab his hand and lead him out of the alleyway. "Let's shift."

Once we have a bit more room, Drake calls his wolf forward first. I watch closely, curious if there are any other differences between us since he's technically a different kind of wolf shifter from me.

Outside of a brief appearance of a shadow around his body, the process is very much the same as mine. Before I shift, I give his wolf a scratch on the head. "You're lucky I still like you after you bit me last time."

The beast growls, but the sound is playful. His tongue drops out and he leans forward. Before I realize what he's going to do, the damn wolf licks the entire side of my face.

My eyes squeeze closed, and I jump back, pulling my shirt up to wipe off my face. "You're..."

I don't even know what to say or do. The action takes me by complete surprise, and when I can see again, he's sitting in front of me, tongue still out and eyes bright.

The little fucker is proud of himself and, honestly, I can't be mad.

He's too damn cute. Though, I don't say that out loud. The *scary* wolf shifter might not appreciate being called "cute."

Instead, I shake a finger at him and feign annoyance. "Bad wolf. No biting or licking when I'm still human. Save that shit for my own wolf."

He lets out another grumble and I hope that's his agreement because I'd love not to be blindsided every time he shifts.

Calling my wolf forward, energy moves through my body, and

I give in to the power of my inner beast. Her presence grows stronger as my muscles and bones start to contort. Within the next second, I'm standing on all fours.

Drake's wolf wastes no time coming over, and in the next second, his tongue laps at my wolf's face. Only she doesn't back away, she starts doing the same to him.

Well, aren't they adorable. Wel,, as long as they keep the tongue-lashings to themselves.

The only time I want to be licked is by Drake himself and much further south than my face.

"That witch is a genius," Kasha says as soon as I finish explaining not only about what Natalia said about my wolf, but everything else we didn't have time to say this morning about Kel. Still, the hybrid doesn't seem fazed by the danger.

She holds the vial within her fingers and grins at me. "I knew there was something different about you. I just hadn't been able to figure out what. You have a very strong energy inside you that now makes a lot more sense."

"But do you think whatever is in there is safe for Spencer?" Drake nods toward the spell from Natalia. He's still riddled with tension that I haven't been able to calm out of him, not even when I've tapped into our bond.

Kasha turns the liquid over in her hands before closing her fingers. Her eyes shut, and there's a hum of power that ripples through the air right before she looks at us again. "Safe as water from a fresh spring. You might be tired afterward, but you'll be okay, even if it doesn't work."

My head tilts to the side as I accept the vial back from Kasha. "Natalia said something about needing to wait until I'm calm, but keeping my cool probably isn't going to happen until Kel is dead. Should I even bother taking this now?"

"You've spent your entire life hiding who you truly are." She points at me. "Even now, there's a wall around you. I think she meant more about that than your overall vibe. If you're not ready to relinquish the security of said wall, then you're not ready. There's not much magic can do about that unless greater measures are taken, but something tells me that's not an option."

Her gaze flicks toward Drake, and I grin. She's not wrong.

I place my hand on his thigh and give it a squeeze. "Doesn't sound like it can hurt to at least give this a try."

"Right now?" he asks, still sounding as if he has reservations.

I nod, because I can't think of any other better time. I suspect tomorrow we will be leaving to head North as Lia advised. Plus, right now, both Peter and my mom are napping. I don't have to worry about freaking them out if something doesn't quite go to plan.

His hand settles over mine, and he presses down firmly. "Let's do this, then."

Kasha claps her hands and stands, but it's Drake's steady gaze that keeps my attention. Any reservations he had just moments ago are gone. I can't even sense anything lingering through our bond.

"If you're sure after talking with Kasha, then so am I," he says with a true smile. "You're going to be fine."

My confidence in this whole thing increases tenfold. It isn't until hearing his support that I realize I've had my own doubts this whole time about not being ready.

As much as I know that by understanding my wolf better, we'll stand a better chance against Kel, Kasha had been right. I've spent my whole life hiding who I am and combining that with Drake's uncertainties, I had no idea what to expect.

But now, I have no doubt that this is going to work. Whatever I've been keeping locked away is about to be unleashed, and I couldn't be more thrilled with the idea of possibly no longer hiding myself. At least, not in the ways I have been all these years.

We step out into the yard where Kasha already waits, and the vial of magic in my hand warms. *I hope you're ready for this, too*, I say to my wolf.

Her responding rumble tells me that she's at least not against the idea.

"What does she need to do?" Drake asks. "Drink it and wait or shift?"

Kasha shrugs. "It's not my spell. I'm only here to watch. The rest is up to your mate."

I grab Drake's arm and turn him toward me. "I'll be fine. I'm going to drink this, and then we wait to see what happens. Natalia would have told me if I needed to shift."

I'm pretty sure anyway.

He cups my face and kisses my forehead. "Then, I'll be right here waiting with you."

My heart swells, and I take a deep inhale, soaking up the strength he has to offer me through our bond.

Uncorking the vial, I don't hesitate in drinking the whole thing in one big gulp. There's nothing to taste. If I didn't know better, I'd think Natalia is fucking with us and that this is just water. Except it's only seconds later that my skin begins to pebble and my legs grow weak.

"I think I need to sit down," I say, my voice a bit garbled.

"Lay on the grass," Kasha says, but she sounds far away. "The earth will help ground you."

Of course, the half-fae would tell me that. Still, I take her advice and, with the help of Drake, lie down on my back and close my eyes.

The sun's warmth covers my body, and my heart starts to slow as every part of me feels weighed down. I try to open my eyes but can't seem to move. Am I sinking now?

It's like half of my body is being pulled into the dirt and the other is trying to stay rooted to the surface, but none of it is painful. A little awkward, but only because this has never happened to me.

Energy swirls within my core like a bright light growing stronger with every beat of my heart. Slow yet steady.

My wolf is there with me, but instead of becoming weaker like I feel, she's only getting more powerful as if taking my life force for herself. The thought should scare me, but I couldn't be calmer if I tried.

In fact, I'm tempted to take a nap right here within the cocoon of the earth, blanketed by the sun's rays.

Not just yet, the voice I know belongs to my wolf says. *We have work to do.*

Hmmm. I want to say more. At least I think I should, but I'm just so tired.

You're not tired, she says. *You're in a state of rest, thanks to Natalia's spell that has allowed me to form a deeper consciousness within your mind.*

Alright. I stretch the word out with a yawn.

Spencer! she snaps with a sharp growl that almost feels as though she's slapped me. *Wake up.*

I shake my head. At least that's what I visualize doing as I sink further into the comforts of the earth around me.

If you keep doing that, you're never going to see Drake again.

This time, her words send a panic through me that clears some of the fog from my mind. *What do you mean?*

You're technically dying right now, she says so casually that I expect her to laugh, but the weaker I become, the more I don't think that's too far from the truth.

What did Natalia do to me? I try to scramble for the surface, to escape the darkness I so easily succumbed to, but the harder I fight against the weight pressing back, the farther away I feel from my mate.

She doesn't understand everything there is to know about us, my wolf says sourly. *Her intentions were sincere, but there is more at play than even she realizes. Because of that, you weren't properly prepared. Though, this really is the only way. It would have happened eventually. I only didn't fight back because I still have an anchor to our reality with Drake's wolf. He's the only reason we're not dead already.*

Well, isn't that just awesome and a fact that makes me want to murder that fucking witch. Her and her *theories.*

Natalia isn't to blame, my wolf corrects. *She must have assumed that you and I are more bonded, but your need for concealing yourself all these years has put a wall between us. It's time to shatter that barrier.*

Another yawn rolls through me. *But I'm so weak.*

I just need you to stay awake and to remember where we belong, she says confidently. *Picture Drake, your mother, and your little brother. Remember how much they need you to stay awake.*

Not that I'm afraid of a little pain, but is this going to hurt? The way she's talking, I feel as though I should be bracing myself for something I'm not prepared for.

Her energy drapes over me, relieving me of any uncertainty. *There shouldn't be any pain. You just need to keep your awareness intact.*

I feel confident I can do that, but then another yawn escapes me, and I tell her to hurry up. I don't know how long I can ignore the inviting nature, waiting for me to join its warmth. Not that I hear any other voices, but whatever waits for me, whatever is calling me farther into the earth... There are promises of peace, and I can't remember a moment in my life where that's truly something I've ever had for longer than brief flickers.

This doesn't mean you can't still have peace, my wolf reminds me, her presence growing stronger. *When I break this wall down, you're going to be consumed by my energy. That should be enough to jolt you back to the surface. Just be ready.*

I have no clue what wall she keeps talking about. I've never sensed a separation between us, but I take her word for it. The faces of my mate and my family rotate through my mind while I ignore the echoes of harshness around me.

The first time I saw Drake and all the pain I sensed in his eyes that had me running away. The day Peter was born and how complete my heart finally felt, but also how terrified I was of the world he was being brought into. The warmth of my mother's smile as she cared for my broken wrist when I was only nine.

Each memory that flashes through my thoughts grows stronger, more powerful, reminding me of the love I have waiting for me if only I can just hang in there long enough for my wolf to—

A shock zaps my chest, and my eyes fly open, only it's not Drake's face that I see, it's my wolf's. She's standing over me in all her glory, not a single part of her being held back.

Her brilliant white coat is glowing with the force of a thousand suns behind her. It should be blinding, but I'm like a moth to a flame, unable to stop myself from reaching for her.

Wolf. The reverence she exudes fills my entire being with pounding energy. She is light, she is strength, she is...pure.

No, we are.

Images flash through my mind that I shouldn't have knowledge of. People I've never met and then my mother. They're strangers, but they feel like family just as my wolf is to me.

I'm inches from grasping her fur, the need to touch her overwhelming, when her paw lifts up and slams onto my stomach. My body folds in half, and I suck in dry air, coughing until I'm choking from the amount of power consuming me.

Fight, Spencer, she reminds me. *Never stop fighting.*

Her light begins to fade, as do the images, and for the first time in my life, I finally know who I am, who we are.

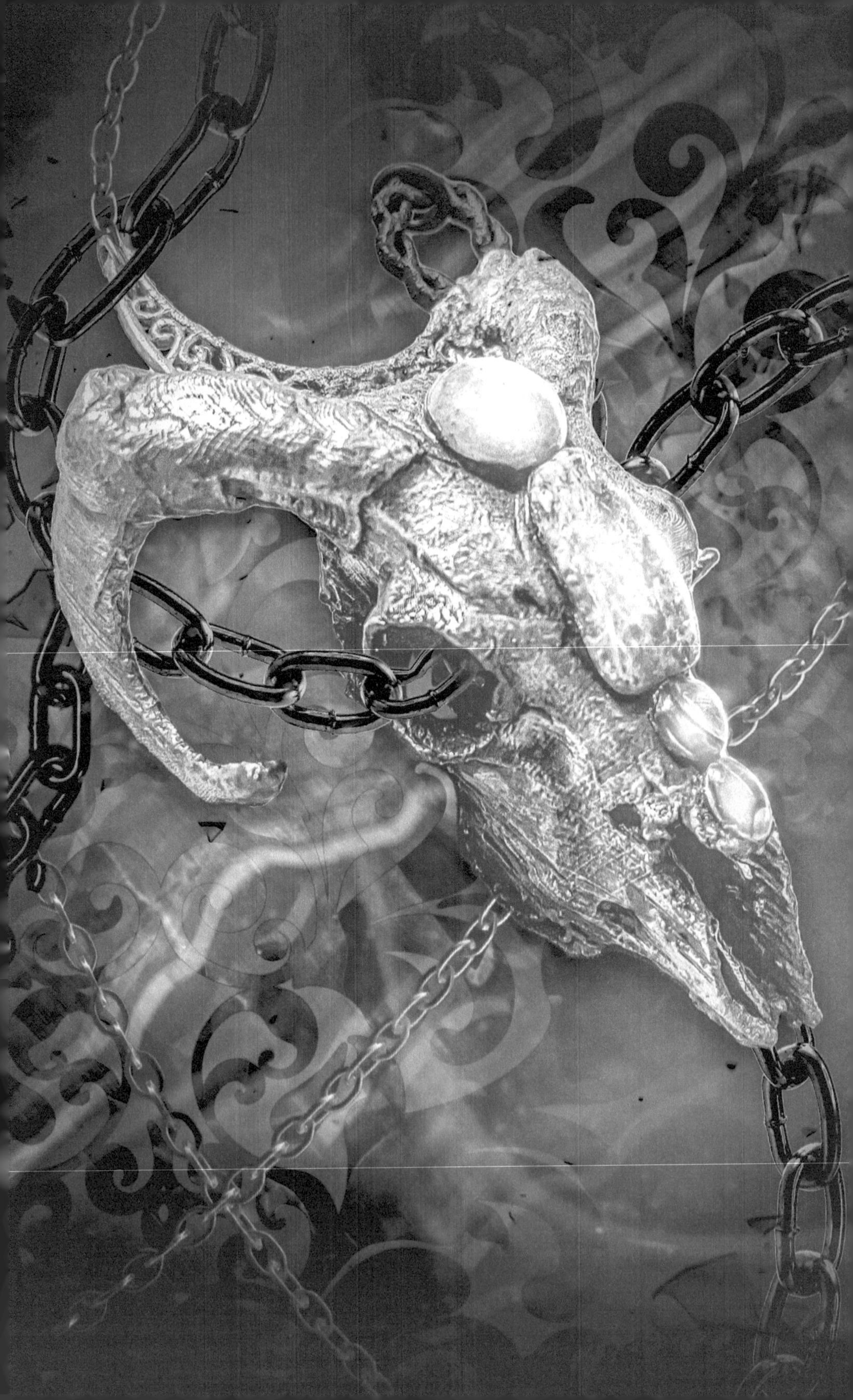

CHAPTER 22

SPENCER

Awareness of the world around me returns, and so does my hearing. Drake is screaming at Kasha, but I don't hear her replies if she even gives any. Rolling over onto my side, I finally catch Drake's attention and he helps me up.

"Fuck, Spencer." He gathers me into his arms. His body trembles, and I can barely breathe from his tight embrace.

"I told you I would be okay." My voice is muffled, but he must hear me because he squeezes harder until I wince.

He gently pulls back. "Are you hurt? What happened to you? I thought you..."

"I'm not hurt." My fingers stroke his cheek, the heat of his skin seeping into me. "You were just holding on a little tight. As far as what happened, my wolf broke the wall I'd apparently built between the two of us, showing me our true power."

Considering I didn't die, I don't see how it would be helpful to tell him that I almost did. It's not like any of it was intentional. At least, my wolf didn't think so.

Speaking of... *Wolf?*

She spoke so clearly in my mind. With the weight of exhaustion pressing in on me, I hadn't been able to enjoy that fact in the moment, and I wouldn't be sad if that becomes something we can always do.

Except, the longer I wait, the stronger the silence becomes.

She's there inside me, more present than ever before, but her voice is gone.

That's okay, I tell her. *We're still going to be okay. Better than okay.*

Her energy blossoms within my chest, and there's a slight rumble in my mind that I take as her agreement.

"Your skin," Drake says, pulling me back to the present, "it was turning grey, like a week-old corpse, and your heartbeat was so faint." He grabs my hands, holding them firmly. "I had no idea what was happening."

I smile and chuckle. "If it helps, neither did I. My wolf did all the work. All I had to do was lie there."

"Sooo," Kasha says from the porch now. "Are you going to leave us in suspense or tell us what you learned so I can decide if it's worth enough to not retaliate against your mate for his inappropriate threats?"

My gaze goes back to Drake, but he only shrugs. "I told you, I'm not as kind as you think I am. At least, not to anyone but you."

That's something I have no problem accepting about him.

"Help me up," I say to him, then add, "Slowly."

While I'm pulsing with new power and strength, I'm still weak from taking on so much all at once. Sleep is what I need next, but I know we have some things to discuss. Though, showing them the changes might be fun as well.

Drake gets me on my feet, and I grab his hand. Energy that transforms to heat moves from my core, up to my chest, then straight to my arm and pools within my palm. I panic for a moment when my skin starts to burn, unsure how to get the power from me to Drake, but I close my eyes and take a deep inhale.

As soon as I exhale, the energy inside me moves through my skin and into Drake's, causing him to come to an abrupt stop next to me. "What the..."

I open my eyes and grin. Even though I can't see my handiwork myself, I have no doubt that it's worked based on the widening of Drake's eyes and how the silver flecks there start to turn white.

"Where the hell did you go?" Kasha says sharply, her eyes narrowed as she searches the yard.

"How did you do that?" my mate asks, seeming to be transfixed with awe.

Kasha's arms cross, and she's now staring at us. "Why can I hear you, but not see you?"

I release Drake and expect her glare to drop, but that doesn't happen. One glance at Drake and his eyes are still glowing with my energy.

Huh. So, I didn't get it all right, but I'm sure I'll figure things out soon enough.

Concentrating, I pull my power back to me, calling it away from my mate and toward the well at my core. My knees want to give out from the extra efforts, but I try to hide my exhaustion.

"Let's go inside and I'll tell you," I say to them with a grin.

Drake's arm wraps around my waist, and I lean into his touch. "You're resting after this. Whatever this is, it took too much out of you."

He's not wrong, and I know we should be prepared for Kel to show up at any moment, but the more open I become, the more I learn, the less I'm worried.

That witch isn't coming here. We're going to her.

Drake half carries me into the house, and Kasha leads us to the couch, which I consider a small mercy because sitting on her wooden chairs in the kitchen sounded less fun than nearly being swallowed by the earth.

Leaning back on the cushions, I sink into their offered comfort and roll my neck. Yeah, I could fall asleep right here in the living room, but I know I have some explaining to do first.

"How about some coffee?" Kasha asks pointedly when I yawn widely. "I have some VitaBrew from Natalia."

I grimace and shake my head. "Just regular coffee is good. I'd actually like to sleep after this conversation. Not two days from now."

She laughs on her way back to the kitchen. "You're no fun."

"What the hell is VitaBrew?" Drake asks when we're alone again.

"It looks and tastes like coffee but is like a drug the humans called crack or cocaine. Well, nearly like that. If you don't know what those things are, you're better off not finding out."

"I'll take your word for it." He wraps an arm around my shoulders, allowing me to settle further into the couch.

Kasha comes back with three steaming cups. "Energy minus the cocaine."

Drake passes, and that doesn't surprise me given what I've just said, but I don't hesitate to take a long pull from my mug. With a sigh, I rest back on the cushion and smile. "That's already better."

"Now, care to tell us why you seem more like an angel to me than a shifter?" Kasha says with unveiled interest.

"Well," I glance at both of them," I kind of am."

Kasha nearly drops her drink and Drake's face goes pale, both of them making me laugh.

"I'm still a wolf shifter, through and through," I confirm, "but an albino wolf is only born when an angel blesses them. I'll have to ask my mother if she remembers meeting anyone unique when she was pregnant with me, but that's my understanding of the whole thing."

"And your camouflage ability?" Drake asks. "You made me disappear out there, but I could still see the both of us."

"You seem to be the exception when it comes to me using my abilities against you, but with the barrier gone between me and my wolf, I'm realizing I can do so much more than hide my wolf when needed."

I place my hand on Drake's thigh and glance between the two of them before continuing. "The moment I was freed from my own restraints, knowledge flooded into me. Things I feel as if I've known my whole life but have been blocking out. What Natalia was telling me about being pure? I understand that now."

"It's not that I'm 'good,' but my energy is original," I continue, my excitement growing with every new revelation that comes to me. "There's nothing else like me on this world. I don't know why the angel chose me or my mother, but I can protect others, hide them from their enemies, just like Natalia has been doing with her spells made from my blood. She unlocked my powers before I even knew they existed."

Drake's grin grows wide, and the silver flecks within his charcoal eyes are nearly as bright as they'd been when I shared my energy with him. "I knew there was a reason I wasn't willing to let you go so easily. You are everything I've never known in this life."

His joy for me radiates through our bond, sending shivers up my spine. How could I have ever thought rejecting him was the best thing for me?

Kasha holds up a hand and starts lifting fingers as she speaks. "So, you're touched by an angel, you can hide yourself and anyone else whenever you feel like it, your blood protects others from their enemies, and you glow like the sun. Anything else?"

My lips press together as I hold a hand in front of me. "What are you talking about? I'm not glowing."

I mean she's not wrong. My wolf does have a glow to her, but that isn't something Kasha should see now.

Even Drake appraises me, appearing to be looking for something neither of us can notice.

"I'm part fae," she states, and I realize I've never even taken the time to learn what she specializes in.

All I cared about was that she left me alone and never brought people around her home that gave me a reason to be suspicious of her, but the time for not caring about others is over.

"What exactly does that mean?" I ask, and because I've never seen her shift, I add, "Do you have a wolf, or do you only have a fae ability?"

"I have a wolf, but our relationship is strained." Kasha grimaces, and when she doesn't elaborate, I don't ask her to. As I've learned, bonds with our wolves can be complicated. "For my fae half, I specialize in wind, but I'm also sensitive to the other energies. Yours has always been strong, but now it's undeniable."

It's a good thing I've already decided that I can trust her, or I'd be more worried about the excitement in her words.

Before I can say anything else, she raises a brow. "Are you going to hide from the witch now that you know what you're capable of?"

This piques Drake's interest, but not mine. I know in my heart that this fight needs to happen. Not only for my peace of mind, but for the rest of our supernatural world. Kel was locked away for a reason and if we can't banish her like those before us did, then she needs to die. Nothing else is acceptable. I won't be responsible for anyone else getting hurt.

"No, we're leaving tomorrow." My gaze goes to Drake. "Right after Natalia finishes whatever spell she's been cooking this whole time."

This has Kasha grinning. "Whatever it is, it's going to be one hell of a banger."

"Why do you say that?" Drake asks, seeming more tense than he was just a few moments ago.

"Nat asked me for viloss dust," she answers proudly. "It's a powerful hallucinogenic made from flowers only grown in the fae realm. If you give that to the witch, she won't know up from down. Though, for how long depends on just how powerful she is."

Interesting and exciting all at the same time.

Kasha gets up. "I have things to do today, but don't worry, your family is still safe here. Nothing has changed where they're concerned, and you're welcome to stay as long as you all need."

I don't know how I got so lucky being introduced to a half-fae who isn't devious or selfish, but I regret not trusting Kasha sooner. I intend to make up for that when all this mess with Kel is done.

When it's just me and Drake left in the living room, I consider getting up and heading to bed, but I'm too damn comfortable to move. The warmth of my mate envelops me, and the cushions of the couch feel like floating feathers lulling me to sleep.

Except I still haven't forgotten Drake's previous rise in tension.

"You know we can't let Kel go, right?" I ask him, closing my eyes and leaning further against him.

His lips press against the top of my head, and he nods. "That doesn't mean I don't wish this wasn't our problem."

I have the same wishes, but there's not a doubt lingering within me anymore. I was made to protect others. While doing so through Natalia's spells is great, I know I'm capable of so much more now.

That's not something I can ignore, and I don't intend to, starting with Kel.

I'm going to wipe her existence from this world once and for all, keeping everyone safe from the danger they likely don't even know is out there, waiting to strike.

Right after I have a little nap.

CHAPTER 23

DRAKE

It takes me several seconds to remember where I am when I wake: on the couch with Spencer, inside Kasha's house. The place is dark and quiet, as is the outside world, but my mate still rests peacefully with her head on my chest, her body laid out next to mine.

My arms encircle her, holding her gently, and I watch the steady rise and fall of her chest. I trail my fingers over her arm, enjoying the feel of her silky skin. A smile forms on my face as our previous conversation comes back to me.

Spencer is a literal angel.

She might technically be a wolf shifter, but now that I know she's more than that at her core, everything else makes sense.

The draw I had toward her, the desperate need not to let her go, the sense of peace I feel with her... Yes, as a shadow shifter, my desire to claim my mate should have been overwhelming, but my wolf was bound when I met Spencer. There was no influence from my inner beast.

Anything that I felt was because of my mate and her alone.

"Hmmm." She burrows closer to me, and I tighten my hold.

Her heartbeat increases as though she's waking up, but she doesn't open her eyes. I kiss the top of her hair and wait, knowing she's been through a lot since the moment we met. Yet, this is the first time I think she's truly rested her mind and body in the last few days.

It's not even a minute later when her eyes flutter open and she looks up at me with a grin on her face. "Well, hello there."

I easily return her smile. "How are you feeling?"

Her hand slowly trails down my stomach. "Like I have a lot of pent-up energy to expend."

A rumble echoes from my chest, and before Spencer can take her next breath, I have her in my arms and am walking toward the backyard. "I can help with that."

She laughs, and the sound warms my entire body as she says, "I had a feeling you could."

Quietly yet with urgency, I get us out the back door and into Spencer's shed. I really hate this space for her. My mate deserves so much better than a shack with a mattress on the floor, and the fact that I can't readily provide more is something I intend to change soon.

Spencer wiggles out of my hold and begins throwing her clothes off, seeming to not care where they land as long as they're no longer touching her body.

Her beauty takes my breath away, and I barely have my shirt off before her hands are on my jeans, helping to move things along.

"If you're not naked in two seconds, I'm going to ruin your new clothes," she says with glee.

I kick my boots off as she tugs my jeans and boxers down my legs. My cock is already wide awake and when her fingers brush over him, he jolts to attention.

"I'm not the only one ready to expend extra energy," she says, wrapping her hand around my length and squeezing firmly as she moves her wrist up and down.

I reach for her, but she moves closer to the ground until she's on her knees in front of me. Her tongue wets her lips right before they part. I inch forward and she guides the head into her mouth. Her resounding moan sends vibrations up my shaft that go straight to my toes.

"Fuck, Spencer," I hiss, grabbing her hair.

She rocks back and forth, sucking my dick with vigor. Her mouth is heaven, but when she reaches for my balls, I see stars.

My fingers get tangled in her blonde strands as I surge forward until she starts to choke. I expect her to pull back, but she takes me even deeper.

I relinquish control for as long as I can, relishing the way she so easily commands me and how much I don't care. This woman owns every part of me, and I'm not ashamed to admit that.

Her tongue swirls as her head bobs, the motions repeating as her hands work their magic at the base. I let myself get lost in the ecstasy until I can't take much more.

"Spencer." Her name is a warning, but she doesn't seem to care.

Though, I do. The need to finally have my taste of her is too strong to ignore. I pick her up, forcing my cock from her eager lips.

Turning her until her back is against the unfinished drywall of the shed, I part her legs as I drop to my knees. "My turn."

My mouth sucks on her clit before she can get a word out. Her fingers grip my hair and she cries out. "Fuck me."

Oh, I will be, but not before I've made her come with my tongue.

Her hips surged forward as I suck and lick with abandon, enjoying as her breathing turns into heavy pants. Her legs are shaking and the hold she has on my hair still is nearly painful. Though, it's easily ignored as I lap at her center, eating up her sweetness as she falls apart for me.

"Oh, Gods." Her strangled cries of pleasure get caught in her throat as she shudders before nearly collapsing to the floor.

I stand to grab hold of her hips and lift her until she wraps her legs around my waist. "I'm not done with you, Mate."

She smirks. "I hope not."

Reaching between us, I grab my dick and rub the head against her waiting pussy. She's dripping wet and trembling with a need that only I can fulfill. One thrust upward and she's crying out my name once again.

The bond between us surges like a livewire, an unnecessary reminder that she means more to me than my own life.

I pound into her, remembering how she asked me not to hold back before. Her hands grab my face, and she keeps her stare on mine. The intensity of our connection nearly takes me down, but I push back, not ready to be done with her.

With one hand still gripping her ass, I use the other to grab the back of her neck and bring her closer. Her mouth crashes into mine, and I kiss her with the force of unspoken promises to never hurt her.

I knew the moment I saw this woman that she was the only one for me, that she is something special I would be a fool to let get away. The more time I spend with her, the more I get to touch her and hold her like this and learn who she really is, the more I know there isn't a day I ever want to spend without her.

My hips surge upward with ferocity and Spencer rips her mouth from mine, her head falling back against the wall as she moans with pleasure.

As I hold her tighter and fuck her harder, her nails dig into my skin, leaving red lines over my shoulders, but it's when her hand covers my chest that heat sears through my heart and a howl echoes through my mind.

With the curse on my wolf broken, there's no tattoo there, but there's still pain. I don't expect it, but more than that, Spencer's touch soothes the aches within, healing what can't be seen.

She doesn't seem to notice my momentary agony, and I don't stop pounding into her. Nothing else matters but her in my arms.

Not the past or what we've yet to face. It's only me and her in this moment, right now and forever.

She brings her head back to mine, our foreheads resting together as she pants and shudders within my hold. "So close," she whispers.

Her ankles tighten around my waist and with refocused efforts, I slam her into the wall, making cracks in the surface. Her cries grow louder, as do my grunts of need. She grabs my face and kisses me again, but this time the action only serves to quiet the sounds of her screams as she explodes around me.

It's only a few more pumps and I'm falling off the cliff right after her. Sweat covers our bodies, and our hearts race in time with one another as we take a few minutes to catch our breath. By the time she pulls back, there's a sideways grin on her face and she chuckles.

"We should do that more often," she says, her fingers playing with the back of my hair.

I hold her tighter and growl. "As often as you'd like, Mate."

She glances back. "But we should probably find somewhere else to fuck before we break Kasha's shed."

"I'll build her a new one," I say with a wink.

Spencer yawns and I expect her to try and wiggle free, but she leans her head against my chest. "I think I could fall asleep again after that, right here in your arms."

"Then, I've done my job right." I chuckle. "Let's get you in bed."

She frowns down at the mattress. "The couch was ten times more comfortable than that."

She's not wrong, but I don't tell her that. "You can sleep on me."

"Then, you won't be comfortable."

My eyes cast down, taking in her naked body. "I think I'll be just fine."

"You're incorrigible." She smacks my chest but makes no move to get away. "And here I thought you were chivalrous just a couple days ago."

"Can't I be both?" My brows waggle as I kneel onto the bed.

"I guess so." She stretches out over me as soon as I lay down. The warmth of her body soaks into mine, and as I drape the comforter over her, she rests her head right beneath my chin. "Best pillow ever."

Her words are already quieting, and I rub her back, lulling her to sleep.

There won't be any more rest for me. Not when there's no forgetting how much is on the line.

In the light of the morning, Natalia will have the spell we need to use against Kel. I'll be taking my mate straight toward one of the most evil witches to ever exist.

As much as I know that bitch needs to die, everything about this plan feels wrong. Yet, the thought of running and hiding for the rest of our lives is just as unappealing.

Considering Spencer seems hell bent on a fight, that's what I want to give her, but that doesn't mean I don't hold her tighter, hoping like hell we're not about to make the biggest mistake of our lives.

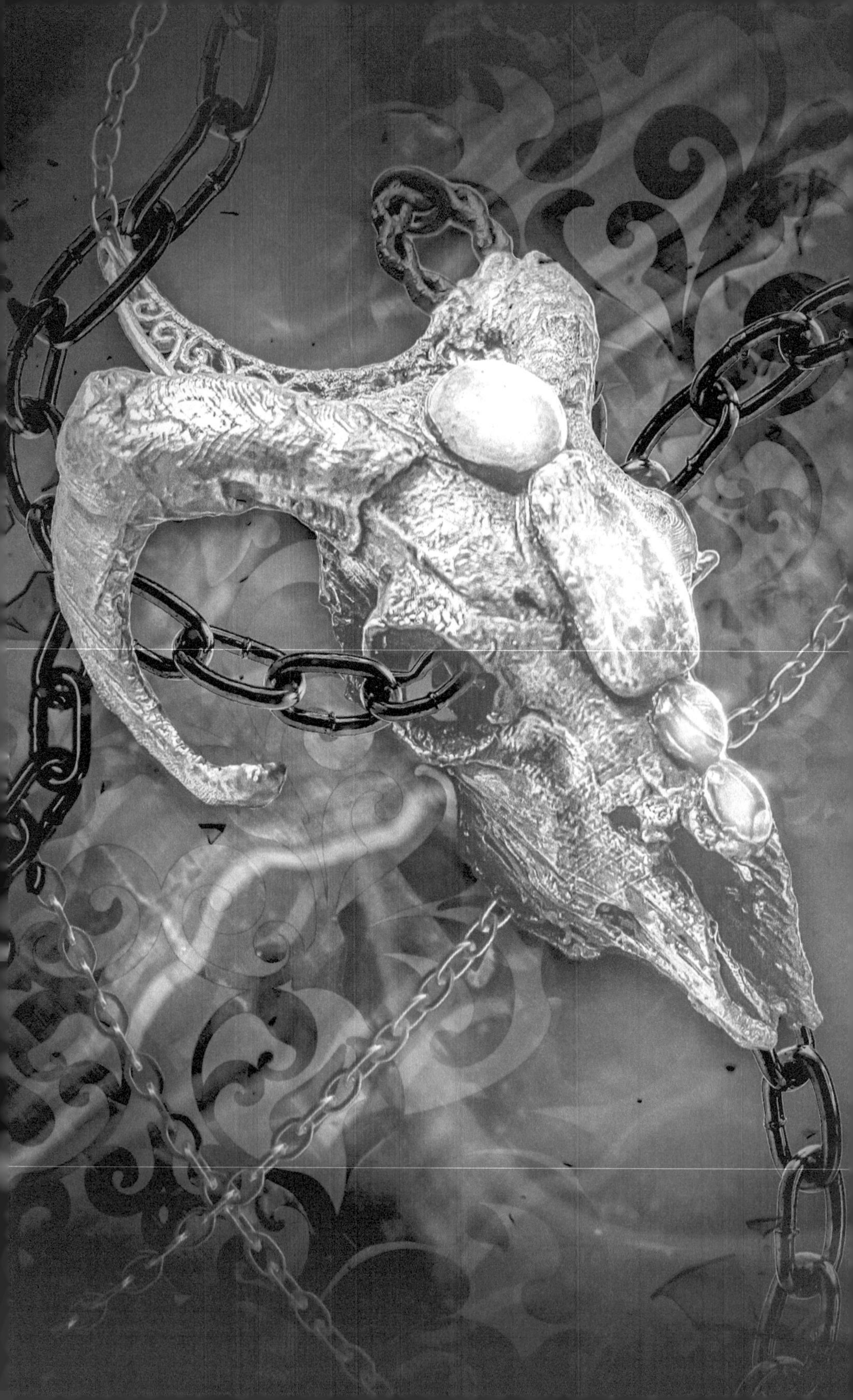

CHAPTER 24

SPENCER

The next morning, I wake at dawn and find myself alone. The sinking feeling in my chest is new, but when I sit up and a piece of paper floats off my chest, the aching eases ever so slightly.

My Dove,
I've gone for a run with my wolf.
If I'm not back before you wake, I will be soon.
Yours,
Drake

I flip the note over, but there's nothing else. I have no clue where he even found something to write on or with, but I tuck the paper into my bag at the corner of the shed before I get dressed.

Today is going to be busy and maybe the end of Drake's living nightmare. I want breakfast and coffee and to have a chat with my mom.

While I'm not afraid of going after the witch, I also have no intentions of underestimating Kel. What she did to Drake and Natalia's fear in the beginning are reminders that we can't be too careful, which means I need to prepare for things not going our way.

It's not something I've allowed myself to think too hard about yet, but I'm leaving my mother and brother behind. I need her to know what resources I have and that she's safe here with Kasha until she decides where she wants to be.

Now that I'm not pushing everyone away, I hope she'll find a home here in Crossroads like I have without realizing it, but if she wants something different for her and Peter then I've prepared for that.

Going into the house, everything is quiet just as it was last night when we went back out to the shed. My shoulders tremble and my lips turn upward, thinking about the way Drake fucked me against the wall.

I really did get lucky with him as a mate. I should also be thanking my mom for not letting me be an idiot and continue on with the notion that my life would be better without him.

Now that our bond has been solidified, I don't want to imagine a time in my life moving forward when I don't have him as my mate and by my side.

There's already a pot of coffee brewed on the counter when I tiptoe through the kitchen. I grab a mug from the cabinet and pour myself a full glass before heading toward the hallway to go peek in on Mom and Peter. I didn't get to see him much yesterday and I don't want to take off this morning without saying goodbye.

Before I can find the room they're sleeping in, Kasha comes out one of the closed doors, dressed in pajama pants, an oversized sweatshirt, and with her hair tossed up into a messy bun. It's the first time I've ever seen her so relaxed with her appearance and I like it. She doesn't say anything as she nods back toward the kitchen.

Curious, I follow her, drinking my coffee as I walk through the peaceful house. She sits at the table, and I take the chair across from her.

"I didn't think you'd be up already," she says with a smirk.

I tilt my head and then realize I didn't put up a cloaking spell before having sex with Drake while everyone else should have been asleep.

Oh well.

"Important things to do today," I reply, not taking her bait.

"That there are." She reaches for the pocket of her sweatshirt and slides a small red velvet bag across the table. "Only open that if things are dire and don't tell anyone that I gave it to you."

I raise a brow and take the offering. "What exactly is *it*?"

"Let's hope you don't have to find out." She grimaces and glances around. "But when Natalia asked me for viloss, I began to wonder about certain things. Just hold on to that and keep it safe. If you don't use it, bring it back to me. Better yet, if you do use it, try to still bring it back if you can."

My fingers play with the string on the small pouch. "And I can't open whatever this is until I'm ready to use what's inside? Will you at least tell me what it does?"

Kasha's fingers drum over the tabletop. "No, you shouldn't look inside. You could jeopardize the..." Her head shakes. "Just don't, okay? As for what will happen when you do open the bag, that depends on a few factors, but just think of it as the ultimate distraction if all else fails."

Hmm, a distraction to run or to finish the job? Something tells me Kasha knows more than she's saying, but she gets up, chugs her coffee, and goes to the sink.

"Cara is waiting for you in the living room," Kasha adds as she rinses the dish.

Well, that works because I was going to be looking for her.

I hold up the pouch as I stand. "Thanks for this."

She lets out a light huff. "Don't thank me yet."

I'm not sure if she's trying to convince me not to use whatever is inside, or if she's really that worried, but either way, I shove the offering into my front pocket, noting that it almost feels like there's a bunch of tiny pebbles inside, and head toward my mother.

She's sitting up straight on the couch and there are dark circles under her eyes that I don't remember seeing yesterday morning.

"Have you been up all night?" I ask her as I sit.

Kasha had said she spelled both Mom and Peter to not be overwhelmed with grief, but maybe whatever magic she used didn't do its job right.

Mom shrugs as she reaches for my hand. Her fingers are cold, and she shivers next to me. "What's going on?"

Instead of answering, she leans her head against my shoulder and presses her side flush with mine. "You're so warm."

"Kasha!" I shout, only staying where I am because I don't want to further upset my mother.

When she enters the living room, she receives my full wrath. "What the fuck did you do to my mother?"

She reaches a hand out to touch Mom's clammy face, and it takes everything in me not to snarl at her.

Kasha must sense my overprotectiveness, because she says, "I need to feel the magic inside her to know what's wrong. The spell worked just fine on Peter, so calm your ass down."

Easier said than done.

With reluctance, I let Kasha inspect my mother who has her eyes closed, resting against me.

"I think it's the bond she shared with your...father," she finally says after a tense minute of silence. "The spell is suppressing the ache of her bond, and this feels as though it's fighting back."

"Well, make it stop," I practically growl, hating that my mother is in pain and there's nothing I can do to help her. Again.

"I've never seen anything like this," Kasha says with awe, "but it's not my magic. It was a potion from Natalia. I can give her a call —wait." She holds up a finger. "I think I have something else that will work."

My first thought is to take my mother and get the hell out of this place, but I'm not supposed to be pushing people away any longer. I have to remind myself that Kasha isn't the enemy. She hasn't tricked me into being here and she's promised to take care of my family.

I feel confident that she will honor that even if it costs her own life.

Instead of stopping her from leaving the room to go get whatever she thinks will help, I hold my mother tighter and brush her hair back from her face. "It's going to be okay, Mom."

"I know," she murmurs. "No matter how bleak things get, you're going to be okay. You're my angel."

That's the first time she's ever called me that and I tense, remembering yesterday's revelations. Has Mom known this entire time that I was blessed by an angel?

I try to sit her up, but she burrows closer to me, seeming to be soaking in my warmth. I call her name several times, but she doesn't respond.

I start to pry her off me, but Kasha returns. "Sorry. I had to search a few boxes, but this is a cleansing spell. It works like a healing one but strips the body of anything foreign. Whatever I gave her before should get taken out by this."

I take the vial of mint green liquid from her and lean my mother's head back onto the couch. She's so cold that her body is almost stiff. My throat tightens as I try not to pay attention or hate myself for not checking in on her yesterday. If I had, maybe I would have...

Shaking my head, I open the potion and part her lips. "You're going to be fine, Mom. I'll make sure of it."

With her not really lucid, I'm not sure how I'm going to get her to swallow, but I don't worry about that too much as I tilt the spell into her mouth. Holding her jaw shut, I watch to see if her body will act on instinct and sure enough, she chokes a little, then I see her throat move.

"How long does this take to work?" I ask Kasha while keeping my eyes on my mother.

"Maybe a few minutes."

I hate to do this, but I release Mom and stand. I need to know my brother isn't having a reaction as well. They were both supposed to be napping together yesterday. If Kasha didn't notice anything wrong with my mother, I doubt she would have with Peter.

"I'm going to check on my brother. I'll be right back," I say to Kasha and without needing to be asked, she gets up and takes my spot.

I move quickly through the house and use my wolf senses to scent for Peter. When I open the door to his temporary room, he's lying on his side, holding a pillow in front of him and the blankets kicked down to the end of the bed.

I grin. Some things never change.

His coloring is normal, and when I press the back of my hand over his forehead, his skin is warm, not cold and clammy like

Mom's. My shoulders relax, but I still bend closer, listening to his heart. The steady beat holds me captive for several seconds as I close my eyes and breathe him in.

Kasha was right before. The bond must be why Mom is having a bad reaction to the spell.

I cover Peter back up and quietly exit the room. Getting back to the living room, I find my mother sitting up on the couch, her eyes shining with tears, but the awareness is back in them and that's most important to me.

"Spencer." The hollowness in her voice slices at my chest and I go to her, wrapping my arms around her.

She cries against my shoulder, and I nod at Kasha, mouthing my thanks.

The fae-wolf exits the room, and I continue holding my mother. Now that I've bonded with Drake and can't imagine living without him, I can better understand her grief.

It doesn't matter that Samuel was our living nightmare. Her heart belonged to him the moment she accepted the bond. What hurts the most and still makes me angry on her behalf is at one point in her life, she trusted him to take care of her and he broke that trust, over and over again.

She deserves better, and I hope one day she finds her second chance at happiness. For now, I won't fault her for grieving not only the mate she lost, but I'm sure the life she never should have been forced to live if he'd been a better partner.

We sit like that long enough for me to sense Drake return, but I assume Kasha tells him what I'm doing because he doesn't come find me. Though, he stays close enough for me to sense his energy. The run did him good. I don't know how long he was gone, but his essence is calmer, which we both need right now.

Mom's tears finally dry up and she sits up, a crooked smile on her face. "I'm supposed to take care of you, but it seems our roles have reversed."

"There's nothing wrong with that." I give her hand a squeeze. "You kept me safe, and now it's time I return the favor."

She sniffles and shakes her head. "It was my honor, but I'm not sure I did you any good by hiding you."

I can't lie and say that there haven't been moments when I've resented her for my upbringing, but not any longer. I make sure she knows as much.

"I've become the person I was always supposed to be," I say with confidence. "I needed to know the risks, and if you'd let me be myself, I might have trusted the wrong people and gotten hurt in the process. But because of you, I've figured out how to put my faith in the right people."

She swipes at her cheeks and nods. "I hate that this hurts so much."

"He was your mate even if he was a piece of shit."

A sob gets caught in her throat, and she covers her face with both hands, but when she pulls them back down, her stare is stronger than I've seen it in maybe forever. "I let you down so many times, but I won't anymore, Spencer. I promise."

"Everything is going to be okay." I offer her a smile because I don't know what else to do. These conversations have never been my specialty, but I know we need to talk about several things. "Crossroads can be the place you start over. I'm not holding on to the past, and you shouldn't either. It's time for us to move forward with our lives. We deserve that. So does Peter."

She nods, squeezing my fingers between her shaking hands. "I think you might be right."

"I'm leaving today, and I might be gone for a day or two," I tell her. "Kasha will take care of you here, but if you need anything, there is plenty for you to trade with in my shed. Take whatever you need."

I can't tell her that there's a chance I won't be back. She's fragile, and I won't put those thoughts on her when I don't even want them myself. But there is something else I need to know before I go.

Looking away because I'm not sure I want to see her reaction, I finally ask, "Did you know an angel came to you when you were pregnant with me?"

She gasps and jerks back. "What?"

At least her shock is genuine.

"I learned yesterday that I was angel-touched," I tell her, finally meeting her wide stare. "It's why my wolf is the way it is."

More tears fill her eyes, and she starts to laugh softly. "How could I have not seen that all these years? Of course you're angel-touched." Her hand covers her mouth, and then she freezes. "Oh."

"Oh? Oh what?" I ask, desperate for any information she can give me.

Her body relaxes, and she falls back onto the couch. "There was a woman. She found me crying in town one day. I don't even remember what I was out getting, but it was the morning after the first time Samuel hit me. I broke a glass and... Anyway, she hugged me and, at the time, I thought my desperation for love was just getting the better of me, but now, I understand. Her touch not only healed my physical wounds that day, but made sure my baby would have the ability to survive the hell we lived in."

Mom's grief is outshined by the memory and, at least for the moment, she's not hurting.

"Thank you for sharing that with me," I say sincerely. I hate to leave her now, but time isn't on our side. We need to find Kel before she gets any stronger or decides to come here. "I'm going to say goodbye to Peter, and then I need to leave, but I'll be back as soon as I can be."

She sits back up and hugs me with more strength than I've felt from my mother in far too long. "I love you, Spencer. You're going to be okay."

It's not the first time she's said that, and I hope like hell she's right, because it feels as if I've only just started living. I'm nowhere near ready to be done.

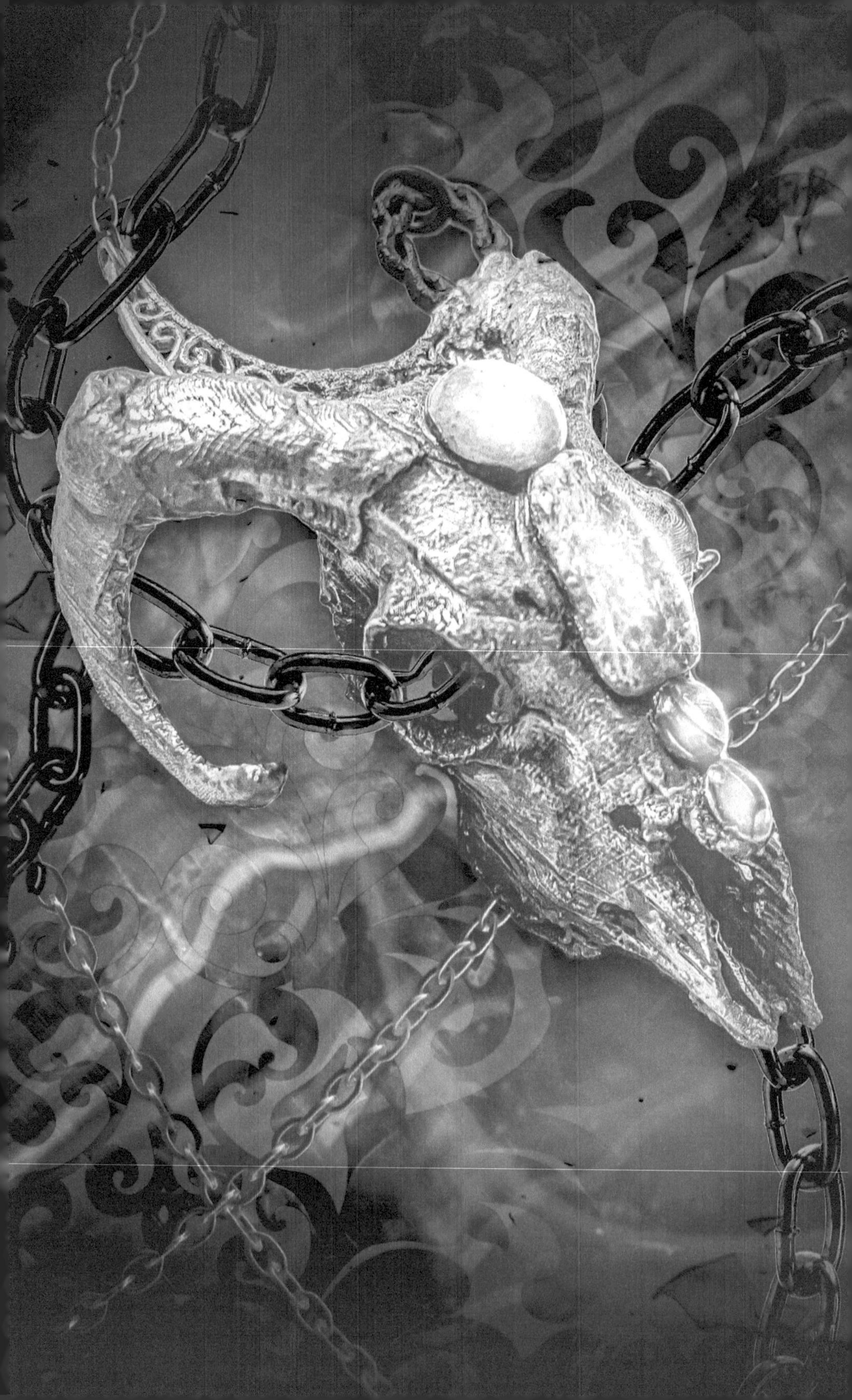

CHAPTER 25

DRAKE

It hadn't been my intention to be gone for so long, but it was the first time in centuries that I was able to run with my wolf on my own. The first time in too long that we were free to be ourselves without my wolf being unsurprisingly distracted by our mate.

The joy that brought me was almost as euphoric as bonding with Spencer. We raced past the city while most everyone still slept until there were only trees around us. The quiet of the night had entranced me, and I have no clue how far we ran, but far enough that the pull to go back to Spencer became too much to ignore even for my wolf.

Hours later, I return, and my mate isn't where I left her. Kasha lets me know where Spencer is, and I gladly give her more time with her mother. I'm envious. I don't even know if mine is still alive, and I tell myself that I don't care, but I would have rather had a parent who gave a damn than one who abandoned me.

I wait outside for Spencer, not wanting to interrupt her time with her family before we go. When the back door opens, I expect to see my mate, but it's Peter who steps out onto the porch.

He waves and has a ball in his hand. "Want to play catch? Mom and Pence are having a grown-up talk."

I chuckle. "Is that what they told you?"

He shakes his head. "I heard Mom crying, and whenever she does that, I get sent to my room because I'm not old enough for grown-up talk yet. But I've been in my room all night and thought I could come out here instead."

Smart kid.

"Well, then let's play," I say, holding my hands up.

He tosses the ball at me and runs toward the other side of the yard. "So, my sister likes you. I kinda thought she hated you. I felt bad for you because Pence can be scary when she wants to be, but I guess I don't need to anymore."

I throw the ball back to him, trying not to laugh because I'm pretty sure he's just making conversation and I don't want him to feel bad, but he really has no filter.

"Sometimes girls are complicated," I reply with a grin. "But yes, Spencer doesn't hate me anymore and I'm very glad, because I like her a lot." I pause, then add with a raised brow, "Is that okay with you?"

He rolls the ball between his hands and stares me down with a stoic look on his face, then he shrugs. "Yeah, I guess. Just don't take her away from us again. That would make Momma sad. Me, too."

Guilt presses in on me, weighing down so heavily that even forcing a smile for the boy takes real effort. If anything happens to Spencer when we go looking for Kel, I don't know how I could ever face her family again. Hell, I'm not sure I could even survive losing her after being alone for so long.

Yet, I know my misery would be the price I had to pay for failing to protect my mate.

Peter throws the ball back to me, and we play catch for a while longer until Spencer finally comes outside to find me.

The smile she sends my way nearly puts me on my ass and distracts me to the point that I don't notice when the ball comes back my way, allowing it to hit me right in the chest.

"I'm sorry!" Peter squeals, hiding his face and dropping to the ground.

Poor fucking kid.

My trance is broken, and I run over to him, gently touching his shoulder. "It's okay, buddy. I'm not hurt and it was my fault. I got distracted."

He's shaking beneath my palm, but then all of a sudden, he throws himself at me, choking me with his arms as they tighten around my neck.

Holding him, I stand and turn toward Spencer, unsure what I'm supposed to do. She watches with shiny eyes as she leans against the porch railing, then gives me a thumbs up before turning back toward the house.

I guess I'm on my own.

"I'm really fine, Peter," I tell him, but his hold only increases.

I've never really been around kids, not even when I was younger. I mostly took care of myself and did what I could for food, but I do know there's nothing wrong with a little bribe to make someone feel better.

"What if we go inside and make hot chocolate?" I ask him.

He loosens his hold ever so slightly. "With sprinkles?"

"Isn't that the only way?"

He pulls back, his eyes wide with delight. "I knew I liked you."

I mess with his hair before putting him back down. "I like you too, kid."

Peter runs for the house, and by the time I enter behind him, he's already standing on one of the kitchen chairs, searching the cabinets as if he owns the place.

Spencer is sitting at the table, still grinning. "I knew you didn't need me."

"Yeah, if I can win you over—"

The glare on her face shuts me right up but doesn't stop me from laughing as I help Peter get everything sorted for hot chocolate.

I'm impressed. He's only been here for two days and already knows where everything is. We heat milk on the stove first before pouring the cocoa powder into the mugs. He sets out five without asking anyone else, and something tells me nobody will reject his offering.

The milk gets hot enough, and I take care of pouring but let Peter do the stirring and pour the toppings. First, the marshmallows, followed by the sprinkles.

"Here you go, Pence," he says, serving his sister first. "Where's Momma?"

"Right here."

Cara enters the kitchen, lines around her eyes that weren't there the day before, and when I glance at Spencer, she shakes her head. I guess we'll talk about it later.

"Morning, Momma," Peter says with a smile that lights up the whole room.

Cara accepts his offering, seeming to force her own grin. "Thank you, sweet boy."

She sits next to Spencer, and I glance around. "Is Kasha still home?"

My mate nods. "Last I saw anyway."

"I'll just leave her cup here," Peter says, putting a mug at an empty chair.

We take our own drinks to the table and sit together...like a family. My stomach churns, and I keep my eyes on the marshmallows that are melting in front of me. I know this is a good thing, to have found my mate and to have people to care about. Yet, I've spent so long on my own that I don't know what to do with this odd sense of peace and belonging.

Spencer's foot nudges mine from under the table. Reluctantly, I look up at her, and she's staring intently. Warmth from our bond flares within my chest, but I can't shake the uncomfortableness within me.

This is a real family. The three of them together, listening to Peter rattle on about nothing and everything all at once. And here I sit, the intruder who is putting Spencer at risk by not having been willing to let her go.

I should leave now. Go to Natalia, get the spell, and deal with Kel on my own. She's my problem, not theirs. Yet, the thought of leaving my mate behind makes the ache within my stomach intensify.

Not knowing what to do brings me back to the early days after I was first cursed. I had no clue how I was going to get free, and the helplessness of the situation had me wishing for death on an hourly basis. Yet, this time, I just want to run away. I want to take this family and hide them away just like Spencer had intended to do before her father died.

But as she continues to stare into my soul, I know she's not that same person anymore. She doesn't want to live in fear any longer, and she shouldn't have to.

I need to find a way to have faith that everything is going to be okay just like she has. She accepted me into her life, trusting that I wasn't going to be the worst thing to ever happen to her like Samuel had been to Cara.

Now, I must believe the same.

"So, Bubby," Spencer starts, and I push down any doubts I have because my mate needs my support right now, not my added stress. "Drake and I need to go do a few things, and it's going to take a day or two. You and Momma are going to stay here with Kasha. Is that okay?"

His little round face scrunches and he sits his mug down. "What are you doing?"

"We need to go find someone," she replies coolly.

"Why?"

She offers him a soft smile. "Because we need to have a little chat with her?"

"Are you going to chat or are you going to fight?" His eyes narrow. "Why does it have to be you?"

She reaches across the table for him and holds his hand. "Sometimes things are too important to let other people handle. This is one of those times. But you'll have fun here, and you're safe with Kasha."

Peter glances over at me, then back at his sister. "You're safe with Drake."

He says the words as if nothing else could be truer, and the weight of responsibility not only to my mate but to her family sits heavily on my shoulders.

"I am, but he's also safe with me." She winks, making him laugh.

"You are pretty strong, Pence." His lips twist. "I wonder who would win in an arm wrestle?"

"As long as it's not done on my table, my money is on your sister," Kasha says as she finally joins us, her long hair damp and face free of any makeup.

Peter's eyes light up. "Can they use the table outside?"

She shrugs. "Sure, but you'll have to help me rebuild it if they break it."

His fist shoots up into the air. "Deal!"

I tilt my head at Spencer. "Are we doing this?"

"Not today, but as soon as we're back, you can count on it." She stands and holds her arms out. "Come give your sister a hug."

His shoulders droop as he trudges around the table. "Do you have to go *right* now?"

"Unfortunately so. There are people waiting on us, and it wouldn't be nice if we disappointed them," she says, holding him tight.

"Yeah, I guess," he murmurs before pulling back, then surprises me when he comes to give me a hug. "You'll come back too, right?"

"Of course, I will." I've never had anyone to make promises like that to, but by saying the words and looking into his wide, hopeful eyes, something twists in my chest. The foreign feeling wipes out my earlier worries. This isn't just about protecting Spencer. It's about keeping their family together and not missing out on the chance to be part of that.

I hug the boy, then catch Cara's stare on me. "I haven't had a vision since we came here, but I know you'll take care of my daughter."

"With my own life," I promise.

"Try not to let it come to that, yeah?"

I hope to hell not. We all have a lot to fight for now. This isn't just about my vengeance any longer. It's about protecting the people in my life and getting the chance to live for the first time in a millennium.

CHAPTER 26

SPENCER

Saying goodbye to my mother and brother wasn't the hard part of the morning. It was once again making sure Kasha will do whatever it takes to keep them safe if Drake and I fail or if things don't go as planned.

I feel confident that she wouldn't accept the responsibility if she wasn't going to do her best, but that doesn't stop me from worrying.

Yet, it also doesn't stop me from walking out the door and heading to Spells once again.

Drake and I arrive just after nine in the morning to find the door locked. I shake the handle and look at him. "It's never been locked for me before."

"Maybe someone else is in here," he suggests, trying to peer through the tinted windows.

No, she wouldn't have other clients at the shop while working on a spell like what we need for Kel. I might not have taken the time to get to know Natalia well over the last couple months, but I do know she honors privacy.

"Why don't we check around the back?" Drake takes a step back from the door, but I stay put. Something doesn't feel right.

I don't answer Drake. I put my palm against the door and close my eyes. A hum of energy moves from the building through my skin and up my arm. There's nothing dark about the magic, but it's also not anything I've sensed here before.

What are you doing, Natalia?

Maybe something went wrong with the spell and the witch is trying to keep the energy contained. It's the only other explanation I can think of besides someone else being in there that shouldn't be. Yet, I don't sense anyone else.

"What is it?" Drake asks quietly.

"I don't know, but we need to get in there." I'm not leaving this shop without that spell. I gave Natalia the time she asked for and one way or another, we're going to find out if she's come through on her promise.

Pressing my hands against the door again, I lean into the glass. Magic snakes up my arms and wraps around me like a blanket, warming my body everywhere the energy touches.

"Spencer." Drake's tone is warning. "You're glowing."

Nothing I can do about that now. Whatever I've found myself locked into has a hold on me, but I'm not being attacked so I stay calm.

The glass starts to rattle beneath my touch, and my heart hammers in my chest as I draw more magic into myself. This is a foreign feeling for me, containing this much energy, but I can't stop. I need to get inside, and the power wants me to unlock this door somehow.

I'm tempted to slam my head against the glass, but I'd rather not get bloody.

Drake's hand settles on my shoulder and, instantly, the magic

I've been absorbing starts to move from my body to his. His grip on me grows tighter and he growls.

"What the fuck is this?"

I try to shrug, but my movement is more like a flinch. "One of Natalia's games. Hopefully." Glancing over at my mate, I grin. "Hey, you're glowing now, too."

Based on the scowl on his face, he doesn't seem too pleased with that revelation, but he should be. With his touch, the power from the shop is now flowing freely, and the weight of it lightens until I can finally lift my hand from the glass again.

My head tilts to the side as I stare at my skin. I'm not touching the door any longer, but the energy is still alive and moving through me. Shivers crawl along my skin, but I'm not afraid. Hell, I'm not even mad about the power boost.

This time, when I pull on the handle to get inside, the door opens without resistance, and the inside of Spells is brighter than I've ever seen it before.

Drake and I step through the threshold together, and the door nearly hits us in the ass as it closes on its own.

"It's about time you showed up." Natalia's voice sounds from behind the curtain.

As she speaks, a soothing chime sounds from above us and I glance up, expecting to see something other than the annoying red-and-black songbird. Yet, it's the same damn one.

"Did you change the ringtone of that thing?" I call out, asking Natalia.

She pokes her head out from the backroom. "Nope. He just finally finds you worthy. That was his test out there, not mine, in case you're wondering."

"You've got to be shitting me," I mutter, glaring up at the bird. "You've been screwing with me this whole time."

He chirps, and I have no clue if he's some kind of familiar or what, but I still want to strangle him.

Drake chuckles next to me. "No wonder you thought it was odd that I enjoyed the sound he made. I wasn't hearing the same thing you were."

I try not to take offense that the bird targeted me and not the cursed shifter from a shadow world, while at the same time, I can't help wondering how many feathers I could pluck from his back before Natalia stopped me...

"I have your spell ready," she says, walking into the bright room with one small pouch.

A frown creases my face. That bag, if you could even call it that, doesn't give me hope that she's going to be offering us much, but maybe big power comes in small packages. Hopefully.

I glance around as we approach the counter. The floating candles don't seem any bigger, yet it's almost annoyingly bright in here. "Did you increase the lighting in here?"

She raises her brow. "Have you looked at yourself? I expected the enlightening spell I gave you to give you some clarity, but I didn't think you'd start showing off your power just because."

If she only knew. Her little spell nearly killed me, but I don't believe that was her fault just as my wolf had said, so I don't tell Natalia just how intense that potion really was.

Instead, I take a deep inhale in. The magic from the glass—or the bird—still pulses inside me. That has to be causing my glow. Yet, I don't know how to release the power.

Drake doesn't seem to be affected any longer, so it's just me as Natalia said, but I have no clue why.

"You've learned to unlock your true self, Spencer, but now, you need to know how to wield the energy you possess if it's to serve you the way you need."

I'm sure the witch knows what she's talking about, but we're out of time for me to learn new things. I close my eyes and do what I've always done, I start to build a wall around my core, keeping the power contained.

Except just when I start making progress, a sharp pain shoots through my mind and I suck in a breath. My eyes open to find Natalia's pointer finger pressed against my forehead. "Um, care to tell me what the hell you're doing?"

She shakes her head and stares intently at my chest for several seconds. Only when I can finally feel my lungs working again does she release me.

"You're not glowing anymore," she says, lines of concern etched around her eyes, "but you're going to want to learn how to truly command your inner power. You can't keep shoving energy like that down. In the meantime, the next time you want to use it, make sure you're prepared to fully unleash your wolf."

Sounds...fun. "Thanks for the help."

She half snorts and huffs. "I seem to be doing a lot of that lately." She slides the pouch closer. "Here is everything you should need."

I pick it up and I feel rather confident the black leather is empty. "Um, thanks."

"Reach inside before you judge," she says with a grin.

Tugging on the thin string, I open the top as far as it will go and just manage to get my fist inside. Wait, my hand should not fit in here.

I hold the bag higher and wiggle my fingers, but the edges of the fabric don't move like they should. "What kind of magic is this?"

"It's a witch's pocket," Drake answers with amusement. "I haven't seen one since I was a kid and tried to steal it from someone in the market."

Natalia chuckles. "I'm surprised you're still alive."

"I'm a fast runner." Drake's fingers brush over the material. "This is going to help."

I have no clue where his confidence is coming from, but I try and fail to mirror it. "I can't feel anything. How do I get the spell out?"

"Call for it," she replies as if I should have already known the answer.

Um, spell, come here.

I've never felt more stupid in my life, yet... Two seconds later, something glass and warm fills my palm.

I pull my hand out and there between my fingers is a glass jar with a silver top, carved with swirling symbols. "Is this it?"

Natalia nods. "Yep. And it's one-of-a-kind. Don't drop that jar or open it until you're absolutely sure you're ready to use it. You'll also find other potions and trinkets in there, along with a few portal spells. Just ask for help and see what you get. The pocket is rather intuitive. I've had that for... Well, let's just say a while."

My skin warms, and I smile at the witch. "Thank you, Natalia. For everything. I know I haven't always been the easiest to get along with, but I truly appreciate your friendship."

She reaches for my hands and holds them between hers. "I knew the moment you walked through my door that you were worth the investment of putting up with."

I laugh and do something I've never done before. I hug the witch, and when she returns the gesture, I nearly melt into her embrace. "You're going to be okay, Spencer," she whispers before we part.

"Thank you," I say again, only because I don't know what other words would be appropriate right now. "I guess we will see you when we see you. I have no clue how long it will take for us to find Kel."

"Just be prepared for the possibility that she'll find you first," Natalia says, and that has both me and Drake tensing.

"We will be," he says gruffly, then looks at me. "Maybe we could find that shifter Lia and see if she has more to share."

Natalia tilts her head. "Who's Lia?"

"No clue," I reply. "She's visiting with her mate Markus, but she said we needed to head north to find Kel, and my wolf trusted her, so that's where we're going."

"Fair enough." She glances between the two of us. "Keep each other safe."

With a nod, we both head toward the door. This time, I don't rush out or glare at the songbird. When my fingers wrap around the door handle, there's a flare of energy, but it's brief and welcoming. Maybe I can finally have a truce with the winged creature.

"Where do you think we'll find Lia?" Drake asks as we step onto the sidewalk.

Spells is only two blocks from the portal, and considering most visitors are here only because of their curiosity in the new world, I take a step in that direction.

"Let's go see what we can find at the portal," I say, then grin. "I promise not to run away from you this time."

His head shakes as he wraps an arm around my waist, his fingers squeezing my hip. "Just like before, I wouldn't let you get far."

The rumble within his words sends a tremor of want down my spine. If only we didn't have a witch to kill.

"Oh," I stop abruptly and reach into my pocket, grabbing the other small bag I've been given this morning. "Kasha gave this to me. She wouldn't tell me what it is. Just that I shouldn't open it unless things are dire."

He takes it from me. "It feels like rocks."

"That's what I thought, but she made it very clear we weren't to open it until we were ready to release the chaos in there." I close his fingers around the small bag. "You keep that, and I'll keep the witch's pouch."

He chuckles. "Pretty sure you're getting the better end of that deal."

"And I'm pretty sure your hand wouldn't fit in Natalia's offering."

Drake shoves Kasha's mysterious offering into his pocket. "True. Now, come on. I'm ready to get this over with."

We continue and once we're at the portal area, we move through the crowds of people out and about. My eyes continue to scan the area, and I search for the unique scent that Lia had put off. Except nothing stands out to me or Drake.

We stay there for about thirty minutes with no luck, and I can't wait around any longer. Walking around in circles when we're supposed to be headed north is making my wolf a little stir-crazy, especially with that spell tucked into my front pocket.

"I guess we're on our own now," Drake says, grabbing my hand and giving the portal one last look.

Since the day that thing opened, I've never had a real interest in seeing what's on the other side, just a draw that I fought like a plague, but maybe I have a reason now.

"When this is all over, if you want to go back, I'd visit with you," I tell him, having no clue if he left anything he cares about behind.

His head shakes. "Tartarus is only a bad memory for me. I'm ready to make new ones here with you."

Damn him and his sweet words. I lean in closer, drawn to his warmth. "Then, we'll do that."

"Spencer?" A familiar voice says, and we both turn around.

"Hello, Corvin." I grin, then nod to his powerful mate. "Styx."

Her black eyes appraise me, and she keeps her chin raised, but there's a flicker of a smile there. "Spencer."

"Who's your—" Corvin starts to ask, but I answer before he can finish.

"This is my mate Drake." I squeeze Drake's hand. "Drake, this is Corvin and Styx. They help guard the portal and have a new pack forming here in Crossroads."

Corvin's brows raise. "Do I finally sense an interest from you in regard to joining?"

I bite the inside of my cheek. I hadn't really thought about it until this moment, but after all that's happened since meeting Drake, a home sounds pretty damn nice.

"Depends," I say. "Do you have room for four shifters? Because I'm a package deal."

Him and Styx share a look I can't read before he answers me. "We're adding cabins to our territory by the river as we speak. There will be more than enough room."

"That's good to know. I'll keep the offer in mind still."

His head shakes as he laughs. "Stubborn through and through. We'll be seeing you, Spencer. Nice to meet you, Drake."

My mate nods but doesn't reply as Corvin and Styx keep walking in the opposite direction.

"He's been trying to get me to join their pack for over a month now," I tell Drake when I start to sense there was something he didn't like. "Seems nice enough."

"His mate," Drake says with tension, watching them disappear down another street. "She's from Tartarus."

Ah, that makes more sense.

"Yes, but she lives here now." Maybe joining the pack still isn't the best idea. "We can build our own home. We don't need a pack."

Drake looks down at me and shakes his head. "Seeing

someone from Tartarus so soon just threw me off. I trust your judgment."

He's really too nice for his own good sometimes.

I turn him until he's facing me. "We won't live somewhere that makes you uncomfortable for any reason, Drake Cage. I promise you that. If you see her again and the same feelings still arise, then we have options. The shed isn't *all* that bad."

He finally cracks a smile. "You're rather incredible, My Little Dove."

"I know." I wink at him, then reach for the witch's pocket. "Now, how about we get the hell out of here and go hunting?"

CHAPTER 27
DRAKE

Once we get out of the main part of town, Spencer retrieves a portal spell from the pouch and takes us about an hour north to a city she's been through before. Though, when we get there, it isn't anything like the one we just left.

There is only one building still standing. The rest are caved in on at least one side or merely a pile of rubble. The paved streets are cracked and have holes every so often that look like bombs went off.

"Huh." Spencer shrugs and holds her head higher. "Some sort of battle must have happened here in the last month, but I don't sense dark magic, so I don't think it was Kel."

Tartarus might be filled with some dark souls, but destruction like this isn't normal. "Why would people destroy homes so thoroughly?"

"This is No Man's Land," she answers. "Home of the House-less, the rejected, the lawless. Crossroads is the exception." Her hand gestures around us. "This is pretty normal unless you live in one of the House territories."

"Why don't you live with a House?" I ask, wondering if they're not as safe as they sound.

"Thanks to my father, I was banished from my pack," Spencer replies. "Though, I don't actually know if the Alpha Supreme Kinsley would let my banishment stand. She's been turning Fire and Fluorite into an honorable House, something that place hasn't been in much too long. We could always go back there and see what happens if you didn't want to be in Crossroads."

Taking Peter back to the place where he killed his father doesn't sound like the best plan, but I appreciate the fact that she instantly caught on to my discomfort and was open to change.

I have no doubts Crossroads will be a good home. I've seen the way people have cared for my mate in their own ways, and I don't want her to lose that. That just isn't how Tartarus was, and living under the command of someone raised in that world gave me pause.

Though, I don't know Styx. Maybe there's a reason she's here and not back in the shadow world. I shouldn't preemptively judge.

"Seeing as how things aren't as I last saw around here," Spencer says, "how about we shift and run for a while? I don't want to teleport too far north and miss Kel if she's headed south."

We just had a long sprint this morning, but my wolf still perks up at the idea of getting out again. I can't blame him and agree with Spencer's idea. Teleporting can only help so much.

"I won't ever say no to a run."

She steps back first, her skin glowing briefly before energy swirls around her. My eyes attempt to watch every part of her shift, but her body contorts so quickly that I feel as if I've missed the whole thing when her wolf appears just a few seconds later.

The stunning white beast stands proudly before me. Her bright blue eyes spark with interest as she comes closer. I hold my hand out, and her head settles into my palm.

"Such a stunning creature," I whisper and lean my head down closer to hers. "Thank you for keeping her safe."

The wolf rumbles in response, then nudges my hand away, making me laugh. "I hear you. You don't want me, you want *him*."

Her tongue rolls out the side of her mouth, and I have my confirmation.

Shifting comes easily, and as soon as my dark wolf appears, Spencer's leaps at him. They nip and growl playfully at each other, but not for long.

None of us have forgotten we're not out for fun. Kel could be anywhere, and the heaviness in my heart only grows as more time passes. I don't know if that's just my dread or a sign that we're getting closer, but either way, we can't let our guard down.

The two wolves begin to run, staying side by side as we move through the ravaged remnants of the town. Our paws kick up dust as we traverse the forsaken road until we leave the destruction behind and reach a main road.

The world around us is eerily quiet as we continue north, scanning the area for any new scents. Miles pass without any signs of life, but as the sun creeps higher into the sky, I have a feeling that won't last long.

Just as I'm about to nip at Spencer, suggesting we stop, she comes to an abrupt halt, her wolf's ears pitch forward, and a growl rumbles deep in her chest.

I don't sense what she does, but I move to stand by her side. When I'm only a few feet from her, the air in front of her tears open, creating a dark void. Six shadows burst from the gaping hole, their snarls echoing around us as they leap to attack without hesitation, their snapping jaws aimed to kill.

My instincts scream to protect Spencer, but one of them barrels into me, its claws sinking into my flesh as we crash to the ground. With a grunt, I push the beast off, feeling the warmth of my blood staining my coat. Still, I'm on my feet in a heartbeat, facing down three menacing adversaries.

A fleeting glance toward Spencer shows me that she's already a force of nature with one enemy down beneath her. I can't help but feel a surge of pride as I launch myself at the nearest wolf, aiming for its throat. He moves swiftly out of my way, but that doesn't stop me from changing focus and aiming for the shifter behind him.

With my teeth bared and claws out, I latch on to the next wolf and rip into his throat. His body thrashes against mine, leaving gouges from his claws in his wake, but I don't relent.

Not until another one jumps on my back.

An ambush from behind nearly brings us down, but we roll out from under our attackers just in time to see the first wolf we struck staggering to the ground, unlikely to rise again.

The other two come after me at the same time. I could run to the side, try to split them up, but I want to be done with this. They're literally bleeding dark magic, which makes me believe this isn't a random attack.

Kel sent them here.

You've always been such a smart man, her voice sounds through my mind, distracting me just long enough for the two wolves to attack without me being prepared.

How the fuck am I hearing her? I assumed when it happened before that it was because the curse had just been broken and she was reaching out one last time before the hold on my wolf was officially broken. This, though? This changes things, and my mate isn't going to like it.

As one wolf lunges for my throat, the other slashes at my

belly. My wolf lets out a loud roar and rolls away from them, but we don't get far.

Did you think you could beat me so easily? Kel taunts. *I've been alive since the beginning of time. There is no stopping me.*

Fuck you, I snarl and start to fight back even as I'm losing blood.

The two wolves above mine are relentless in their attempts at killing me, but my wolf shakes our head back and forth, barely avoiding a deathly blow.

A roar tears from me, a sound of determination as I evade another strike to my neck. My wolf kicks our back legs out and takes one of our attackers by surprise. There's a brief reprieve, and we use that to finally stand back up, but our limbs are shaking, and each step sends shooting pains across our spine.

A deep growl catches the attention of the two wolves stalking closer to me, but they barely get the chance to glance left before Spencer's wolf is on them. She's covered in blood, but the scent isn't hers. The ferocity in which her wolf fights the remaining two beasts is awing.

Her teeth rip into the first one as if he's being served to my mate on a platter for lunch, and the second one goes down with a few swipes of her front paw. When she's done and looks at me, the fury pulsing off her is the only thing that keeps me standing.

Spencer's white wolf approaches mine, licking some of his wounds as they slowly begin to heal. I don't believe I've lost enough blood to fear for my life, but I'm definitely going to need rest.

Only I have no clue if rest is coming.

I search for the presence of Kel in my mind, but she's nowhere to be found. I can't seem to communicate with her like she's just done to me.

Spencer shifts first and her rage is no less palpable when she's standing before me on two feet. "I'd kill them again if I could."

She pulls the witch's pocket from her jeans and opens it. A second later, she has a jar of salve in her hand. "This should help you."

Opening the small container, she dips her fingers into the creamy substance and walks around my wolf, placing the balm over the wounds covering him. Each spot burns from whatever concoction she's using, but then there's relief.

Not entirely, but enough that by the time she's done, I feel as though I can shift back without worry of further injury to my wolf or human half.

I step back from Spencer, not wanting to hurt her during my transformation. The change takes longer than normal, but in under half a minute, I appear on two feet, fully clothed.

With a silent thanks to the ring Natalia gave me, I go to Spencer, wrapping my arms around her. She trembles in my arms, gripping me so tightly that I expect there to be holes in my t-shirt when we part.

"I thought..." she starts to say but doesn't finish.

"That certainly wasn't good, but you did incredible," I say. "Kel underestimated you."

She pulls back, a frown between her eyes. "How do you know that was her?"

I've yet to tell Spencer that I heard the witch in my head even before, and I don't suspect it's going to go over well, but after that attack, I know I can't keep this from her.

"She spoke inside my mind and—"

"She what?" Spencer's roar makes my ears hurt. "How?"

I reach for her hands, hoping my touch will calm her, but she only shakes harder. "I don't know. I thought Natalia stripped any hold Kel has on me, but she was there in my head somehow."

"Could she control you?" Her tone is cold as her eyes darken.

I shake my head. "Not even my emotions. And I don't sense her now. It doesn't seem to be a two-way communication."

"Too fucking bad, because I'd love to tell her a few things right now." Spencer growls. "Though, she'll be dead soon enough and we won't have to worry about her screwing with your mind."

I fucking hope so.

She gives me another onceover and pokes around my collarbone. "You need more medicine. The wounds were so severe that the bruises carried through when you shifted." She grabs my hand and leads me toward some trees.

"Where are we going?" I ask. Though, it doesn't really matter. I'd follow her to the ends of this Earth.

"You need to rest, but we need to be out of sight." She glances around. "Kel isn't the only psycho out here that we need to worry about."

After passing through that town, I wouldn't assume so.

"Maybe there's a cloaking spell in the witch's pocket," I suggest, but Spencer doesn't slow.

"We still want to be out of sight. I don't want to risk something not working against whatever creation that was back there."

I wasn't the only one who noticed those wolves weren't regular shifters. They might have been at one point, but whatever Kel likely did to them was dosed with dark magic I don't miss from all the times she used to try to sway me.

I used to wonder why she never forced my hand. Considering she was capable of sending those wolves to attack us, I have no doubt that she could have manipulated my thoughts into believing I cared for her.

My stomach viciously churns at the thought of what my life might have been if she had manipulated me. I guess that's one thing I can be grateful for. The witch at least had *some* lines she wouldn't cross. Or maybe her ego is really that big that she can't fathom someone not wanting her on their own and that still has her unwilling to leave me alone. Unfortunately for us, it's likely the latter.

We find a spot between a close grouping of trees, and I lay down on the overgrown grass. Moisture from the earth soaks my back, but the coolness soothes the aches there.

Spencer is kneeling beside me and wastes no time taking care of me. I watch as she rubs more of the salve on my wounds, lifting my shirt and checking over my ribs. Every touch sends tremors along my skin, and before I realize what I'm doing, my fingers are roaming over her body.

"I'm supposed to be helping you, and you're distracting me." Her words are sharp, but she can't hide her grin from me.

"You've done such a good job, I feel the need to repay the favor." I grab her hips and tug until she straddles me.

Her brow raises and she sets the balm down, rubbing whatever is left on her hands onto her jeans. "Is that so?"

"Hmm, yes."

Her hips move over my hardening cock and any thoughts of wicked witches and possessed wolves are long forgotten.

CHAPTER 28

SPENCER

We really shouldn't be considering sex right now. Nothing of the sort. Yet, the moment Drake lifts me up and I straddle him, that's the only thing on my mind.

The wolves that attacked us came out of nowhere and nearly killed my mate. Seeing him hurt and barely able to stand ignited a fire within me that could only be quelled by the blood of the monsters.

I don't know where they came from or how Kel got to them, but my wolf wasn't going to be beat. Once they were down, I almost didn't think my wolf was going to let me shift back—her rage over Drake being hurt stormed inside us both—but he needed to be healed, and there was no way for her to do the job.

Thankfully, his injuries weren't as severe as they looked, but he still should be resting now. Not looking at me like his next meal.

"We shouldn't get distracted out here," I finally say even though I'm already primed for him.

His hands slide up and over my shirt, gripping my breasts through the thin fabric. "Too late."

He's not wrong about that.

Taking a moment, I close my eyes and extend my senses. I'd meant what I said before. Kel isn't the only person we should be concerned with. I've spent my fair share of time in the less-civilized parts of No Man's Land.

The supernaturals out here live for power. Taking an albino wolf and a shadow shifter would be the pay day of the century to some of these people.

I search the area, drawing my wolf forward and enhancing my abilities. Nothing to smell or hear, but still, I know we shouldn't do this. Not now.

Yet, when I reopen my eyes and find Drake's heated gaze on me.

Fuck it.

"Only take your pants down to your knees," I tell him. "And don't kick off your boots. This is going to be quick and dirty."

He chuckles as I sit up to shimmy my jeans over my hips. Only I realize I won't be able to be on top unless my bottom half is free of restraints. This really is a bad idea, but knowing that doesn't stop me from getting sort of naked.

Especially when I see his cock spring free, begging to be ridden.

I practically jump on him, and he groans, his eyes pinching closed for a moment. "Gentle, My Dove."

Quick and dirty, not rough and tumble. Got it.

My hands rub over his chest as I grin. "I'll make you forget about your aches."

His smirk turns into an "O" when I sit up again and stroke his erection, rubbing the head over my center.

"Fuck," he murmurs, then gasps when I slam down over his cock, taking him in one go.

My body tries to tense, but I breathe deeply and relax, settling into position. "Better?"

He nods, a moan escaping from between his lips. "Nothing could beat my dick inside you."

Placing my hands beside his shoulders, I lean forward and nip lightly at his lower lip. "Good."

I start to move my hips, still mindful of his injuries as I lift up, then go back down until I've taken every inch of him again. Repeating the action over and over again has my body heating, but so does the risk we're taking.

At any moment, we could be caught with our asses out, and the thrill of that has my pulse pounding and my need increasing.

Drake's fingers dig into my ass cheeks, and while I'm still riding him like the last bull of the night, he starts to counter my movements, forcing my hips to also move in a circular motion.

Every time I go down and he does that, I can barely breathe. Every nerve ending inside me is ignited, and I can't hold back much longer.

Knowing he needs to finish with me, I reach back with one hand and find his balls. The lightest touch of my fingertips has him stiffening beneath me.

"Spencer," he warns.

My smirk is all evil. "Quick and dirty, remember?"

Still fondling his sack, I ride him harder, grinding over him and enjoying as I watch his jaw tighten. He's close, but so am I.

I pull my hand back and lean forward until I can capture his lips. I want to taste him as he comes inside me.

Drake doesn't disappoint. Even with his legs still trapped within his jeans, he moves beneath me, hitting deeper and harder as I start to fall off the edge of the most glorious cliff.

My toes curl and my body begins to coil with seductive tension. Fuck, I'm so close.

Drake's tongue sweeps across my mouth, and one of his hands grips the back of my head, pulling on the long strands of my loose hair. "Come for me, Dove."

Those four little words have me crying out and tremors rapid-firing through my body. I fall over him, breathing heavily and panting. "Quick and dirty is really nice."

"Nice?" His chest rumbles, and he grasps my hair tighter. "That was *nice*?"

My laughter vibrates through the both of us. "You know it was more than that. Forgive my poor vocabulary. My brain is muddled."

"When you say it that way, I guess 'nice' will do." He lifts my chin and kisses me again. "We should probably get up."

Yeah, we probably should.

I'm on my feet as quickly as my ravaged body will let me. As I reach for my pants, I do another cursory glance around the area. There isn't anything new to sense out there, which is good, but also not what I expect.

If Kel sent those wolves after us, I would have expected a backup plan. One that included sending more when the others failed.

"We should teleport to the next town before shifting into our wolves again," I tell Drake. "I don't want to *run* from Kel, but if she targeted us here, she has the upper hand in this area."

Then, I unfortunately remember that bitch can speak to Drake through his mind. "Have you heard anything else from her?"

If she spoke to him while we were fucking, I will kill her. Twice.

His head shakes, then he lowers his eyes. "I'm really sorry, Spencer."

I step toward him as I button my pants. "*You* have nothing to be sorry for."

"You didn't want any of this, and everything has only gotten worse," he says with a growl. "I thought I could just forego my vengeance because you're all I need. I didn't want to bring you into this mess."

"And you didn't," I tell him sternly, holding both of his hands. "I volunteered. This nightmare will be over soon. Just focus on that."

He nods, but I know he's still upset. As much as I love that he cares so damn much, he needs to concentrate on the vengeance he was just speaking of. That rage he had when he exited the portal is what we need to win this fight.

Fear and regret won't get us anywhere. Pure, unfiltered determination to murder that bitch is key.

Once I'm finished redressing, I start to say things I really don't want to but feel are necessary to the situation.

"Kel stole your life, Drake. She took your home, your freedom, your time. If her spell hadn't basically frozen you in time, you'd probably be dead. Remember that, and don't for one second think I regret signing up for this. I might not have known how bad things were, but I knew enough, and nothing has changed since bonding with you."

His shoulders rise as he takes a deep inhale, but he still keeps his gaze averted.

I go to him and lift his chin with a finger. When I can finally see his eyes, they're filled with silver sparks and I smile. "There's my mate."

"I don't want to be angry."

"And I don't want you to be, either, but sometimes it can't be avoided," I say softly. "Let's show that witch bitch she fucked with the wrong wolf."

"As long as you know this isn't who I am." His hands cup my face. "I would never hurt you."

Damn him. He's too fucking good for me, and it seems I'm the only one that knows it.

"I know and that's exactly why I'm here and ready to fight for the life I know we will have."

Our foreheads press together, and our bond thrums with an intensity that tastes of a sweet smokiness.

Nothing will take this man from me. Not a pack of rabid wolves or a psychotic witch. I'm going to make damn sure of that.

"We should go," he says quietly.

I know he's right, but I take an extra minute to hold him close. I'm not ready to let go just yet.

When I finally pull back, the tight lines around his face break my heart a little, but I know he needs to stay focused on the end game. Nothing else matters outside of ending Kel. Ending her control over him and whatever terror she intends to cause.

"I'll use another portal spell," I tell him, digging out the witch's pocket. This thing has really come in handy. I'm going to figure out how I get one for myself since it didn't seem as if Natalia has any intentions of letting me keep hers.

A rift forms in the air in front of us and without hesitation, we step through, hand in hand. On the other side, the sky is still blue from the afternoon sun and this town isn't as run down as the last, but it's still eerily quiet.

I glance behind us to make sure the portal is closed and then turn to Drake. Except my fierce mate doesn't seem as if he's doing so well.

His shoulders are hunched over, and his eyes are squeezed closed as he holds his stomach with both arms.

"What's wrong?" I ask and look around, but there isn't

anything here. Hell, there aren't even any supernaturals. That could be a good thing, but considering there should be, I don't think it is.

"My head, it's pounding and if I open my eyes, everything around me is moving." Drake's voice is pained, but I have no clue what I'm supposed to do for him. That doesn't mean I'm not going to try and figure it out, though.

I wrap an arm around him. "Let's go sit down."

The building nearest to us is a café. The windows are busted out, and so is the door, but it's at least somewhere to sit.

Just as I usher him inside, he stumbles and starts falling forward. Even with my increased strength, his dead weight feels impossible to hold up on my own. I lean him toward the wall and help as much as I can to get him on the ground without hurting himself.

"She's close," Drake murmurs, his eyes still shut and face pinched.

"How close?" I take a deep inhale, but I don't scent anything sinister.

His head shakes. "No!"

"Is she talking to you?" I snarl. "Get the fuck out of his head," I add, even though I doubt she can hear me or that my words would make a difference.

"Run, Spencer." Drake lets out a strangled breath. "Just run."

"Not fucking happening." Using the witch's pocket, I reach inside and call for a cloaking spell. Maybe this will block Kel out. At the very least, it should at least hide us, so I can call Natalia and ask her what the hell I'm supposed to do.

I open the cloaking spell and pour the vial out around us. My eyes stay on Drake, but the pain he's radiating with doesn't lessen.

His head slowly raises, and he opens his eyes. They're all black this time, and his voice doesn't sound like his own.

"You can't hide from me, Spencer."

"Fuck you," I snarl. It's time to end this bitch once and for all.

CHAPTER 29
DRAKE

Howls ricochet within my mind as my wolf fights against the dark energy of Kel. Her nails feel as if they're digging right through my skull, and I can't hear above the roars.

Fighting back feels futile, but I refuse to give up. I won't let her hurt Spencer.

In my mind, I'm thrashing around, but I have no clue what's happening on the outside. Parts of me feel frozen again, as if I'm back in Tartarus, invisible to the world.

Dread fills me, weighing down over my body, only making me feel even more confined. I won't let this happen again. I'd rather die.

Spencer! I shout in my mind.

I know she can't hear me, but I need her. I won't be trapped again. I won't lose my mate after only just finding her.

Minutes seem as if they turn to hours. My wolf finally quiets, but so does everything else until I hear Spencer's voice.

"What the fuck am I supposed to do, then?"

I groan, but no words come out, and then her hands are on me. "Drake? Can you hear me? Wake the fuck up!"

The terror in her voice makes my heart crack. I hate that I've done this to her, put her in this position. I should have let her reject me.

"I have the cloaking spell up," Spencer snaps. "I just told you that."

I have no idea who she's talking to, but I need to get my shit together and help her.

My heart pounds, and the faster it beats, the more tired I feel, but I refuse to pass out. Kel will not beat me this time. I might think Spencer would have been better off without me, but that doesn't mean I'm going to give up now.

I can't change the past, but I can do my damnedest to make sure it doesn't repeat.

Forcing my body to relax, I breathe deeply and settle my mind. Spencer wanted me to be angry earlier and I understand why. Rage is better than fear, yet I can't shake the feeling that there's something else I'm missing.

I focus on my breathing, slowing everything down until there is only calm. As soon as that happens, a glow begins to grow within me.

The bond.

Kel might still have some of her magic within my mind, but she isn't my mate. She doesn't own my heart.

I draw on my connection to Spencer. My thoughts remain only on her and our connection and the strength I draw from that.

When Spencer and I completed our bond, it wasn't only her that glowed. My body had taken in some of her energy, and I don't believe it ever left.

I can use her pureness to fight back against Kel. I won't be at that witch's mercy, not ever again.

The tether that connects me to Spencer warms and brightens. I tug on the link until it's taut, then change my focus back to my mind.

There are dark spots there I mistook for my previous wrath, but that's not all they are. Kel wanted me to break. She wanted to unleash a monster, but I won't be her puppet. Not today or any day after.

With the light energy from Spencer, I push the remnants of Kel from my mind and clarity returns. My body no longer feels trapped within itself, and I can sit up on my own.

We're in some sort of diner, and Spencer is pacing in front of me with the witch's pocket in her hand.

Before I can say anything, she stiffens and turns around. "Drake."

Her shoulders drop, and she's on the ground next to me before I can take another breath.

My arms wrap around her, and I kiss her forehead. "It's okay. She's gone from my mind."

She drops her phone and chokes before her words finally come. "I didn't know what to do. Natalia didn't have anything for mind control because she thought you were free of that, and the only thing I could think to use next was whatever Kasha gave us, but I didn't want to accidentally kill either of us."

I chuckle at her rambling and rub a hand over her back. "I'm okay, and you did exactly what you should."

Releasing her, I start to stand, and she tries to help me, but it's not necessary. My muscles pulse with new energy, and my heart beats steadily in my chest. There's no fury within me, only determination to protect those I care about most. With my mind right, I've never felt stronger.

Spencer's head tilts. "You're different."

"I'm finally tapping into our bond." The back of my hand brushes over her arm. "We're going to be fine."

"I'll take your word for it," she grumbles and glances toward the outside. "I think we might be trapped in here."

The sky is darkening, but it's the middle of the day. I can't sense Kel, but that doesn't mean she isn't coming.

"Get Natalia's spell," I tell her. "There's no reason to fight. When Kel shows her face, we use it and end this."

Spencer opens the pouch and frowns. "I was looking forward to at least a little fight, but your plan is probably better."

I shake my head and grin. Of course she was.

I start to say something else, but my words are cut off as an inky shadow starts to form within the diner.

"What the fuck?" Spencer growls. "So much for a cloaking spell."

A cackle echoes through the small space. "There isn't a witch in existence that can keep me from where I want to go, and that includes your little friend who will soon pay for trying to kill me."

She's here.

Months have passed since I've seen Kel. Days filled with ire and the desire to spill her blood, and now that the moment is here, none of that surfaces. I don't want to be the monster she held captive.

One look at my mate, and I know more than anything else, I want to be the man she deserves.

"You're not going to hurt anyone else, Kel," I tell her with my eyes focused forward, waiting for her to take form.

The shadows she's created begin to fade and, in their place, there stands the witch. Her short ebony hair curls in around her face and her fair skin stands out against the ruby red of her lips. Her hands slide up the sides of her one-piece black leather suit as she raises her arms up into the air.

"Doesn't it feel good to be free, Drake?" Her dark-green eyes leer at me. "I've quite enjoyed myself, but it's time for you to come home with me."

"He's not going anywhere with you, bitch." Spencer throws the spell from Natalia just as we talked about and I prepare to shift to give the killing blow, but Kel's laughter stops me.

"It's quite charming that you thought you could beat me," she taunts, brushing a hand over herself as if the supposed-to-be-lethal spell is nothing more than dust before her glare settles on Spencer. "I was going to leave you alive as collateral for Drake to do what I want, but I think it will be more fun to kill you just like I've sent others to do to your family."

Spencer tries to launch herself at the witch, but I grab her waist and pull her back toward me. I won't let my mate give that witch what she wants.

"That's right. Keep your bitch on a leash." Kel waves a hand around the lingering flickers of Natalia's spell. "I have to give credit to the other witch. She may have nearly beat me if I wasn't prepared. Having a lock on your mind sure did come in handy when you weren't pissing me off for being a pathetic man."

She's been listening this whole time.

My heart sinks and I grind my teeth together, but Spencer is raging enough for the both of us. I have to keep my mind calm.

"If there's even a scratch on my family, I will bring you back from the dead after we're done with you just to kill you again," Spencer spits out, but she's at least no longer fighting against my hold.

Kel shakes a finger. "You shouldn't make threats you can't follow through on, pup. You might be strong, but your energy isn't enough to beat me. Now, roll over and die or fight me, then die. Either way, your life ends today. But look at the bright side, you'll see that mother and brother of yours soon."

Spencer's growl is deep, but mine drowns hers out within an instant. "You won't hurt any of them."

Maybe there's a balance between what Spencer thought I should be and what I've been trying to be. I'm about to find out.

I reach into my back pocket and grab the *gift* from Kasha. If they're at risk back at the house and Natalia's spell isn't going to work, then I believe we've officially become desperate.

CHAPTER 30
SPENCER

I could sense Drake's calm. I was trying to give him the benefit of the doubt and try things his way, but the moment that bitch threatened my family, I lost all sense of control. My wolf trembles just beneath the surface, and I don't want to hold her back any longer.

We're both craving the blood of this witch and we're going to get it.

Right before I shift, Drake reaches for me, but I step away from him, not wanting to accidentally hurt him. My wolf pushes forward in a rapid transformation that sends a jolt through my entire body. Bones break and skin shreds before everything comes back together in the shape of my white beast.

She stands tall on four legs, head down, eyes narrowed, and jaw snapping.

Right before we leap for Kel, Drake catches our attention. Or more accurately, what's in his hand does.

He has the pouch from Kasha. We have no clue what's in it,

but this might actually be a good thing. The fae did say to use it if we were in a dire situation.

When he opens the velvet top, my wolf's ear twitch. There's a ringing coming from the bag that's high pitched, but not enough to hurt our head.

Allowing myself the brief distraction, I watch as Drake turns the pouch over and out come tiny glowing...flies? I don't know what they are exactly, but they seem to be waking up and the more they move, the louder the ringing becomes.

Kel screeches. "What the hell is that?"

I grin internally. *Thank you, Kasha.*

The fluttering beings start to circle and turn into a swarm that gets bigger before they start to form into a cone directed right at Kel.

Before I charge in, taking advantage of her distraction, I catch Drake dropping to his knees and holding his ears.

My wolf goes to him, nudging his shoulder and growling. She wants him to shift.

His head shakes and his eyes are closed, but she doesn't relent, nipping at him, leaving small tears in his shirt. It isn't until she starts scratching at his legs that he finally roars.

We back up just in time for his wolf to burst free. A wolf that isn't as shadowy as he once was. His dark charcoal fur has layers of white woven throughout, almost like highlights.

He's absolutely stunning.

His continued snarls remind me that the time for admiration isn't now, and my attention goes back to Kel.

The swarm from Kasha is covering the witch, and I smell blood. I have no idea how they're hurting her, but it's our turn now.

My wolf lunges forward, claws out. We slice across Kel's stomach, but the sharp tips barely leave a scratch in the leather bodysuit she's wearing.

Her hands thrash, trying and failing to get the...bugs away from her, but still, she lets out a taunting laugh. "I already told you. You can't hurt me."

The fuck I can't. Her clothes might be tough as steel, but that doesn't mean the rest of her is, proven by the fact that she is bleeding. Though, I can't see where.

I go for her again, but Drake beats me this time. His wolf is right there, jowls wide and canines out. He aims for her throat, but only manages to bite her arm before a surge of power bursts through the room and sends my mate flying over tables and crashing into the counter.

A snarl builds low within my wolf, and we scrape our paw over the peeling laminate. *Go!* I tell her, but she's already charging forward.

With every step we take, the light around us grows brighter and it's almost as if my wolf is getting bigger. The power I've been keeping shoved down my whole life comes to the surface, eager to be unleashed. Our muscles coil, preparing to spring forward. Just a little bit closer.

A black smoke starts to billow around Kel, and I growl. That bitch isn't getting away. No, we're finishing this now.

Just as we leap for her, the smoke attacks, dropping us to the ground like a sack of rocks midjump.

The glow around me flickers, but I'm not even close to done. She won't beat us. She won't hurt my family or have my mate.

Drake is back up and moving faster than I am. Through our bond, I sense his worry for me, but more than that, I can taste the smokiness of his vengeance. His need for blood now matches mine and I'm here for it.

Forcing my wolf back to her feet, I concentrate on our connection to Drake and the power I hold within myself that I'm pretty sure I'm also sharing with him.

I may not understand exactly what I'm capable of yet, but I know that I'm more than a wolf shifter. I'm a woman who has been fighting for her life since she was born. I'm a mate who just wants to feel and give love. I'm a daughter and sister who can't lose her family. Not like this.

And right now, I'm not only fighting for them. I'm fighting for myself because I deserve more than the brief glimmers of happiness I've had as of late. I deserve to thrive in the new life I can see for myself. One where I no longer have to hide who I am and can quit pushing everyone away.

I deserve that and so much more and I'm going to have it. This witch won't take that from me.

Kel might be more prepared and powerful in her own ways, but my motivations are stronger because they're pure.

I am pure, and that's how we're going to win.

Pure determination, pure power, pure strength.

Focusing on our bond, I send as much of my energy to Drake as I can push through the tether between us. The more I do, the brighter his coat becomes and the louder his rumbles are.

He stalks toward Kel, wrath in his glowing eyes, but as he attacks, she's ready for him.

The tiny beings from Kasha are still attacking the witch, but she's created a shield around herself, stopping the worst of their... I have no fucking clue what they're doing, but they've at least bought us time and hopefully weakened her.

Drake's wolf bites Kel's exposed hand, going right through the opaque shield around her. She wails and digs the sharp nails of her other hand into his neck. "That's not you being a good boy, now is it?"

With a tight hold on his scruff, she somehow easily casts his couple hundred-pound wolf to the side as if he's nothing, but I'm already charging forward.

My wolf takes advantage of her distraction and we hit her in the side, forcing her to the ground. We don't ease up. Our claws scratch furiously at her body, hitting her exposed hand and chest, drawing more blood.

Just as I suspected, her bare skin isn't protected, which means we need to go for her neck.

She tries to reach for me like she did Drake, but my wolf is prepared for that and bites her non-injured hand clean off.

Take that, bitch.

My wolf licks her lips and her eyes focus on Kel's neck. Before the witch can get back up, we place a paw on her chest and expose our razor-sharp teeth. We go to chomp down, but her remaining hand pushes against our side and sends a bolt of electricity through my wolf. Muscles seize and it's as if a few thousand needles are assaulting us, jabbing into every inch of our skin. Our vision falters and our head pounds, but there is no option of giving into the agony.

We have to win.

Being unable to keep our position over Kel, she gets up, holding her bleeding arm over her chest. "I'm going to make a welcome mat out of your pelt." Her booted foot slams into our ribs, breaking at least one of them.

Damn it all to hell.

But Drake is right there, having recovered from his last blow. His eyes are glowing that deep orange I remember from before, and he doesn't hesitate in attacking the witch.

His claws swipe across her face, ripping open her cheek and she lets out a wail. "Nooooo!"

Fucking yes is more like it.

My wolf's body still trembles, and getting up feels impossible, but that doesn't mean we can't be helpful. Once again, I push energy through the bond to Drake. He hits her again, only her mangled hand gets in the way.

I'm pretty sure I see a finger fly through the air as Kel conjures magic within her bleeding palm. A black orb grows, and she smacks it against Drake's wolf head. "I should have taken your mind years ago."

My heart stops. What the fuck does she mean by that?

The quakes rocking my wolf start to cease and we stand, but my connection to Drake flickers. The magic from the orb starts to cover his fur, but the little... Holy shit. Are those fairies?

Whatever they are, they change their focus to my mate and it's almost like they start consuming the dark energy trying to take Drake from me.

With a shake of his head, he snarls at Kel. Oh, how I wish I could hear what he's thinking right now.

She takes a step back, eyes wide. "That's not possible."

Drake goes for her remaining hand, his teeth cutting through her wrist with ease before he spits out the body part. My wolf is already moving in to help finish the job, but just as we prepare to leap into the action, Drake's wolf pins Kel to the ground.

Silence fills the small space, and it's like the rest of the world has gone quiet.

One moment, Kel's head is attached to her body, and in the next, with a swing of Drake's right paw, I watch with glee as it tumbles toward my feet.

Her eyes are still open, and I'm sure she's dead, but my wolf isn't pleased. She leans forward and rips into the bitch's face with her teeth, making the witch unrecognizable within seconds.

By the time we look up again, Drake has shifted to his human form, and he's standing over Kel's body. I start to shift back as well, wanting to go look for matches or something to set fire to the corpse, but when I'm back on two feet, she's already...disintegrating?

"What the hell?" I mutter, making my way toward Drake.

"I think they're eating her." He points and I notice the fairies, or very tiny beings with bodies and faces I can't actually make out, are burrowing beneath her leather bodysuit, cleaning up the mess.

Kasha mentioned me hopefully returning them, but there's no way I'm fucking with those things.

More importantly, we don't have time for that.

Kel sent those wolves after us before, and I have no doubt that she was being serious when she said my family was being attacked.

"We need to go," I tell Drake, already digging out the witch's pouch for another portal spell.

His eyes stay locked on the body. "It's over. She's finally dead after all these years."

I open the portal and place one hand on his back. "We can celebrate soon. I promise."

He nods stiffly, then tilts his head. "I think they're all sleeping."

My jaw tenses. Waiting a second longer to jump through that portal makes my chest ache, but I do anyway.

Sure enough, the fairies as I've deemed them are lying around the bodysuit, still as dead flies.

Drake pulls the velvet bag from his pocket and bends down. "We shouldn't leave them out here."

He's probably right. Okay, I know he's right, but I really want to fucking leave. Yet, the thought of going without my mate isn't something I can fathom this soon after thinking there was a chance that we were both going to die today.

He sweeps them into the pouch carefully, but I can sense his urgency, which makes the painfully passing seconds slightly more manageable.

As soon as he stands, I grab his hand and jump for the portal without warning him. The moment we reappear in Kasha's yard, my knees go weak.

Her house is gone. Not as if it's disappeared. No, it's been decimated. All that's left is a concrete foundation and a few pipes sticking up. Everything else is...gone.

My hands tremble, and my throat feels as if it's closing up, but not quickly enough to hold in my scream. A deep guttural sound that rattles my body and brings me to my knees.

I cover my face and shake my head. "No, no, no, no."

Drake's arms wrap around me, but even his warmth can't penetrate the soul-deep cold I feel. My heart is freezing over with every final beat.

It no longer matters that Kel is dead. We lost. So much more than I was willing to sacrifice.

Sobs rip from my chest, and Drake holds me tighter, but no amount of support can keep the pieces of me from falling apart. There is nothing left inside me that—

"Pence!"

I choke on another scream and lift my head, but I'm still frozen on my knees.

"Pence, you should have seen it," Peter begins to ramble, having no clue my heart is still shattered even though I can see with my own eyes that he's okay. "Kasha blew up her own house!"

My emotions can't catch up. As he comes to a screeching halt, confusion gracing his face, I cry harder.

Twice in one week, I've thought I lost my family. That's twice too much.

His little hands cup my face as I try to rein in my emotions. "Did something happen?"

I shake my head. "As long as you and Mom are okay, then no. I just..."

"Had a moment?" he fills in. "That's what Momma called them when I couldn't control my wolf."

A strangled laugh leaves me. "Yeah, Bub. I had a moment."

Mom and Kasha approach. One shared look with Mom and I see the terror in her eyes. I wasn't the only one frightened. Yet, they'd kept the worst of whatever happened here from Peter and for that, I'm grateful.

"Is it done?" Kasha asks hesitantly.

Drake nods as I hold Peter, still needing to feel the warmth of his body to calm myself.

"And did my offering help?" she asks, a smirk on her face.

He tosses the small bag to her. "We almost left them behind, but I figured it was safer if, whatever the hell those things are, aren't left unattended."

She holds the pouch up to her ear. "They're nice and full. Good job, my babies."

"More like flesh-eating termites," I mutter, finally standing.

Kasha chuckles. "You're nearly right."

I hug Mom next. "What happened here?"

"Kasha had some unexpected visitors," she says, eyes flicking toward Peter. "They weren't being very nice, and she had to show them what happens when they don't listen."

"You should have seen it, Pence," Peter exclaims. "There was a tornado, and once me and mom snuck out the back, Kasha fed the rude men to it, but then her house accidentally went with it. That sucked."

Kasha grips his shoulder and smiles. "It's more important that we're all safe. I can always build another house."

He stands taller. "I'll help you."

My eyes close briefly, and I take a deep inhale. For just a

moment, I breathe in the people closest to me. They're okay. We're okay.

Drake's fingers entwine with mine and I look up at him, finally smiling. "We're home."

"Home is wherever you are, Mate."

EPILOGUE

SPENCER

Two Months Later…

For over twenty years, I wasn't sure I would ever feel at home somewhere, or that I would be able to allow myself that kindness. I was afraid to be myself, afraid of the unknown, but no longer.

Not only do I have a home, but I'm no longer in hiding.

Over the last month, since we officially joined Corvin's pack, I've stopped concealing my wolf. The fear my mother instilled in me for so long is gone and, even better, she hasn't had a vision of my death since Samuel died.

We'll never know if he was the only danger to me, or if me finding Drake made the difference, but either way, the peace we both have is something I'm thankful for every day.

"Where's my dove?" Drake calls from the front door of our new home.

"The kitchen." I put the last of the silverware into the drawer and turn toward his approaching footsteps.

It's our move-in day at Corvin's pack. Mom and Peter have been living here since a week after Kasha's house was destroyed, but I wasn't keen on staying in the pack house with my new mate, opting to wait until my mother and brother had their own place and for one to be available for Drake and me.

The shed had suited me just fine for months and somehow survived during Kasha's windstorm, turned tornado. I figured that was a sign for us to stay a bit longer.

Drake enters the kitchen carrying more boxes. "Natalia sent these. She said 'Your mate needs a new wardrobe. Fill her closet with these.' I haven't looked inside, and I wasn't going to tell her no."

My big, wolfy mate is such a softy.

I grab the top box and open the flaps. To my surprise, it's filled with jeans, a pair of new boots, and plain tees. Just my style. I really do adore that witch.

"Drop them in the bedroom," I tell him. "I'll put those away next."

Another knock sounds at the door that opens before we can reply. "Anyone home?" Corvin announces, and I shake my head.

He knows damn well we are seeing as how he's our alpha and has a direct link to us, but I don't bother to remind him of that. Especially when he's been so kind to my family.

"I was just checking in on Cara and Peter and thought I'd stop by," he says, standing near our new-to-us table. "Is this cabin going to work for the two of you?"

I glance around at the one-bedroom place. There's a place to cook, somewhere to eat, a couch to relax on in front of a fireplace, and a bedroom that I get to share with my mate. I don't think that I could ask for much more.

"It's perfect," I tell him. "Thank you."

He rocks back on his feet. “Good. As soon as you’re settled, let me know.”

His tone tells me there’s more he wants to say, but like the good alpha I’ve begun to know, he’s trying to be patient.

“I know what I signed up for, Corvin,” I say with a grin. “If the pack needs help with something, unpacking can wait.”

Even when I lived within Fire and Fluorite, I never felt like I had a home. Yet, even before moving onto the pack lands, Corvin has gone out of his way to make both Drake and I part of his growing family. We’ve been invited to nighttime runs, a few group dinners, and he’s made sure we’ve had everything we need.

Repaying that kindness is no hardship for me and based on Drake’s increased interest, I’d say the same for my mate.

“There’ve been some disturbances at the portal,” Corvin says. “Nothing major, but we thought having a shadow shifter there for the next couple of nights might help stave off any further misconduct.”

I glance at Drake, and he’s already nodding. “Count me in.”

“Thank you,” he says, then nods back at the door. “I’ll see myself out. Make sure to let me know if you need anything to make this place feel like home.”

A laugh bubbles up inside me. “I’ve been living in a shed for six months. I’m pretty sure we’re good here.”

Drake wraps an arm around me and kisses the top of my head as Corvin lets himself out. “He’s a good leader. I wasn’t sure with him only being half-shifter, but he’s proven himself a worthy alpha.”

That he has.

I glance out the window in front of the table next to us and sigh happily. Peter is out front, playing with one of the other pups within the pack. They have sticks they’re using as swords and giggling as children should.

Kasha's adjustment to his emotions has since faded, but he's moved on with life since killing his father, eager to live without the fear he'd only ever known.

He and Mom live in the cabin next to ours. She hasn't been leaving much, but I know she's trying and one day she'll get there. Maybe she'll even meet someone new to piece the shattered bits of her heart back together.

Drake holds me tighter. "You did good, My Dove. You're everything I thought you would be and more."

"This wasn't all me." I turn in his arms and look up at him. "I might still hate the world if you hadn't forced your way into my heart."

"I would grovel at your feet for millennia if that's what it took to win you over." His lips brush lightly over mine. "I'm just grateful you didn't make me wait that long."

The door opens again, but in unison, we both say, "Go away."

"Try again," a familiar voice replies. "We have plans and you're not canceling." Kasha stands in the doorway. "Now, quit sucking face. We have a girls' night planned."

Another revelation in my life. All the people in Crossroads who had tried to befriend me when I first arrived have slowly come back into my life.

I glance at the clock in the kitchen. "It's only five. *Night* isn't for another few hours at least."

She rolls her eyes and sighs. "You are the worst at checking your phone. The plans changed. Now, let's go. Styx and Sin are already waiting at the pack house."

Drake releases me with a smile so sweet I nearly melt at his feet. "Have fun, and don't come back before midnight."

"You suck." My lower lip juts out.

He leans as if he's going to kiss my cheek and whispers, "No, that's your job."

I grip his shirt and move to capture his mouth, but Kasha throws a pillow from the couch at us. "Seriously. You can get laid any other night. Let's *go*."

"I'll see you soon," I say and reluctantly part from my mate. "Don't have too much fun at the portal tonight without me."

"I'll do my best." He blows me a kiss, then I'm yanked out the front door.

"You are such a lucky bitch." She shakes her head. "You and Styx with your too-sweet-for-their-own-good men. Though, Raegan can't really complain either with her broody, knows-he's-a-God mate."

I pat her back and shake my head. "We need to get you laid at the minimum."

She huffs. "Preach."

But she also isn't wrong. I know exactly how lucky I am, and I make sure Drake knows how much I appreciate him every day. Better yet, I know that nothing in this world will tear us apart.

Our bond is forever and so is our love, something I'll never take for granted again.

Checking my phone, I see there are more than just the text updates about girls' night.

Tori: Legion's stuck at work and I slipped through the portal. Let's get into some trouble.

I grin. My other fae friend.

I haven't yet invited her to hang out with the others. Half because she moved to Tartarus and half because I'm still adjusting to actually having friends and I think she might be, too, after the hell she recently went through, but maybe this is the perfect night.

"I'm going to invite my friend Tori," I tell Kasha as we walk toward the pack house.

"Tell her to meet us here. We're still waiting on Raegan and Clara."

I've yet to meet those two myself, but the former has been talked about enough that I feel as if I already know her.

I text Tori back with the details and before my phone is even tucked back into my pocket, she replies.

Tori: I'm in.

This night is either going to make me wish I stayed a loner or it's going to be one I won't soon forget. Only time will tell...and maybe a few drinks.

Three hours later, the sun has only just set, but I can barely see straight, and my cheeks hurt from laughing so much.

"I'm a God and your mate." Raegan crosses her arms and glowers, deepening her voice. "You will stay with me or else..."

"And then you fuck his brains out and everyone lives happiler ever after." Clara hiccups and laughter echoes around from all of us as her cheeks redden. "Happiler? Happily? Whatever."

Raegan drops the façade and shrugs with a wicked grin. "I mean, he *is* a God."

"Gods aren't the only ones with talented cocks," I mutter behind my glass, and all eyes turn toward me.

Shit, did I say that out loud?

Tori raises an eyebrow, her green eyes on me. "Do tell."

"Yes, please," Kasha whines. "I need to live vicariously through all of you. My vagina is starting to shrivel up from lack of use."

"Oh!" Sin holds up a finger as she finishes off her drink, then her gaze lands on Raegan. "Bruno."

"Bruno?" The unicorn shifter cocks her head to the side. "What did he do now?"

Sin's smirk grows. "It's more like *who* he's going to do."

Kasha perks up. "Tell me more. I'm not afraid to admit I'm desperate and willing to take a set-up, or even a pity fuck."

"I'm sure we can find a shadow shifter to devour you," Styx chimes in, sipping on her whiskey and maintaining the most control over herself compared to the rest of us.

My fae-wolf shifter friend waggles her brows. "Why can't I have both?"

More laughter fills the room, and a warmth grows within my chest.

This is the life I always wanted, but never thought I could have. A mate who not only consumes me, heart and soul, but would burn the world to protect me, my family safe and sound and close by, and the most badass group of friends a woman could ask for.

I never expected any of this, but now that I'm finally living my life, I'm more thankful than ever before to just be me. I can be myself not only with my mate, but with these women.

I never have to hide who I am or what my wolf is. Not ever again. That alone has me grinning and raising my glass.

"To having everything we want and more!"

The End.

Thank you for reading *CAGE ME*! I hope you enjoyed Spencer and Drake's story. Want to read more about some of the other characters you've just met or continue with the world? Make sure to pick up:

Forbid Me—The next book in the series
Mate Me—Raegan and Caius
Shadow Me—Corvin and Styx
Ignite Me—Lia and Markus
Hunt Me—Tori and Legion

STAY IN TOUCH

Find Heather on Facebook:

Reader Group

Want to talk all things books and get updates before anyone else?

Come hang with me in my reader group:

Heather Renee's Book Warriors

Author Page

Teaser and big updates are also posted here:

Heather Renee Author

Newsletter:

I send this out sporadically, so don't worry. You won't ever be spammed by me and you get a couple goodies when you sign up!

http://smarturl.it/HeatherReneeNL

ALSO BY HEATHER RENEE

Paranormal Romance Books:

Mystics and Mayhem World—Series are connected by characters crossovers, but not the plots. You can read them in any order.

Broken Court

A complete New Adult Urban Fantasy series featuring an unconventional and anti-heroine leading lady, a broody love interest, and a fae kingdom with a vile king.

Luna Marked

A complete New Adult wolf shifter series (dual POV) featuring a strong-willed leading lady and a patient, yet fierce alpha male.

Scorned by Blood

A complete New Adult Vampire series featuring a supernatural hunter and the sexy vampire bound to protect her no matter the cost.

Fated to the Wolf

A complete New Adult Witch and Wolf series (dual POV) featuring an abandoned witch, a rogue wolf, and their broken bond.

The Hidden Realm

A complete New Adult wolf and dragon shifter series (dual POV) featuring a feisty wolf shifter just looking for her freedom and a broody dragon trying to save his world.

A Pack Christmas

A Christmas weekend in the East Texas Pack filled with ten different POVs, mayhem, laughs, a new mateship, and so much more!

Fractured Mates

A standalone second-chance fated mates novel featuring a food obsessed wolf shifter with trust issues and the protector she never asked for, but can't help falling for.

Individual Series

Raven Point Pack Series

A complete Upper Young Adult Paranormal Romance series featuring wolves, witches, vengeance, and fated mates.

Shadow Veil Academy

A complete Upper Young Adult Urban Fantasy Academy series featuring shifters, elves, witches, and more.

Elite Supernatural Trackers

A complete New Adult Urban Fantasy series featuring witches, demons, a smart-mouthed female lead, alpha males, and a snarky fairy sidekick.

Royal Fae Guardians

A complete Young Adult Urban Fantasy series featuring fae, magic users, a sweet romance, along with snark and humor.

Standalone Books

Ignite Me - A spicy wolf shifter story featuring a lost heir, the mate who doesn't want her, and the enemies who wish them dead.

Marked Paradox - A Young Adult fae story about a realm divided and one fae to bring them back together.

Contemporary Romance Books with Harper Reed:

The Wicked Duet

A mafia romance with enemies-to-lovers, forced proximity, and a happily-ever-after after more than a bit of unaliving...

Ruthless Truths

Tangled Deceit

The Unexpected Series

A Spicy RomCom trilogy featuring three best friends and their happily-ever-afters!

A Mutually Beneficial Proposal

A Mutually Beneficial Mistake

A Mutually Beneficial Secret

Standalones

A Royal Oops

A Spicy RomCom with royal antics, an epic second chance romance, and a kingdom that needs their new queen.

ABOUT THE AUTHOR

Heather Renee is a USA Today Bestselling author who lives in Oregon. She writes Paranormal Romance and Urban Fantasy novels with a mixture of romance, humor, and sass. Her love of reading eventually led to her passion of writing and giving the gift of escapism.

When Heather's not writing, she's spending time with her loving husband and beautiful daughter, going on their own adventures. She loves to hear from her fans, so visit her website: www.HeatherReneeAuthor.com and check out the Contact Me page for ways to connect.

www.ingramcontent.com/pod-product-compliance
Lightning Source LLC
Chambersburg PA
CBHW020458310726
48979CB00016B/2709/J
* 9 7 8 1 9 5 7 7 3 1 2 8 5 *